Macady

A Novel

by

Jennie L. Hansen

Covenant Communications, Inc.

Published by Covenant Communications, Inc.

American Fork, Utah

Copyright © 1995 by Jennie Hansen

Printed in the United States of America

First Printing: August 1995

01 00 99 98 97 96   10 9 8 7 6 5 4 3 2

ISBN 1-55503-820-4

Hansen, Jennie L., 1943-
    Macady: a novel/by Jennie Hansen.
        p. cm.
    ISBN 1-55503-820-4
    I. Title.
PS3558.A51293M33 1995
813' .54--dc20   95-19135
                                                                      CIP

Acknowledgements

For the love of my life, Boyd Hansen. He's my husband and best friend. Without his support and sacrifice, I wouldn't be able to follow my dreams. Thanks, too, to some other special men in my family: Jed Smith, David Smith, Darrell Henson, Steve Little, and to the Twin Falls County Sheriff's Department for all their help in researching the background for this book.

CHAPTER ONE

It was unbearably hot. With one hand Macady unbuttoned the top two buttons of her denim shirt, then pulled her old brown hat from her head. She used the hat to gently fan her face and neck as she squinted at the hills around her. Shimmering waves of heat rose from the desert floor. Off in the distance, a dust devil whirled toward the black lava rock, then lost its momentum and collapsed into the stillness.

She should head back. She'd promised to return by one to relieve Mary at the store, but the sun felt good. It had been a long time since she'd ridden through the sweet smelling brush that stretched from her mother's store near the freeway to the South Hills and beyond to the Sawtooth National Forest.

Tasha shifted uneasily beneath her, drawing Macady's attention to the mare. The horse was generally placid, but this morning she'd shied several times. Right now her ears stood erect. She flicked her tail and took a few mincing steps sideways. Macady jammed her hat back on her head and tightened her grip on the reins. Carefully she scanned the brush for twenty feet around, expecting to see a snake, but the only wildlife she spotted was a lizard sunning himself on a rock.

"Okay, Tasha, just to the top of the ridge, then we'll start back." She patted the horse's neck and urged her forward toward a swell where the brush was thick and taller than the horse. The faint path twisted through the sage and gradually ascended to a rocky outcropping which overlooked a dry creek bed.

Part way up the incline, Tasha stopped. Macady pressed her

knees against the sides of the horse and tried to coax her to keep moving. "What's the matter, old girl? Have I been away so long you've gotten lazy?"

Tasha jerked her head up and back down sharply. Her hooves moved in a nervous crabstep.

"Easy. Easy." Macady leaned forward to whisper soothing words in the mare's ear.

A sharp crack broke the silence and a high-pitched whine sang over Macady's head. A soft thwack and flying splinters showed where a bullet had lodged deep in a thick, twisted sage trunk. Macady's heart thumped and her pulse began to pound. She didn't have time to dwell on her fear as Tasha bolted back down the trail. Macady had her hands full trying to stay in the saddle. She kept her head low against the horse's neck in case the fool fired again.

"It's okay," she attempted to calm the frightened animal. "It's just some idiot hunting rabbits and not watching where he's shooting." Tasha had never been any good to take out hunting. She hated loud sounds, especially gun shots ever since Macady's cousins had terrified the young mare with firecrackers. Uncle Carson had been furious with his boys, said they'd ruined a good horse, and gave her to Macady since neither she nor her mother hunted.

Another shot rang through the still summer air. A little puff of dust flew up in front of the running horse. Tasha neighed in terror and reared wildly in the air. Macady dropped the reins as she struggled to stay on the frightened horse's back.

"Stop shooting!" She shouted, knowing full well there was little chance the hunter could hear her words, but perhaps he'd recognize a human voice and stop firing into the thick scrub.

Two more shots followed in rapid succession. Fear and anger fought for supremacy as Tasha reared again. The horse's hoofs hit the ground with a bone-jarring thud and she was off in a maddened frenzy. Sagebrush scraped against Macady's thick denim pants and clutched like grasping fingers at her shirt. A branch dealt her face a stinging slap. Ahead, the brush opened up onto a rocky plateau. As Tasha's hoofs clattered across the rocks, Macady struggled to right herself in the saddle. Surely now the jerk with a rifle would be able to tell he was firing at a horse and rider, not a rabbit or an antelope.

Tasha slowed and Macady heaved a grateful sigh as she looked around. She turned slowly in the direction the shots had come from, back toward the ridge. A tiny figure stood on the top of the rocks, clearly outlined against the blue sky. A flash of light reflected off the barrel of the rifle he held at his shoulder. Macady reached for her hat. Slowly she waved it back and forth. There was no doubt he could see her as clearly as she could see him.

Tasha stepped on the trailing rein and stumbled, pitching Macady sideways. At the same time Macady felt her hat ripped from her hand. Tasha whirled crazily before bolting again into the brush. Macady lost a stirrup and clung desperately to Tasha's mane with both hands. She felt her hands slip and clutched at the saddle, but she couldn't prevent her downward slide. She met the ground abruptly and lay still, winded, for several minutes, listening to the receding sounds of her horse crashing through the brush.

Macady knew she should get up. She wasn't hurt. If something were broken, she'd know it. It was a long walk back to her mother's store, at least five miles in the desert midday heat, and she knew she should get started.

She tried not to think the one thought that kept trying to scream its way past all the others, but it wouldn't be denied. The man on the ridge had deliberately fired at her. He wasn't an irresponsible hunter. The shots were no accident. He'd seen her, taken aim, and fired his rifle.

Slowly Macady opened her eyes. Tasha had dumped her in the brush. At least she wasn't exposed to her attacker by lying on the rocky plateau. Macady wiggled her toes, scooted deeper into the brush, and tried to think. Her head ached. It was nothing serious she suspected, just a reaction to the tension.

She lifted one hand and pushed damp tendrils of her cropped brown hair off her neck and face. She winced as her hand brushed against a scratched cheek. She looked at her hand and saw streaks of blood across the back of it. Her shirt sleeve was torn, too, and a couple of long scratches on her arm were spreading a steady stain across what was left of the material there.

A crazy man with a gun had shot at her. Incomprehensible. She might not be loved by everyone who had ever met her, but Macady didn't have any serious enemies either. She didn't have a clue why he'd selected her for a target; however, she had no intention of hanging around and providing him with another chance to shoot at her.

The man had stood on the highest point around for miles, and sagebrush didn't provide a lot of protection. If she could work her way to the dry stream bed, would it hide her until she could reach a deeper fissure? Or would she be an easy target in the narrow gully? Two miles to the east it dropped into a narrow canyon, a miniature of the mighty Snake River canyon a few miles further north. If she could make it to the canyon, she knew she'd find better cover.

Macady certainly knew she couldn't stay where she was. The man might come to see if he'd hit her. She felt her chin quiver, but she wouldn't allow herself to cry. She hadn't cried since the summer she was fifteen and her father had asked her mother for a divorce.

She hadn't cried when he left, not at first. It was later when Uncle Carson brought Tasha. She'd ridden the little chestnut mare out onto the desert and stopped on the top of a low butte. She'd slipped from the horse's back and stood with her face buried in the mare's mane and cried until there were no more tears. Then she'd prayed. She'd told God she didn't have a father any more, but she had heard a quiet whisper in her heart tell her she still had a Father in Heaven.

That's how it had been ever since. When she had problems, she'd turned to her Heavenly Father. She didn't need a father or any other man. Once she'd thought she needed Brian, but he was just as incapable of fidelity as her father had been. With the help of God she could handle anything.

But she'd never been in this much trouble before. Macady closed her eyes briefly, then ordered her trembling body to start moving. She slid several feet flat on her stomach before stopping to add a quick postscript to her prayer. "Please don't let me run into any snakes." She shivered and dug one elbow and a knee into the soft desert sand to scoot herself forward.

Aaron flattened himself against the rocky ground and pressed his field glasses to his eyes. Taking care to avoid any reflection off the lenses, he searched the area on the other side of the dry stream bed. Nothing. Yet the feeling persisted. He wasn't alone out here. Right after he'd left the tiny concealed airfield an hour ago, he'd felt eyes watching him. Playing it safe, he'd worked his way into heavy brush, leaving his horse in a hidden wash, then crawled to this high spot.

He lifted the glasses again and paused. A man stood on a knoll a little more than a half mile away. He held a rifle and he was watching something through the scope of the gun. Aaron let his eyes drift down the slope until he saw a slim, denim-clad rider on a chestnut horse emerge from heavy brush. A brown felt cowboy hat slouched low on the rider's head hiding his features.

Aaron sucked in his breath sharply. He barely had time to register that from a distance the rider could be his double before the first shot cracked in the still desert air. Two more shots followed in rapid succession.

Aaron let the glasses drop and reached for his .40 Smith & Wesson. It was useless at this range, but he drew it anyway. He didn't doubt the bushwacker on the hill was the unknown presence he'd felt following him, and it confirmed his suspicions regarding the small airfield he'd found earlier. Someone didn't want the location of that field to make its way back to Twin Falls. That someone was about to kill an innocent kid because at six hundred yards he resembled Deputy Aaron Westerman.

The unknown rider disappeared into the brush. Aaron lifted his binoculars in time to see the gunman disappear behind a rocky ridge where he continued to fire at the beleaguered rider.

Aaron ground his teeth in frustration. There was no way he could reach a point where he could see the gunman or offer aid to his unknown double in time to prevent a tragedy. Nonetheless, he began sliding down the hill, headed for the dry creek bed.

He was almost to the lip of the gully when he spotted movement directly across from him. To his horror, he saw the rider break free of the brush, pull the horse to a stop on a bare rocky promontory, and remove his hat.

"No! Get out of there," Aaron shouted, but the rider made no indication he'd heard. The faint crack of a rifle reached Aaron's ears and the horse went crazy. He could see the figure clinging to the side of the frenzied animal as it disappeared once more into the brush. Moments later the horse reappeared, streaking across another open spot. There was no sign of the rider.

Aaron slid feet first down the steep side of the dry wash. He didn't doubt for a minute that the gunman would come to check his handiwork. Aaron had to get to the kid first. He might be injured or even dead, but he wouldn't be alone when his ambusher came poking his nose around.

Aaron didn't know why he thought the rider was a kid. It wasn't just his slenderness. Aaron was accustomed to being frequently mistaken himself for someone a lot younger than his twenty-eight years because of his own frame. Perhaps it was the way the rider moved and the tenacious way he'd clung to his horse.

The dry soil crumbled between Aaron's fingers and his boots slipped in the loose dirt as he scrambled up the other side.

Sheriff Blacker had been madder than a wet hen when he'd given Aaron this assignment. Someone was using his county to slip millions of dollars worth of cocaine into the state, and Blacker took that as a personal affront. From Twin Falls county the illegal drug was fanning out across the entire Northwest and Nelson Blacker wanted it stopped. He only had four range deputies to cover an area as large as some eastern states, but for two weeks they'd crisscrossed the sage-covered desert, the steep canyons, and the slopes of the South Hills. Federal agents from the Drug Enforcement Agency were working the area, too.

Today Aaron had struck pay dirt. The glint of sun off glass had been the tip-off. The site had appeared abandoned at first, but Aaron had gotten close enough to determine a small plane shrouded in brush stood at the end of a narrow slice of bare ground. The landing strip was part of an old firebreak carved out of the rocks and brush by the Bureau of Land Management two years ago when range fires had devastated the area to the south. He suspected the remainder of the firebreak served as a rough road for heavy four-wheel drive vehicles. Aaron hadn't explored further because he was afraid to tip his hand before he could get back to the sheriff and bring in a team of investigators.

Keeping low, Aaron worked his way to the plateau where he'd last seen the rider. He skirted the open area and moved cautiously toward the spot where the horse had re-entered the brush. An object caught his attention and he reached out to retrieve a brown felt hat, identical to his own except for the hole through the top. The gunman had caught it dead center.

Aaron pulled his own Stetson lower to protect his eyes and glanced back toward the ridge where the shots had been fired. The gunman was gone, but he'd had a long, clear shot at his target. Aaron feared the kid was dead or lying wounded under a clump of sagebrush.

He found the horse's tracks and followed them. A few yards in, he found where the rider had fallen. Broken brush and a deep impression in the powdery dirt told its tale of impact. But, there was no body; that meant the rider was alive and moving away from the spot.

Aaron checked the ground for boot marks, but found none. He did find several damp spots, small round dots in the dirt he

7

knew were blood. There was no way to tell whether they came from the horse or the rider. The kid had to have crawled away, but Aaron wondered if it was to keep a low profile, or if he were too seriously injured to stand.

Aaron puzzled over the marks in the sand. He had to get to the kid quickly, before the gunman did. Where had he gone? Was he following his horse or had he crawled off to hide? Taking a piece of the broken sage, Aaron carefully wiped out all traces of the rider's fall and his own boot prints. He studied the ground where the horse had continued its flight. At a ninety-degree angle from the horse's path, he found what he sought. A shallow impression in the ground gave evidence a weight had dragged its way into the brush and headed toward the dry creek bed. He smiled in satisfaction and began to follow.

Aaron kept low as he followed the depression in the sand. Frequently he paused to listen but picked up no tell-tale whispers of sound from the downed rider. He was glad of that; if he couldn't hear the kid, his pursuer couldn't either.

As the ground grew rockier, the faint trail he followed disappeared. Aaron felt certain he was headed in the right direction, so he continued on. He estimated that by now the ambusher must be about two-thirds of the way to the clearing where the rider was last seen. Aaron would have to hurry to reach the dry gulch before the gunman started searching the area. Fortunately, through luck or fear, the rider was staying out of sight. But Aaron had to find him.

When he reached the dry creek, there was no sign of the kid. Aaron couldn't tell whether he'd gone over the edge or was following the winding course from above. He searched for a spot where someone might have slid downward, but saw nothing. Finally he chose a rocky point and made his descent, taking care to leave no sign.

At the bottom he began a careful jog in the direction that would be downstream when spring run-off or a heavy summer storm provided water to flow along the stream bed. As he passed a jagged outcropping of rock, a slight movement caught his eye seconds before a well-aimed missile struck his shoulder. The split-second warning saved him from a blow to the head, but the momentum of the object sent him stumbling back a step.

Recovering his balance, he lunged toward a figure scrambling up the rocks, intent on a hasty retreat. He didn't dare call out, but he couldn't let the kid suddenly pop up at the top of the gulch. He left the kid's hat behind as he leaped after him. Ignoring the bite of the rough rock cutting into his fingers, Aaron scrambled up the slope and closed the distance rapidly, but not fast enough. He'd have to jump. A flying tackle could send them both tumbling backward onto the sharp rocks below, but the risk was better than a bullet.

He bunched his muscles and threw himself forward to land on his objective's back. His hand immediately circled the kid's head to cover his mouth and prevent any sudden outcry. The body beneath his bucked frantically, and he could feel teeth attempting to find a hold in his hand.

"Hold still!" he whispered fiercely. "I'm not going to hurt you, but you've got to keep quiet."

An elbow caught his midsection and the air left his lungs. A leg tangled with his and nearly threw him. He grabbed for the blue shirt and got a handful of brown hair. He took advantage of his hold to shove his opponent's face into the dirt. With one hand nearly choking off the boy's breath and the other immobilizing his head, Aaron held his captive until he stopped struggling. He slid forward to sit astride the kid's back and leaned down to speak directly into his ear.

"All right," he hissed through his teeth. "Just listen. I didn't shoot at you. I'm a sheriff's deputy and I'm trying to help you. I'm going to turn you over and remove my hand. Don't make a sound."

Aaron released the fistful of hair he held, slowly withdrew his hand from under his prisoner's face, and raised his weight off the body beneath him. One deft twist of the tense form and he found himself eye to eye with wide brown eyes, almost the same shade he stared at in the mirror each morning. At the same moment he recognized the face he stared at didn't belong to a boy, he became aware the body he straddled was feminine soft.

A woman! A young, beautiful woman, his stunned brain amended. Feelings he thought Alicia had destroyed forever made him painfully aware of his position. His first instinct was to remove himself and apologize, but his training took over. This woman was in danger and he had to not only keep her quiet, but also get her out of sight as soon as possible.

"We're going back down. Move quickly and keep quiet."

She glared mutinously at him for several long seconds, then slowly nodded her head in acquiescence. He rolled to his side and started along the side of the gulch with the woman beside him. At the bottom he picked up her hat and handed it to her.

With both of them standing now, he noticed she matched his own five feet ten and their clothes really were the same. Only their boots were different. She wore brown riding boots, while his roper boots were black. Whereas he suspected his face betrayed that he hadn't taken time to shave that morning, hers appeared soft as silk except for a series of scratches on one cheek. Bloodstains on her shirt sleeve had dried, indicating no serious injury.

The gap where she'd left one too many buttons undone on her shirt reminded him forcibly that though their shirts might have been cut from the same bolt of cloth, they certainly didn't fit the same. He felt annoyance at the reaction she stirred in him. Women didn't interest him, not since Alicia.

The woman stared blankly at the hat he handed her, then gingerly, almost as though she expected something terrible to happen, she pressed one long, slim finger through the hole. Her eyes met his and she whispered, "How did you get my h—?"

"Sh-h, not now. We've got to move. I'll buy you a new one when we get out of here." He took her arm to urge her on when some sixth sense sounded a warning. Pulling her with him, he dived for the shelter of the rocks she'd hidden behind earlier.

Cautiously he raised his head enough to scan the opposite side of the gully. A man was moving steadily toward them. He hadn't seen them yet. His eyes were lowered, and his hat brim concealed his face as he searched the creek bed from the bank above. Something about the man seemed oddly familiar, and Aaron wished he could catch a good look at the man's face.

Aaron shifted slightly and pressed his companion behind him more firmly into the rocks. Aaron's eyes returned to the approaching man. He was tall, probably several inches over six feet, and dressed in denim much like Aaron and the woman were wearing. His face was averted, leaving Aaron only a glimpse of a dark beard and hair a little too long. He carried a lot of weight, and it didn't look like fat.

Aaron turned to check on the woman. She stared right past him and when he heard her gasp, he whirled back to face the intruder in time to see him standing with the rifle at his shoulder. His arm blocked Aaron's view, but Aaron suspected the woman had seen the gunman's face before he raised the rifle. Had she recognized him or was it the rifle pointed their direction that had startled her?

Aaron reached for the woman's hand and gave it a squeeze to reassure her. The intruder hadn't seen them; he wasn't even aiming the rifle toward the gully. He was using the gun as a telescope to scan the surrounding brush-covered landscape.

After several tense moments while Aaron scarcely dared breathe, he saw the man lower his gun and reach for something on his belt. A cellular phone! The creep was calling in reinforcements!

For just a moment Aaron considered using his own gun to take the other man out. That would buy him enough time to get the woman to safety and contact Blacker, but he couldn't do it. If he and the woman were discovered, then he'd resort to deadly force if necessary, but not until. Besides, he couldn't risk an exchange of fire when he had a civilian to look after.

"He's leaving." The woman's hushed whisper barely reached his ears.

Aaron nodded his head and watched as the man disappeared back the way he'd come. Aaron waited several minutes after the gunman was no longer in sight, then grabbed his companion's hand.

"Come on. Let's move." He hustled her abruptly down the creek bed. She didn't argue or hesitate and he was glad of that. Alicia would have been in tears long before this, Aaron mused.

The woman stumbled a few minutes later, then righted herself. Aaron reached for her arm, but she brushed away his help. "We can travel faster if we move independently," she whispered.

He nodded his head and released her arm. "Don't talk," he warned, though her whisper had barely reached him and he sensed she fully understood the necessity for silence.

She was right. They would both have better balance and control if he didn't have to help her along. He hoped she was really as tough and savvy as she appeared, but he wasn't willing to test her needlessly. He slowed his pace. A twisted ankle about now could cost them their lives, and if his suspicions were right, they didn't have much time. He glanced uneasily at the sky and made a few quick calculations. The truck and horsetrailer were a long way from here. They could probably reach his horse before anyone caught up to them, but then they'd be in the open and exposed if they tried to ride it anywhere. They couldn't stay in the gully either. As hiding places go, it was much too obvious.

Aaron slowed to a walk and felt, more than saw, the woman ease her stride beside him. He scanned the steep banks on either side of them until he spotted a place where the brush grew thick along the top. It would have to do. He pointed up the bank and started climbing.

CHAPTER TWO

Macady followed Aaron Westerman up the crumbling bank. He was hampered by his pistol, but still he moved quickly. At the top of the rise, he poked the gun into the holster at his waist, then slithered on his belly into the brush. Macady dived in right behind his boots. They lay motionless and silent. Macady sensed a tenseness in Aaron as though he were listening intently. She couldn't hear anything but the chirping of a cricket.

When Aaron reached for her hand, drawing her forward to lay snug against his side, she didn't resist. He placed his mouth next to her ear and his breath sent a tickle down the side of her throat. She felt her heartbeat accelerate. "We've got to move away from the wash and hide until dark."

She wasn't about to argue. She figured if anyone could get her out of this mess, it was Aaron Westerman. She hadn't seen him for years. He and her cousins Zack and Slade had been in high school while she was still in elementary. She'd grown up listening to Uncle Carson brag about their exploits and knew there wasn't a man anywhere who knew his way around sage brush deserts, old lava flows, or Idaho's rugged mountains better than her cousins and Aaron Westerman.

Moving deeper into the brush, Macady thought briefly about the risk of ticks crawling beneath her clothes, but decided to worry about that later. The powder-like dirt covered them both and a picture of a cool shower with plenty of shampoo flitted briefly through her mind. She ignored the thought and concentrated on crawling, sometimes on hands and knees and sometimes flat on her stomach. Her hand scraped across a prickly pear and she gasped, quickly swallowing her reaction to the sudden pain. With her other hand she pulled out the slender needles and bit her lip to prevent the sharp exclamation that rose in her throat.

Anger exploded inside her without warning. Since the first crack of the rifle, she'd done what she had to, first to stay on Tasha and control the frightened animal's panic, then to put as much distance as possible between herself and the maniac with a gun. There hadn't been time to think or feel. Every muscle in her body should be protesting her physical ordeal. Instead her stomach churned with rage. She wanted to strike back, make the sniper pay.

"Why didn't you shoot him?" she blurted out.

Aaron stopped and turned his head toward her. She could see the disapproval on his face and immediately regretted her outburst. She didn't want anyone shot; not herself, or Aaron, not even the man pursuing them. Silently, Aaron pointed toward a clump of brush beside a group of black boulders a short distance ahead. He moved forward again.

Her anger melted away as swiftly as it had arrived and was replaced by a terrible weariness. She sighed and scooted herself along, but much more slowly.

Aaron stopped short of the spot he'd indicated and broke off a stack of gray sage branches. When she paused beside him, he searched her face and frowned. "I don't think we have to worry about someone hearing us any longer, but we should play it safe by keeping our voices down." He indicated a sandy spot on the east side of the brush. "Let's start digging there."

"Digging?" Macady raised her eyebrows and looked sideways at Aaron.

"We're going to bury ourselves and wait for dark."

Dark? It wouldn't be dark for hours. The sun was forming short shadows on the east side of rocks. It was now afternoon, a long way from night. Macady sighed and started digging with the flat of her hand. It would take her until dark to dig a hole deep enough to crawl into, but since she couldn't think of a better plan and Uncle Carson had once said Aaron Westerman would be his first choice for a partner if he ever found himself stranded in rough country, she'd do whatever Aaron told her—for now anyway.

Aaron removed a hunting knife from a leather sheath on his belt and dug with rapid movements. She wished she had some kind of tool. Her hand brushed her waist and she realized she did have a tool she could dig with. Macady unbuckled her belt and grasped the large square buckle in her hand. Her cousin Ben probably never envisioned it being used for a shovel when he gave it to her.

She paused to wipe perspiration from her face and was startled when Aaron shoved her into the hole she had dug and began covering her.

"Aaron, what is it?" There was a kind of frenzy in his movements. He threw himself in his own hole next to hers and scrambled to pull the remainder of the dirt and brush over them.

"You called me Aaron." He sounded puzzled, but she suspected he was avoiding answering her question. She could just make out his face through the cover and saw his brows raised as though he'd asked a question. "I must have missed introductions back there."

"Aaron Westerman, are you saying you don't know who I am?" She wasn't certain whether he really didn't know who she was, or if he might be trying to distract her. "Uncle Carson misled me. He said you were the smartest of the Westerman boys."

"Uncle Carson! You couldn't possibly be the little Jackson girl!"

"I am. Macady Louise Jackson, and I'm not so little."

"No, you're not. But the last time I saw you was before your father—"

"Your mission farewell is the last time I remember seeing you." She ignored his unfinished statement. She never talked about her father.

"You remember? What were you, about ten years old?"

"Thirteen."

He chuckled softly. "What have you been doing since then?"

"Mostly going to school. I graduated from college a few weeks ago and accepted a temporary job with the *Times* so I can be near Mom this summer. How about you?"

"I finished college and went to work for the Forest Service, got married—" He stopped speaking, and held his head as though listening to something. Goosebumps crawled across Macady's skin.

Was the gunman coming? Had they disturbed a rattler sunning himself on the rocks? She cocked her head. Then she heard it, too—the steady beat of rotary blades. A helicopter! From the sound, she knew it was coming in low. No doubt looking for her. And from Aaron's reaction, she knew it didn't belong to Search and Rescue.

Aaron tensed as the chopper reversed directions and swept slowly back up the length of the dry wash. He and Macady hadn't gotten as far from the old stream bed as he had hoped before the aerial search had begun. There was no telling how many pairs of eyes glued to binoculars were sweeping the brush searching for them. Actually the men in the helicopter were probably looking for just one person. He didn't think they knew their man on the ground had fired at the wrong person. Poor Macady, it had been her misfortune to be in the wrong place at the wrong time.

He turned toward her. He could see one side of her face. It was still and showed no emotion. If he could see her eyes, he bet they'd be full of terror. Maybe not. Not once had she reacted as he had expected. She'd gotten herself away from where the gunman had expected to find her. She'd been prepared to go on the offensive to protect herself, and she'd matched him stride for stride as they'd moved down the gully. Even now she was lying motionless beneath enough dirt and brush to send most of the women he knew into hysterics. He winced, trying to picture Alicia beside him, or his sister-in-law, Denise.

He couldn't believe little Macady Jackson had grown up to be this tall, cool-headed woman. They'd been in the same ward when they were kids, and her cousins had been his best friends. Zack and Slade had had a lot of little brothers, six of them, and he could remember all those little boys sitting on the front bench in the chapel with Macady smack in the middle. He had a vague recollection of ruffles and lace with curls hanging down her back. From where he and the older boys sat, he would see her pinch one of her cousins. Before the deacons were through passing the sacrament, the whole row would be pinching, poking, and giggling until her father would reach over the bench and pick her up. She'd spent the rest of the meeting curled in his lap as sweet and innocent as could be. The next Sunday would be the same.

The curls had been for Sunday only. The rest of the week she wore her hair in two fat braids and the ruffles and lace were exchanged for shorts or jeans. A smile twitched the corner of his mouth as he thought of Macady, a skinny little girl with her hands on her hips and her elbows akimbo shouting her indignation at one of her cousins for shooting a couple of rabbits. The cousin had tossed back some insult, and she'd blacked his eye and bloodied his mouth before Slade managed to pull her off his little brother.

Aaron's peripheral vision picked up a distant movement to the right. He strained to see better and wished he dared to pull out his field glasses. Seconds later he watched one antelope leap over brush, then another. The chopper had scared up a small herd that he hoped wouldn't come too close to his and Macady's hiding place. If the animals spotted them and panicked, their behavior would be noted by the men in the helicopter. He watched, holding his breath, until he could no longer see them without raising his head and was satisfied their paths wouldn't cross.

The afternoon stretched out, long and hot. He was thirsty and knew Macady must be too. There was a canteen hanging on his saddle, but it wouldn't do them any good. He wondered if the drug runners had found his horse. He'd left him ground hitched.

Chances were the helicopter had scared him out of the draw and he'd headed for home. That should stir up some excitement if Macady's horse made it back to the store and his to her uncle's ranch, both saddled, both riderless. Ben, the youngest Jackson boy, had been the only one home when he'd borrowed the horse. The boy was seventeen or eighteen, old enough to know to call the sheriff's office, Aaron hoped.

"You okay, Macady?" he spoke softly.

"Yes. You?"

"Sure. I wish I'd brought my canteen instead of leaving it with my horse, though."

"The dirt and brush help. I'm glad you picked a shady spot to bury us."

"Glad to please. I always wanted to be buried with my boots on, but I hadn't expected it to happen this soon."

He thought he heard a faint giggle, then Macady was quiet for a long time. He listened to the throb of the chopper approaching and receding once more. It wasn't following the creek bed anymore, but seemed to be sectoring the vast area on either side of the wash.

"Do you think Tasha made it back to the store?" Aaron had to strain to hear Macady's voice.

"Your horse?"

"Yes."

"Most horses head for home if they lose their riders. Mine should be traveling the same direction. I borrowed him from Carson."

"I don't know if Tasha was hit. With the reins trailing, she could trip and hurt herself."

"We can only hope they both make their way safely back." Aaron noted that she hadn't voiced any concern about her own predicament, but she was worried about her horse. As a child she'd been tender-hearted where animals were concerned, so he shouldn't feel this sense of surprise. He knew Alicia would be crying uncontrollably by now, and it wouldn't be her horse she'd be worrying about. He squirmed a fraction; he shouldn't compare Macady to Alicia. Alicia had never shown him much loyalty, but he'd never felt that that diminished the loyalty he owed her.

"I've been in your mother's store quite a few times since I came back to Idaho. How come I haven't seen you?"

"I've only been back a week."

"Oh, I assumed you still lived with your mother."

"I guess I do, but I've been away at school. Mom needs help right now. I interned with the *Twin Falls Times* last summer, so I was able to get on there again part time."

"Are you a reporter?" That's all he needed. First he'd been spotted by the drug runners and forced to hide out all day in the desert giving them plenty of time to move their operation. Tomorrow he'd see the whole fiasco in print.

"No, I'm in advertising. I sell ads, then I design and lay them out."

Aaron expelled his breath softly. Maybe there was a chance she'd see reason. "I'd rather you didn't tell anyone at the paper about this little experience," he began carefully.

"I'm not anxious to see this in print either," Macady took her time, "but this is too serious to go unreported. I assume the man who shot at me and the ones hunting us in the helicopter think they have a good reason for their action, a reason that's illegal. I got a good look at the gunman in the gully; I never saw him before in my life. Don't you think the public should be warned there's someone out here who shoots at strangers?"

"He wasn't shooting at you. Not really. He was shooting at the law."

"What?"

"I told you, I'm a deputy. I discovered something our friend would rather we didn't know about. You were just unlucky enough to appear about the time I disappeared, and from a distance you looked like me." Macady didn't make any response and Aaron's mind had drifted to plans for making their way to his truck when she finally spoke.

"I won't tell anyone about this experience. I don't want our names in the paper before you put those men in jail."

"Good choice. They don't know there are two of us, and you'll be a whole lot safer if they think the only witness to their little operation and attempt at murder is me."

"I don't like the idea of anyone trying to shoot you either." Macady's voice sounded strained. "Whatever made you decide to be a cop?"

"Originally I meant to be a forest ranger. Right after I got out of college I got a job with the park service in Yellowstone, but Alicia hated West Yellowstone and refused to live there. Her parents lived in Colorado, and I took her back. I couldn't find a forestry job, but there was an opening for a game warden so I took it. I'd had some law enforcement training, so I took some more classes and discovered I liked it. Then I went to work for the sheriff's office in Boulder. Later I applied for a job with the Twin Falls county sheriff's office."

"Is Alicia your wife?"

"Is. Was. I don't know how to answer that question. She died a year ago, but we were married in the temple so I guess she's still my wife."

"I'm sorry, I didn't know."

"It's okay. I've put it behind me. It's the future that matters. I've got a four-year-old daughter, Kelsey, and it's her future that concerns me."

"You have a daughter?" Aaron could hear the surprise in Macady's voice.

"Why does that surprise you?"

"I don't know. I guess because I remember you as a teenager with my cousins, then today. It's hard for me to think of you as a father."

"It's almost dark." Aaron was glad to change the subject. Even after a year he found any discussion involving Alicia difficult.

"I haven't heard the helicopter for quite a while. Do you think they've given up?" Macady's voice sounded hoarse and Aaron wished again he had water to give her.

"I don't know, but I doubt it. They may have gone to refuel and will be back with a search light. They might be packing up and moving, or they might have dreamed up some new tactic to cut us off before we can make it back to civilization."

The helicopter hadn't reappeared by the time Aaron decided it was dark enough to move. After lying still so many hours, his muscles protested as he crawled out of his hiding place. He could see Macady was having the same problem and he reached down to give her a hand. She'd taken a fall from her horse as well and was probably hurting worse than he was. She let go of his hand and sat down on the ground.

"Do you think you can walk?" They'd be in real trouble if she couldn't.

"Sure, just give me a minute." She reached her fingers toward her toes, then turned over and assumed a crawling position. She straightened one leg, lifted it and pointed her toes, then lowered her knee to the ground. She repeated the action with her other leg.

"What are you doing?"

"Stretch exercises."

"You better consider your muscles stretched. We've got to get moving." But he took a moment to flex his shoulders and twist at the waist a couple of times before stepping into the brush. Macady was right behind him.

The desert was quiet, too quiet in Aaron's opinion. He decided against returning to the creek bed. It would provide easier walking and be darker, give them better visual cover, but it was also the most likely place to stumble into a trap. They'd have to avoid open areas and seek out the heaviest ground cover. With the setting of the sun, the night had turned cool, and they would no longer have to watch for snakes.

The closest telephone would be at Hazel Jackson's store, a distance of about five miles, but to get there they'd have to cross the gully and a lot of flat rocky ground with little cover. It was also the most obvious direction to take. They'd have to try to reach his truck, five miles in the opposite direction, and hope it hadn't been discovered.

His admiration for Macady grew the further they hiked. She kept up with him and never complained. She displayed a natural affinity for disappearing into shadows and avoiding high spots where she might be silhouetted against the softer black of the sky. She was obviously in good physical condition; her knowledge of exercise and the easy way she moved indicated regular workouts of some kind.

Aaron made sure they rested at regular intervals, but they couldn't afford long stops. They had close to five miles to cover over rugged terrain.

At long last, a slight rise ahead looked familiar. His truck should be on the other side, about a quarter of a mile down a hill. He'd left it in a juniper grove well off the dirt road which wound through the foothills.

Aaron dropped to the ground to approach the crest at a crawl. Macady didn't have to be told to do the same. For some reason that pleased him. He signaled for her to stay back when he peeked over the top. At first he saw nothing but the side of a brush-covered hill, just like dozens of hills they'd already crossed. A few high, distant stars and a tiny sliver of moon didn't provide much light which Aaron considered an advantage, all things considered.

At the bottom, he could just pick out a darker shape. He carefully swept the area with his eyes, then repeated the motion. There didn't seem to be anyone about, but he'd have to get closer to be certain. He'd go down and check it out, then if everything was clear, he'd come back for Macady. If it were a trap, the people pursuing them might get him, but they'd still be ignorant of Macady's presence.

He scooted back to her side and explained in low tones what he planned to do. To his surprise, she shook her head.

"You'll be safe here, and I won't be long," he argued.

"I'm going with you."

"I don't want you taking chances." She'd cooperated fully until now. What could he say to convince her to stay put?

"That's an order," he growled.

"I don't take orders."

"You will this time." He knew immediately he'd handled this all wrong; he shouldn't have mentioned orders to a Jackson, and he had a hunch this female Jackson was even less inclined to take orders than her male cousins.

"And if I don't, what are you going to do? Arrest me?"

"No, of course not. I didn't mean to get high-handed. I just want to keep you safe."

"Aaron, we can keep each other a lot safer if we both go down. I can't see anything from up here, and down there two sets of eyes are going to see more than one. You said they're only looking for one of us, so if we both go down, the element of surprise will be on our side."

He didn't like her argument, but they couldn't stay flat on their bellies on the top of this hill arguing all night.

"Okay. See that clump of brush on the right about half way down the hill? You go that far and no further, got that?"

"Unless there's trouble."

"Especially if there's trouble. Even if you hear gun shots, don't come looking for me. Stay out of sight until these people are gone. They don't know about you, so they won't hang around if I'm out of the picture."

Aaron jammed his hat lower across his brow, checked his gun holster, then slid forward. Once over the top, he remained crouched below the height of the brush. Macady didn't make a sound, but he could feel her right on his heels.

Aaron moved a few yards, then stopped. He had a premonition something wasn't right. He'd experienced the feeling before and had learned to listen to this silent call for caution. He wasn't certain whether he enjoyed the sixth sense some lawmen were reputed to have or whether the warnings he sometimes sensed came through the Holy Ghost. Either way, he trusted the feeling. Slowly he surveyed the dark patch of trees ahead for any sign of trouble.

"There!" Macady's hand grasped his arm. "To the left of the trees, about forty feet."

He strained to see what she saw. Finally he picked out a spot that appeared more dense than the brush. It might be just a rock. But it wasn't. A tiny point of red told him all he needed to know. Someone was waiting a short distance from the truck, and while he waited he'd decided to have a smoke.

CHAPTER THREE

They'd traveled all this distance for nothing. There was no radio and no water waiting for them. He felt Macady tug his hand and the movement snapped him out of his black disappointment. He wasn't giving up. They were alive and still undetected—he'd get them out of this mess yet.

More than ten miles separated them from Carson Jackson's ranch, and they'd already hiked over five. They were both young and strong. They'd make it, but they'd have to use the old foothill road so they could move quickly. Otherwise the sun would catch them before they were halfway there. He'd have to be particularly alert in case the drug smugglers had someone watching the road. He squeezed Macady's fingers, ducked low, and led her back over the crown of the hill.

Macady wished she had on running shoes instead of boots. She had a hunch she had blisters on top of blisters. Pride was the only thing keeping her from limping. She glanced enviously at Aaron's boots; they sported a lower heel than her fancy riding ones and the toes weren't pointed. They resembled motorcycle boots, only shorter. With her next paycheck, she'd buy herself a pair like Aaron's that wouldn't cripple her if she had to take another long hike. She hoped she'd live long enough to need another pair.

She could imagine the worry and fear her mother must be experiencing about now and how helpless she would feel. The moment Tasha appeared without her rider, Mom would have been frustrated because she couldn't ride out to search for

Macady. She hadn't even been able to attend Macady's graduation ten days ago thanks to a gallstone that had landed her in the hospital two days before the big event.

Macady's heart twisted painfully. She'd never thought she'd be thankful for her mother's physical problems, but now she was glad there was no way she could stumble into the same situation she and Aaron had.

It seemed like they'd been walking all night. At least they could stand up straight now and that helped, though she understood how much more vulnerable it made them. Aaron said speed was what counted. They might have to run part of the way in order to beat the sun, but she doubted she could go any faster than the pace Aaron was setting just walking. If she had a drink and her running shoes, she'd love to see if she could outrun him. She had been collecting trophies and T-shirts for both sprinting and distance since junior high. If she survived this night, it would be a while before her feet healed. She sighed.

"What's the matter?" Aaron sounded concerned.

"Nothing. I was just thinking about my mother and wishing there were some way to let her know I'm alive and on my way."

"We'll make it."

"I'm counting on it. How about you? Will your mother be worried?"

"No. Mom and Dad aren't around. They're serving a mission in New Zealand." Macady's reference to her mother had annoyed Aaron for some reason he didn't understand, unless it was because he'd found himself thinking about Alicia several times since he and Macady had been thrown together. He'd resented the way Alicia's first thought had always been for her mother.

"I wonder why Mom never mentioned your parents' mission?"

"She might not know. They don't live around here anymore. When Dad retired, they moved to southern Utah."

"Oh—I think Mom did mention they'd moved quite a while

ago. What about your little girl? Where is she?"

"My brother Matt's wife, Denise, keeps her while I'm at work."

"Won't they wonder why you didn't come for her?"

"Not really. They know I sometimes have to work a double shift. When that happens, I don't pick her up until morning."

Macady thought about what Aaron had said, not the words so much as his tone of voice. There was a hint of anger. No, anger wasn't the right word. He sounded defensive. There was love and pride when he spoke of Kelsey, but there was something else too. It must be hard to raise a little girl alone, and he probably felt guilty about all the hours he had to leave her with his sister-in-law.

"Macady," Aaron's gravelly whisper sounded harsh to her ears and brought her back to an awareness of her surroundings and the deep fear that hid beneath her thirst and sore feet. "The bridge is just ahead. I think we'd better find another way across the canyon."

Of course! If their pursuers were still searching for them, the bridge would be the ideal place for an ambush, but how else could they get across the narrow canyon? Like the Snake River canyon further north, this smaller canyon had been etched out of stone by running water. A small stream, ideal for fishing, traversed its length and eventually plunged over a stone ledge to join the Snake.

"Let's hope they don't know this country as well as we do," Aaron continued, "and that I can still find the trail your cousins and I always used to get down there to fish."

"It's this way." Macady stepped off the road. She'd forgotten about the trail, just as she'd forgotten about a lot of the places where her father used to take her. He'd betrayed not only her mother, but Macady, too, and she had tried to put him completely out of her mind. That included all those places that had been "their places" back when she'd believed her family was a forever family.

The trail wasn't as difficult to find as she'd feared. Perhaps her cousins still came here. She peered over the rim of the canyon into blackness. As she remembered, climbing the trail in broad daylight was risky enough. Doing it in the dark didn't bear thinking about.

"Ready?"

"Yes," she answered, and prayed it was the truth.

"I'll go first. Turn around."

She knew the routine. Descending backward, her balance would be more natural and she could use her hands as well as her feet to secure her position.

A rock slipped beneath her boot and rattled its way down the slope. She held her breath and sensed Aaron's tension as they waited for a reaction to the sound. When none came, they moved on. Macady grasped for finger and toeholds as she worked her way downward. The distance seemed much further than she remembered.

When they both finally stood at the foot of the cliff, Aaron whispered, "We need water. I don't think we should risk drinking out of the stream, but there's a spring almost under the bridge. It's probably safe; I've been drinking out of it all my life."

"At this point I'm willing to risk giardia."

"Okay, let's go. We'll get a drink then backtrack to here to cross the creek."

He didn't have to say they shouldn't talk, not even whisper, as they approached the bridge, but she knew that's what he meant. He moved cautiously across the rocks and she moved soundlessly beside him.

"He must be part cat," she thought as he moved unerringly through the blackness. She stumbled once and he grasped her arm. He stopped and listened, then clasping her hand, he led her upward a few feet. She couldn't see the water but heard the faint tinkling sound. He indicated she should kneel.

Gratefully she scooped up a handful of water and pressed it to her lips. Swallowing was pain and pleasure like none she'd ever experienced before. Hastily she reached for another handful. As much dribbled off her chin and ran down her neck as trickled down her throat. She wanted more, but knew Aaron was thirsty, too, and he couldn't reach the water until she moved.

They took turns drinking until Macady felt Aaron's hand come down on her shoulder, drawing her back. He stood still with his hand circling her upper arm for several minutes. His rigid body communicated tension and she strained to hear whatever he'd heard. It didn't take long until she too caught the rhythmic tread of footsteps on the bridge. Whoever was up there wore soft-soled shoes, not boots.

Another sound reached her ears like the metallic clatter of an aluminum can bouncing across rocks. More than one person waited on the bridge above. Macady could feel her pulse pounding against the point where Aaron's hand grasped her arm. One kicked rock, a cough, or just a second's bad luck could give away their position. Adrenaline pumped through her veins and when Aaron moved, she matched him step for step.

Slowly he eased their way down to the stream. Macady forgot to breathe as they passed under the bridge. Aaron's steps never faltered as he led the way close beside the stream where the ground was softer, less likely to betray the sound of their boots. They were more than a quarter mile from the bridge when Aaron stepped onto a rock in the ankle deep water. He still held her hand and she followed him across the stones.

There were a few hardy bushes on this side of the narrow canyon and the shadows appeared deeper and darker. Macady remembered the canyon curved slightly at this point. They would soon be beyond where even the beam of a searchlight could catch them.

The climb to the top of the canyon wasn't as steep now, but the knowledge that their pursuers were nearby heightened the tension.

Aaron did some quick mental calculations as he crawled out of the canyon onto the desert floor. They were a good eight miles from Carson's ranch with only a couple of hours of darkness left.

They'd have to circle away from the bridge for some distance, then cut back to the road. That would add another half mile. They'd practically have to run to even reach the irrigated part of the ranch before dawn, let alone make it to the house. He turned back to offer his hand to Macady to help her over the rocky canyon lip, but she was already beside him, moving right with him.

It was rough going until they made their way back to the road. Avoiding it altogether would reduce their risk of detection but slow them down, and Aaron knew they couldn't stay holed up on the desert without water. The drink from the spring had helped, but it wouldn't carry them through another day. He approached the road cautiously, and when all seemed peaceful, he stepped onto the dusty track and increased his pace.

An hour passed and he estimated they'd covered a little more than half of the distance. A faint hint of color began to show to the east, and Aaron wondered if Macady could handle a faster gait. He wasn't sure he could, but he hadn't come this far to not give it his best shot.

"Aaron." The whisper was so low he almost missed it. "I've got to take my boots off." Macady sank down beside the road and began tugging at a boot.

"You can't!" He dropped down beside her and reached to still her movements. "We can't quit now. We've only got another three or four miles to go."

"It's going to be light in a half hour," she responded calmly. "We're two miles from the first hayfield, but we can make it if we run. I can barely walk in these boots."

"You're going to take them off and run?" His voice was incredulous. He glanced down at her feet and winced. He hadn't given a thought to her western riding boots. How had she made it this far? But barefoot?

"It will be okay. The road is soft dust until we reach the irrigated land where it's packed and hard, or muddy. I can make it."

Aaron felt a wave of helpless fear wash over him. No one

should be out on the desert without boots, but she was right; she couldn't possibly run in high-heeled, pinch-toed riding boots. He wished he were a bigger man and could carry her, but trying to carry Macady would be absurd. He'd already noticed that when she stood before him, her eyes were level with his own. Reluctantly he withdrew his hand from her arm and knelt to help her draw them off.

"Hide them under a bush," she whispered. She couldn't carry them in her arms, so she'd have to abandon them.

Aaron let Macady set the speed and was hard pressed to remain at her side. This woman could run, he thought admiringly. He found himself wishing he could abandon his gun, binoculars, and the weight of his boots, too.

Streaks of pink and gold were setting the sky ablaze when he saw a familiar butte. The road wound around its base, and on the other side were Carson's hayfields. They were going to make it. Once they reached the green field, they would have cover and shade, transportation and water, too, if one of the Jackson boys turned up to set the sprinklers or start mowing.

He glanced at Macady. He could see her clearly now. Fatigue showed on her face and in every line of her body. A wave of tenderness welled in his heart, but he quickly dismissed it as admiration for a job well done by someone who had shared a traumatic experience.

A sound reached his ears and he lunged for Macady to pull her into the sparse brush beside the road. His eyes searched for rocks that would provide some protection. There, twenty feet off the road stood a pile of boulders. Without boots, Macady would be next to helpless off the road, but she didn't hesitate to move in the direction he indicated. Before they could conceal themselves, a wall of riders rounded the butte and rode straight for them.

Aaron drew his gun as he stepped in front of Macady. The riders were immense dark silhouettes against the rising sun. A hasty count showed nine horses. The front rider cradled a rifle in the crook of his arm and the outline of gun scabbards could be seen on every saddle.

"Macady!" A gruff voice barked and Aaron heard her gasp behind him. Then she was off and running full tilt toward the nearest horse. Aaron tightened his grip on the Smith & Wesson and took a step after her before the voice registered. Carson! Old Carson Jackson and all of his boys—Zack, Slade, Web, Daniel, Will, Jeremiah, David, and the youngest, Ben—had come after Macady. He should have known they would. The Jacksons looked after their own. Even though Carson's younger brother, Spence had divorced Macady's mother Hazel, the rest of the Jacksons still considered Hazel and Macady part of the family.

"That you, Aaron?" A tall man with hair just beginning to recede stepped forward to clasp him in a fierce bear hug. With bleary eyes and aching muscles, Aaron returned the bruising embrace his old friend gave him. He'd only seen Zack once, and then only briefly, since returning to Idaho. Zack had spent most of the past year expanding the family holdings into Owyhee county. He and Mary had only recently returned to their newly built home on the Jackson ranch.

"How'd you lose your horses?" Slade, taller than Zack and wider through the shoulders, looked at Aaron with narrowed eyes. Slade had made it clear he didn't wish to renew their old friendship. He'd barely concealed his hostility on the few occasions their paths had crossed since they'd found themselves once more in the same community. "Only time I ever knew a man to lose both horses when he took a lady riding was when he was up to no good."

"Where are your boots, girl?" Carson roared.

The man stood six and a half feet tall and with his huge barrel chest easily intimidated most people, but Macady didn't even flinch. She grinned and answered saucily, "You're the one who taught me to get rid of excess baggage." Standing on her toes, she gave her uncle a resounding kiss on his leathery cheek.

"You didn't tell me you were taking Macady," Ben approached

Aaron. "You said it was official business."

"Monkey business, most likely," Slade's voice cut in.

"Hey, wait a minute." Aaron didn't like the innuendo he was hearing in Slade's voice. "Macady's been shot at, buried in the desert, and hiked more than fifteen miles with blisters on her feet and had nothing to eat or drink since yesterday. Don't you think the explanations can wait?"

"Shot at?" Carson's big, shaggy head came up and a dark scowl covered his face. "Who shot at Macady?" His sons turned silent stares toward Macady, then Aaron.

"Drug runners." Aaron knew there'd be no pussyfooting around Carson. The old man was big as a grizzly and honest to the bone, and he didn't let anyone else get away with anything less than the truth either.

"Let's go, Uncle Carson," Macady cut in as her uncle began to bristle. "They're still out here looking for us. We'll explain everything when we get to the ranch."

"The first thing you'll do, young lady, is call your mother." Carson boosted her into Ben's saddle as he scolded. The boy climbed on behind her and Aaron rode double with Zack. "Daniel! Web! You two ride ahead. Slade, ride up that butte and take a look around." Carson bellowed and Aaron smiled. Aaron represented the law, but it would never occur to the old man to defer to anyone else on Jackson land. If anyone was waiting to ambush them, they'd think twice before they took on Carson and his army of sons.

"Is Tasha safe?" Aaron heard Macady ask and Carson answer, "'Course she's all right. That horse has better sense than some people I know." Then Aaron found himself battling to keep his eyes open and stay upright in the saddle until they reached the ranch house.

When they stopped at the corral behind the barn, Aaron slid to the ground on unsteady legs. He could see Macady had fallen asleep with Ben's arms securely wrapped around her. When Aaron moved to take her from the boy, Slade beat him to it, and

Aaron felt a tug of annoyance as Macady curled in the big man's arms and snuggled against his chest. For the second time in one night, he found himself wishing he were as big as the Jacksons, all of whom topped six feet by at least a couple of inches.

The sun was setting when Macady awoke. She struggled to a sitting position and gazed around the room, owlishly blinking her eyes to clear her sleep-befuddled head. A mortar board with a "Class of '95" tassel hung from one post at the foot of the bed, and a letterman's jacket was draped across the other. A shelf at eye level mixed rodeo, basketball, and seminary memorabilia. She recognized Ben's bedroom and remembered she hadn't called her mother. She must have slept all day.

As she stood, she noticed she had on an unfamiliar nightgown, presumably one of Aunt Lucille's. On Aunt Lucille it most likely reached her ankles, but on Macady it left a long expanse of bare legs. There wasn't any sign of her own clothes. They were probably being washed, and Macady was stuck with nothing to wear but a too-small, paper-thin, cotton nightie.

Macady sighed and moved toward Ben's closet. She pulled out a T-shirt which sported an oversize pickup truck with huge balloon tires. She rummaged for sweat pants. She hated to borrow first and ask later, but she needed to call her mother. Of course, Uncle Carson had already told Mom she'd been found, but Mom would worry until she actually talked to Macady. The sweat pants bagged around her ankles and the shirt nearly reached her knees. If she had to borrow men's clothes, she wished they were Aaron's. His would probably fit. The thought of wearing Aaron's clothes gave her an odd feeling. She quickly shook it off as she went in search of a telephone.

Macady walked down the stairs and stepped through double doors into a large family room. She stopped. The whole family was there: Uncle Carson, Aunt Lucille, the cousins, the married cousins' wives, and half a dozen toddlers. Mom was there, too.

"Macady!" She turned to her mother who was ensconced in

Uncle Carson's favorite Lazy Boy. Her mother held out her arms and Macady ran to her. She struggled to keep her emotions in check as her mother hugged her. It had been years since she'd cried, but now she had no idea if she or her mother was responsible for the river running down their cheeks.

When Uncle Carson cleared his throat, she gave him a watery smile. She looked around at her cousins and gave them each a smile. Then her smile faltered. There was one too many people in the room. Standing at the back beside Aunt Lucille and three cousins' wives was her father. She quickly averted her eyes. Why was he here? She didn't want to be in the same room with him. She knew he sometimes visited Uncle Carson, but she'd always been careful that her visits never coincided with his.

"Well?" Uncle Carson folded his arms and indicated his patience was at an end.

"Well, what?" Macady kept her eyes on her uncle and avoided the area where her father stood.

"What happened out there?" Uncle Carson scowled and jerked his head in the direction of the desert.

"Were you hurt?" Her mother questioned softly.

A lump rose in Macady's throat. She wanted to tell her mother and Uncle Carson and even her cousins what had happened and that she loved them, but she didn't want her father there. She'd felt so comforted and wrapped in love until she'd seen him.

Her eyes moved from face to face, carefully avoiding one intent pair of eyes. With a start, she realized she was looking for someone. "Where's Aaron?" she blurted into the expectant silence.

"Sheriff sent a car for him. Said he had work to do." Zack answered her question with a minimum of words.

"Young scamp didn't have much to say," Carson growled. "Said he'd leave the tellin' to you while he went after some folks that needed their butts kicked all the way to jail. Blacker told me some weeks ago that Westerman's about the best deputy he ever saw, so how come he let some riffraff take a shot at you?"

Macady told them then of being shot at and her trek across the desert with Aaron. She repeated Aaron's request that they not talk about their experience until the man who shot at her was behind bars.

"Did you get a good look at him?" Carson demanded to know.

"Yes, he took off his hat and wiped his forehead with the back of his hand while Aaron and I were hiding in the gully. I saw his face clearly."

Ben and Slade wanted to get their rifles and go hunting, but Carson insisted Aaron and the sheriff have their chance first. Macady shivered. She didn't like thinking about Aaron going back out there, and she certainly didn't want her cousins meeting the sniper.

"We've got Macady back," boomed Uncle Carson. He walked over and put a beefy arm around her shoulder. "She's safe, but I don't believe it was all her and that Westerman kid's doing. They were strong and plucky, but I expect the Lord had a hand in their escape, and I've a mind to thank him proper." He sank to his knees. In seconds the whole family joined him.

Macady's mother didn't leave her chair, but she tucked her hand in her daughter's as Macady knelt beside her. From the corner of her eye Macady saw her father slip quietly out the door. She was glad he hadn't tried to talk to her.

CHAPTER FOUR

Macady wiped the glass of the cooler where sandwiches and soft drinks were displayed in her mother's store. She looked up when the shop door opened and smiled to see Aaron walk in. It had been three days since their shared adventure, and she'd found herself thinking about him with alarming frequency.

The little girl clinging to his hand had to be Kelsey. Her long dark curls were the color of unsweetened chocolate and her face appeared to be all eyes. Macady thought she looked small for a four-year-old and there was something about the child that made her want to protect her, though what she needed protection from Macady had no idea.

Her glance went to Aaron. She could see a resemblance between the two, but not so much anyone would automatically assume they were related. Aaron's eyes twinkled and Macady felt her heart beat faster. No, that couldn't be. Aaron was an old friend, nothing more. Even if he was the best looking man she'd ever met, she didn't need him or any other man in her life. She only imagined some invisible link between them because of their desert ordeal a few days ago and their shared childhood.

"Hi!" Aaron grinned. "I just thought I'd drop by and make certain you've recovered." He lifted a couple of soft drink cans from the cooler and popped the tab on one before handing it to his daughter.

"I'm doing fine. How about you?"

"After drinking a gallon of water and sleeping the clock around I'm great."

Macady laughed. "That's all I did for forty-eight hours—sleep and drink. I still can't seem to get enough liquid." She put away her towel and walked to the counter where Kelsey had wandered. She crouched down beside the child and said, "My name is Macady Jackson. If it's all right with your daddy, I'd like to show you something in the barn behind the store."

Kelsey looked toward her father, then back to Macady, but she didn't speak.

"It's all right, punkin," Aaron smiled his encouragement. "Macady is an old friend of Daddy's."

"He pulled my hair when I was about your size," Macady whispered in a loud aside to the girl. Kelsey frowned uncertainly.

"No fair," Aaron laughed. "You have to tell her the whole story. Tell her how you hid up in the apple tree and pelted me with green apples, then ran." He turned to his daughter. "I was trying to catch her and when I almost caught up, I grabbed, and all I got was a handful of her braids. She told her big cousins, Zack and Slade, I'd pulled her hair, and they knocked me down and sat on me."

"Did they hurt you?" Kelsey looked worried.

"No, honey." He picked her up in his arms and gave her a hug. "They just liked to remind me real often that they were bigger than me. Now let's go see what Macady has out back to show you."

"Mom, could you watch the store a few minutes?" Macady waited for an affirmative answer from Hazel before leading the way out a side door. Not far from the house stood a small barn and a couple of acres of pasture. She walked toward the structure with Aaron and Kelsey beside her. When she opened the barn door, four kittens raced to meet her.

"Kitties!" Kelsey squealed with excitement and demanded to be let down. She picked up one after the other to bestow hugs and kisses. Macady was pleased to see how gently she held each one.

"Are they all yours?" The little girl turned wonder-filled eyes toward Macady.

"Yes, they're mine." She turned questioning eyes to Aaron. He shook his head and mouthed 'no.' "Denise is allergic to cats," he clarified.

Macady understood. Kelsey couldn't have a pet that would be left alone every day while she went to her aunt's house.

"See that big cat over there?" Macady pointed to a large calico cat stretched out on a feed bag. "She's the mama cat. She doesn't mind if we come visit her babies, but she doesn't want us to take them away. She knows they're still too little to go away to live with someone else. When the kittens are bigger, I'll find homes for three of them. The other one is yours. It can stay here and live so its mama won't get lonesome, and you can come visit it anytime your daddy can bring you."

"It's mine? Really?" Kelsey's face shone with excitement.

"Whichever one you like."

Macady cast Aaron an amused glance as Kelsey tried to decide which kitten should be her very own. His answering smile told her he approved of the gift she'd given his child and that he appreciated the avoidance of a problem with Denise. They stood companionably, watching the child play with the kittens, until a beeper sounded. Macady looked at Aaron and was startled to see him remove a pager from his belt.

"I'm off duty, but—" He shrugged his shoulders. "Mind if I use your phone?"

"No, go ahead." She watched long strides carry him back to the store, then she knelt beside Kelsey to discuss the merits of each kitten.

In moments Aaron was back and Macady sensed something was wrong. The indulgent father and the dedicated lawman were on a collision course. He wasted no time filling Macady in on his predicament.

"When we returned to the airfield in the desert, I found everything gone. The only sign that I hadn't imagined the whole thing was an empty oil drum, a lot of tracks, and spent shell casings on the ridge where you were fired at. The drug runners have apparently abandoned the landing strip. Sheriff Blacker said one of his deputies found something important near where I had parked my truck, and he wants me to meet him there."

She read the question in his eyes and answered before he asked. "Go ahead. Kelsey can stay here with me until you get back."

"Are you sure?"

"Just go." He smiled his thanks and stooped to tell his daughter the sheriff needed him and that he'd back as soon as possible. Macady watched him race for the gray Ford F150 parked in front of the store and felt a small hand slip inside hers. Why did it feel as though that hand had slipped inside her heart?

Aaron slowed for the bridge and remembered the terror that had gripped him when the men waiting to ambush him or Macady had revealed their presence. As a lawman, protecting innocent civilians was his business, but there had been something personal that night in the feelings that swamped him. He'd felt a need to keep Macady safe, much the way he'd felt a compulsive wave of protectiveness for Kelsey the first time he'd held her and again when Alicia died, leaving his little girl motherless.

The feeling disturbed him. Macady disturbed him. His thoughts had been of her too often the past three days, and he didn't like it. He didn't want to think about a woman, not even one as different from his wife as Macady seemed to be. Though on the surface, Macady seemed to be nothing like Alicia, in one way they were alike. Both had strong family attachments—and Macady had an awful lot of family.

Aaron adjusted his dark glasses and let his eyes drift ahead. He marveled at the quiet serenity of the desert. It was hard to believe that such a short time ago it had been the scene of a massive manhunt, and he had been the prey—he and Macady.

He slowed when he spotted the sheriff's vehicle. In minutes he was parked a few feet from where he'd unloaded his horse and left his truck that fateful day. He thought briefly of the chestnut he'd ridden and was glad the gelding and Macady's mare had made their way safely back to Carson's corral, alerting the Jacksons to the fact he and Macady were in trouble.

He scowled, thinking of Slade's suspicious reception. Of course, Macady was the only girl in the Jackson clan and the whole bunch had always been fiercely protective of her, but Slade had known him all his life and should have shown a little more confidence in Aaron's character.

He glanced toward the two waiting men as he stepped out of the truck. Blacker had been sheriff of Twin Falls county for twenty-six years. He stood six feet tall and his corpulent frame and silver sideburns gave him an authoritative air. He had a reputation for being blunt but fair, and Aaron liked working for him. He got along well with the other deputies in the department, too.

"Blacker. Rodriguez." Aaron acknowledged the other two men as he strolled toward them. "What's this possible piece of evidence you've found?"

"I don't know if it's important or not. A lot of hunters and campers go through here. Anyone could have lost it." Blacker held out his hand. Nestled in his palm was a ring, the kind high school seniors buy to commemorate their graduation.

"It hasn't been out here long," Rodriguez spoke up. "It's not tarnished, and there's no dirt imbedded in the design."

"We found it along side a coke can and half a dozen cigarette butts over by that big rock." Sheriff Blacker pointed in the direction where a pinpoint of light had served as a warning three nights ago.

A sick feeling crept into Aaron's stomach as he stared at the ring. He didn't want to touch it, but a stronger compulsion had him reaching for it.

"Ever seen one like that?" Blacker asked.

"Yes," Aaron answered slowly. "I have one just like it in a box in the top drawer of my dresser." He held the ring up to the light. There, on either side of the red stone, were the numerals 1985, the year he, Zack, and Slade had graduated from high school. His graduating class hadn't been large, and he'd known each of the other young men well. They'd played ball together, gone to church together, fished and camped. Surely none of them were involved in smuggling drugs or shooting at Macady.

Reluctantly he turned the ring. He had to look inside. They'd all had their initials inscribed inside the band. He stared at the fancy scrolled letters. How many had initials S.J.? There was Sean Jaramillo, Steve Jennings, Stuart Johnson—and Slade Jackson.

Of course the ring couldn't be Slade's. His name shouldn't have even popped into Aaron's head. What about the others? He'd seen Steve a week ago. They'd both been standing in line at K-Mart when Aaron spotted his old classmate trying to pick up some girl in tight denim shorts. He didn't seem to have changed much since high school, still the same cheerful flirt. Aaron had no idea where the other two were. There might even be others with those initials; he'd have to check his old yearbook.

"Want me to follow up on the ring?" he asked the sheriff. Blacker nodded his head.

Kelsey stopped to gaze longingly back at the kittens and Macady smiled. "It's their lunch time. Their mama wants them to drink some milk and have a little nap. We can visit them again later. By that time you might know what you want to name your kitten."

"I already know."

"Oh?"

"Her name is Sandy."

"Sandy? Why did you pick Sandy for your kitten's name?"

"Because Daddy said everyone should have a Sandy."

Who was Sandy? Did Aaron have someone special in his life called Sandy? Macady suspected asking Kelsey questions just might be prying, so she changed the subject.

"Would you like some lunch?" she asked.

Kelsey's brow wrinkled and she appeared to be studying the proposal in great depth. "Do I have to eat everything on my plate?"

"Not unless you want to," Macady laughed.

"Are you sure?" Kelsey appeared genuinely concerned.

"I'll tell you what." Macady reached for the girl's hand. "You can help me fix lunch, and you can put just what you want to eat on your plate."

"Are you going to make peanut butter sam'iches?"

"I can make you one if that's what you want."

"I don't like peanut butter." Kelsey looked so forlorn Macady was tempted to hug her.

"Well, goodness, if you don't like peanut butter then I won't make peanut butter sandwiches. What would you like?"

"Aunt Denise says I have to eat peanut butter sam'iches 'cause they're good for me. Grandma says they're full of po-teen, and I should always clean up my plate." Kelsey sighed and shrugged her shoulders as though they carried the weight of the world. "Grandma cooks lots of po-teen and vitamins."

Macady laughed and squeezed Kelsey's hand. "Follow me. I'll bet we can find something you'll like." She led the child up and down the aisles of the tiny store pointing to first one thing, then another. After making their selections they joined Hazel in the family's living quarters behind the store.

A smile twitched the corner of Macady's mouth as she looked at Kelsey's plate. If Aaron was as much of a stickler for proper diet as Denise and his mother-in-law appeared to be, she was in big trouble. Kelsey's plate held a banana, a cup of pudding, a dough-nut, a slice of microwaved pizza, four strawberries, and a carton of chocolate milk.

The bell over the front door rang and Macady jumped up and returned to the store to see to the customers who had entered. When she was done and came back, she could hear Kelsey's soft giggle before she stepped into the room. Hazel had moved her chair closer to their small guest and was threatening to steal her strawberries. Kelsey promptly popped one into her mouth, then giggled when Hazel pretended to cry. Macady could see at a glance that Kelsey had eaten almost all of her unorthodox lunch.

Macady turned to her mother. "Are you going to lie down for a while, or would you rather sit in the front room and read?"

Hazel smiled at Kelsey. "Would you like to come sit with me? I think I could find a story to read to you."

Kelsey's eyes lit up. "A story with pictures?"

"Certainly!" Hazel smiled. "What's a story without pictures? Macady, don't you still have some picture books on the bottom shelf of your bookcase?"

"Yes, let's get you both settled in the recliner and I'll run and get them."

There was just enough room in the big chair for Kelsey to snuggle against Hazel's side, and after Macady returned with several books, Macady returned to the store.

Almost an hour passed before Macady found time to check on her small charge. She stepped into the living room to find a peaceful scene. Kelsey had moved to Hazel's lap, and they had both fallen asleep over a picture of a big strawberry and a little mouse. A tendril of dark hair clung damply to a rosy cheek and Kelsey looked content snuggled in Hazel's arms. The little worry lines around her mother's eyes had been smoothed away and Macady smiled. It seemed she wasn't the only one charmed by their visitor.

Macady tiptoed from the room and swallowed a sudden lump in her throat. There was something about the little girl that touched her in an unexpected way. She'd never spent time around children and hadn't given much thought to having any of her own. She'd never once thought her mother might enjoy, even look forward to being a grandmother. Macady considered sacrificing motherhood a small price to pay in exchange for living her own life, free of the demands and disappointments of marriage. Now she wasn't so sure.

She didn't hate men. In fact, she loved Uncle Carson and his sons dearly, but she didn't want a life like Aunt Lucille's. Her aunt was shy and unassuming. Her whole life revolved around the needs of her men. She spent from early morning until late at night cooking and cleaning, doing huge batches of laundry, weeding her garden and preserving its harvest. Though she was happy and cheerful doing those things, that wasn't a life that would satisfy Macady.

Three of Macady's cousins were married and their wives seemed to be cut from the same cloth as their mother-in-law, seemingly content to wait on the big lugs they'd married. Their idea of a girls' night out was the four of them, Lucille and her three daughters-in-law, traveling into town together for home-making night. She supposed Uncle Carson was faithful to Aunt Lucille, but she wasn't sure about her cousins, especially Web. He was awfully good-looking, and he'd always had a generous supply of girlfriends in high school.

Macady's mother was nothing like Aunt Lucille. She'd held an important corporate position in Seattle before she married. She was bright, fun, and dressed well. She hadn't wanted to move to southern Idaho, but her husband did, so she had come. He'd inherited the store, but it had been Hazel who managed it and turned it into a success.

Once Macady had adored her father and believed her family was perfect. Her parents had been married in the temple, and she'd assumed they would be a family forever. Disillusionment had cut deeply.

Macady refilled the soft drink machine and tried to shut out the thoughts in her head. She didn't like thinking about her father. She couldn't think about him without remembering his betrayal. She glanced out the window, hoping a car full of tourists would arrive to keep her too busy to think. The parking lot remained empty.

Kelsey's peaceful trusting face haunted her, reminding her that she too had trusted her father when she had been a child. He'd been her best friend. Then one afternoon he'd come to her room. He had looked sad and ill at ease, but he wanted to talk to her. He said she was almost grown up, old enough to understand. But she hadn't.

He said he'd made some mistakes and he and her mother had drifted apart. They no longer wanted the same things, and he'd met someone else. He hadn't gone looking for another woman he assured her, but he and Carol had been together a lot at work and in their ward callings. She'd needed advice and encouragement, and he'd spent many hours trying to help her. They hadn't planned to hurt anyone, but it had happened.

He had tried to assure Macady that she would be fine, and he would see her often. Her mother was strong and capable. She could handle this, he told Macady. But Carol really needed him. Carol was going to have a baby, and though he would love it, it would never take Macady's place. He'd always love his little girl, his Macady. But Macady was nearly grown while a tiny baby needed a father.

Inside her head, Macady had screamed and cried and thrown things. Outwardly she'd calmly told her father she hated him and never wanted to see him again. She'd stood like a frozen statue, neither speaking nor hearing until he left. To her he was dead. Perhaps that explained the pull little Kelsey exerted on her heart. She too had lost a parent.

The bell jangled and Macady looked up in surprise. She'd been so engrossed in her thoughts, she hadn't heard tires crunch across the gravel. Aaron stood in the doorway, a hesitant smile on his face. He looked tired and disheveled. With a touch of horror, she quashed a desire to go to him and offer him comfort. He glanced around the room, and Macady realized he was searching for his daughter.

"She fell asleep. I'll get her." Macady caught herself almost running from the room.

She didn't try to awaken the little girl, but gathered her in her arms to carry her to her father. The moment she stood with the weight of the child crushed against her breasts, she knew she'd made a mistake. Kelsey felt too right in her arms. From somewhere deep inside her swirled an intense desire to hold and treasure this child forever. Her arms tightened. At a sound from the doorway, Macady lifted her eyes to meet Aaron's. Something sharp and swift passed between them. Hesitantly, she made herself walk across the room and transfer Aaron's sleeping daughter to his arms. Their eyes collided once more, and Macady felt a stab of pain.

"Daddy?" Kelsey stirred, then opened her eyes. Suddenly she was wide awake. "I want to show you my kitten. I named her Sandy." She struggled to be let down, which he did. "Come on, Daddy."

"We have to go now, punkin." Aaron resisted his daughter's tug on his hand.

"Macady said I could see the kitties again."

"Go ahead." Macady whispered to Aaron, then wondered why she was whispering.

"Thanks for watching her," Aaron began.

"We enjoyed her visit."

"I really do appreciate ..."

"Daddy!"

"Go on, take her to see the kittens." Macady smiled brightly, but inside she felt like the fine film of ice that formed on the horse trough in early winter, as transparent as glass, but more brittle and delicate, ready to shatter at the lightest touch.

Tonight she'd fill out the application form for that advertising position in Portland. As soon as Mom was strong enough to look after the store, she would leave.

CHAPTER FIVE

"Macady, is that really you?" Macady turned at the sound of her name, and saw an attractive woman coming toward the restaurant table where Macady had stopped for a quick lunch. Sylvia Ashcraft! A few years older than herself, the other woman had been Macady's sitter when her parents had gone out in the evenings when she'd been a little girl. Later Sylvia had gone steady with her cousin Slade until he'd graduated from high school and gone away to college.

"Sylvia, how nice to see you." She gave the other woman a bright smile. Sylvia was just what she needed to get her mind off Aaron and Kelsey. The pair had been occupying her thoughts too much. "Please join me ... unless you're with someone."

"I'd love to. Sid and a friend were going to join me, but evidently they've been held up." Sylvia slid into the vacant place across from Macady.

"Sid?" Macady wrinkled her brow, trying to remember if he was someone she knew.

"My brother," Sylvia interpreted her puzzled look correctly. "You probably don't remember him. He's quite a bit older than I am."

"No, I don't remember meeting him." Macady set down her sandwich and took a long swallow of her chocolate shake. "M-m-m, that's good," she murmured.

Sylvia laughed. "You haven't changed a bit. You always liked to eat and lucky you, it never showed."

"If there was a compliment in there somewhere, thank you,

but it looks to me like you're the 'slim 'n trim' one. You look great."

"You'll notice I'm eating a salad while you've got two sandwiches, fries, a shake, and a large soft drink. Good grief! You have a glass of ice water, too. How can you drink all that?"

"I'm thirsty," Macady admitted. "I've been running all over town this morning, and it's so hot I feel like I'm out on the desert."

"Have you been out on the desert lately? I remember how crazy you used to be about riding for hours out in all that nothing."

"Just once." Macady knew her peeling nose was a dead giveaway. Self-consciously she covered it with her hand. "I stayed out longer than I meant to."

"You're not only sunburned, that's quite a scratch on your cheek. What happened?"

"I … uh … fell off my horse."

"Not you! You never fell off a horse in your life!"

"I was careless." She shrugged her shoulders.

"You never used to be careless."

Macady squirmed uncomfortably. "Something came up, and I couldn't get back when I'd expected to. My horse was spooked."

Sylvia looked at her, encouraging her to go on, but Macady took a large bite of her sandwich and followed it with a long, cool sip of Sprite.

"Tell me about yourself," Macady invited Sylvia, to change the subject. "I always thought you were headed for the big city and a trend-setting career. How come you're back in Twin Falls? Are you married? Do you have children?"

An expression Macady couldn't decipher crossed the blonde's face, and it was almost as though the temperature had dropped ten degrees. "I did head for the big city when I left here, but living in San Francisco is expensive. So is Los Angeles. Anyway it was the other coast I always dreamed of. I was married to a jerk who did his thinking with his fists, so I divorced him. No children, thank goodness. Anyway, since Dad died and left the business to Sid and me, I decided to come home and make certain I got my share."

She stared out the window at Blue Lakes Boulevard and drummed her fingers on the table. With a quick gesture, she reached into her handbag and placed a package of cigarettes on the table. Her long fingers played with the cellophane-wrapped package several seconds. She tapped it to extract a cigarette, then changed her mind and tossed the package back into her bag.

"How about you?" She turned her attention back to Macady.

"I'm single and plan to stay that way." Macady suspected she'd spoken a little too emphatically. "I'm just here for the summer. Mom had surgery a few weeks ago. As soon as she's well again, I'll be on my way to Portland."

"Do you have a job there?"

"Sort of. I have a friend who runs an advertising agency, and she asked me to come interview as soon as my obligations here are cleared up."

Sylvia toyed with her salad for several minutes. Macady finished her milk shake and drained her soft drink.

"Do your cousins still live on that ranch out by you, or are they all married and scattered now?" Sylvia leaned forward and her long hair fell across her face, shielding her eyes from Macady's view.

Macady felt a twinge of sadness; she knew what Sylvia was really asking. She'd always suspected Sylvia's feelings for Slade had gone much deeper than his had for her. Aloud, she responded, "Zack, Web, and Daniel are married. All three built their own houses on the ranch. Slade splits his time between the ranch and flying for a private courier service. Will is going to BYU. Jeremiah just returned from a mission, and David is leaving next month. Ben graduated from high school this spring and still lives with Uncle Carson and Aunt Lucille. He's planning a year at CSI before going on a mission, too."

"I suppose they all still show up every Sunday morning for

church in suits and ties and take up the first two rows, front and center."

"They do." Macady laughed. "Only now there are six more boys, all preschoolers, three wives, and an occasional girlfriend, so we need three benches these days."

Sylvia shuddered. "Don't you ever get tired of all that preaching? After what your father did, I would've thought you'd want nothing more to do with the Church."

Macady pinched her straw between her fingers in an alternating pattern. Finally she spoke. Her voice was soft, but clear. "I've never blamed the Church for what my father did."

"But he was in the bishopric."

"... And breaking every rule the Church set up for leaders who counsel someone of the opposite sex." The old familiar anger rose in her throat. She didn't want to talk about her father. How had the conversation taken such a detour? She attempted to turn the talk back to Sylvia. "Are you telling me you aren't active anymore?"

The other woman shrugged her shoulders. "I guess I outgrew it." Macady felt sympathy for her. Sylvia's childhood hadn't been easy. She'd been left out of most of the activities the other kids had participated in because she'd had to help her father after school. The domineering old man had expected her to work as hard as her brother in his barrel and salvage business, but had seen no reason to pay her. Her only spending money was what she had earned babysitting.

Macady suspected her old friend had seen more bad times since leaving home, and instead of turning to the gospel for help, she'd turned her back, maybe even blamed the Church for her troubles. If the package of cigarettes she carried in her purse was an indication, Sylvia had changed a great deal in the years since Macady had last seen her.

It had been at Slade's homecoming after he returned from his mission. He had stopped dating Sylvia several months before he'd gotten his call, and since she didn't live in the same ward as the Jacksons, Macady had been surprised to see her that day. Sylvia had sat in the back alone, then slipped out early in tears.

Perhaps a little cousinly matchmaking to rekindle an old flame was in order. Slade was still single. On the other hand, if Sylvia wasn't committed to the Church, she'd never do for her cousin. Perhaps that was why they'd broken up all those years ago.

Macady finished her lunch while Sylvia picked at hers. Then together they emptied their trays into the garbage and walked outside. They stopped beside Macady's sporty red Toyota Paseo.

At that moment a sheriff's truck pulled in beside her car and the driver stepped out. Macady's mouth fell open at the sight of the uniformed officer.

"Hello, Macady, Sylvia." Aaron touched the brim of his hat. The heavy black gun belt around his waist and the star on his chest added an aura of danger to the beguiling grin he flashed their way. He'd told her he was a deputy, but he hadn't been in uniform that day in the desert or the day he'd brought Kelsey to the store. The way he looked in the smartly tailored black and gray uniform made her pulse accelerate.

"Aaron! Good to see you again." Sylvia's voice dropped nearly an octave to a throaty purr. For some reason that annoyed Macady, but she couldn't think of anything clever to say. Actually she was having trouble saying anything. It wasn't fair for Aaron to have this kind of effect on her. She'd driven across town, picked the noisiest fast food restaurant she knew, and here she was right back where she'd started—with Aaron on her mind. And him standing a little too close for comfort.

"I didn't know you were in town," Aaron spoke to Sylvia. "Have you seen any of the old crowd ... Sean Jaramillo or Stuart Johnson?"

"I heard that Sean finished law school and is practicing in San Diego. I bumped into Stuart in Sun Valley a few weeks ago. He's assistant manager of the King Sol Inn. Divorced twice now. Most of the girls we used to know are married or have moved away." Her voice indicated she didn't care which.

Keeping her head bent, Macady picked at the seam running

down the leg of her white linen slacks. Occasionally she peeked through her lashes at Aaron, but he was absorbed in reminiscing about the past with Sylvia who had been just a year behind his class in high school. Sylvia tossed her long blond hair over her shoulder and leaned forward to say something to Aaron. Macady became aware the other woman was wearing a low-cut tank top. One glance at Aaron told her he'd noticed, too. That annoyed her. Telling herself she was being silly, she attempted to join their conversation, but being six years behind Aaron and her two oldest cousins in school, she hadn't known half the people Sylvia and Aaron discussed. As they talked, they both seemed to forget she was present.

On the other hand, maybe it was just as well. She needed to get back to work—and to put some distance between herself and Aaron.

"Excuse me." She reached for her car door.

"Are you on your way home?" Aaron stretched out a hand to hold the door for her.

"No, I'm working today. Lunch hour's over." He seemed disappointed and Macady's heartbeat picked up a tiny bit.

"Kelsey's been begging me to take her out to your place to see her kitten. I'm off this afternoon, and I thought ..."

"Mom's there. Zack's wife, Mary, is helping out, too. So it would be all right if you wanted to stop by." Macady kept her voice level. She didn't want Aaron to suspect she was disappointed she couldn't spend the afternoon with him and Kelsey.

"I was hoping we could do a little shopping before picking up Kelsey." Aaron's crooked smile hinted at a secret.

"Shopping?" Macady couldn't imagine why Aaron wanted to take her shopping.

"There's a little matter of the hat I promised you."

"You don't owe me a hat! You aren't the one who put a hole through it."

"A hole that was meant for me," Aaron responded softly. She didn't know what to say, so she said nothing. For long minutes they simply looked at each other, reading memories of that awful day and night in each other's eyes. Sylvia, who up to this point had stood by silently, looked at Aaron sharply.

With a more businesslike tone, Aaron added, "That reminds me, Sheriff Blacker would like you to come down to the office and look at some pictures." Macady shuddered.

"I'm sorry," Aaron spoke softly and touched her arm. "It won't take long and it might help ... since you are the one who can identify him. I'll take you shopping afterward. No argument. I promised you a hat and a hat you're going to get."

"I have to get back to work."

"Okay. Tomorrow afternoon?"

"All right."

"You two have something going?" Sylvia spoke up at last and Macady jumped guiltily. Both she and Aaron had completely forgotten about Sylvia, who watched them with a thoughtful expression on her face. Her eyes hardened and she spoke brusquely, "It's okay, I can take a hint." She moved rapidly toward a row of cars parked at the far side of the lot.

"Sylvia, wait." Macady started after the other woman.

"She won't believe you." Aaron clasped her arm to stop her from rushing after her old friend. "Does it matter anyway?"

Macady shrugged her shoulders. Did it matter? No, it really didn't, but Macady didn't like that kind of misunderstanding. It made her feel as though she'd told a lie, even though she knew she hadn't.

Aaron waited while Macady settled herself behind the wheel of her car, then returned to his own vehicle. He watched her pull into traffic, then continued to watch until her bright red car was out of sight. He was glad he'd spotted her leaving the restaurant. It was a good chance to talk to Sylvia about old classmates, he told himself. Nevertheless, it was Macady's smile that lingered in his mind.

He still planned to speak to Zack, but the information Sylvia had given him provided a place to start his investigation, and a little more space to think about the strange suspicions that kept creeping into his head.

Aaron was reluctant to talk to Zack or Slade about the class ring Blacker had found. He, Zack, and Slade went back a long way. The two brothers were barely ten months apart, and the way their birth dates fell, they had started school the same year, along with Aaron. Even though Slade seemed to have a burr under his saddle where Aaron was concerned, he knew Slade was a good man. Slade wouldn't be involved in anything as nasty as drugs—and he definitely wouldn't shoot at Macady—but then he couldn't have known Macady was anywhere around. Still, the man doing the shooting was about Slade's size. No, Aaron shook his head. His suspicions were way off base. And Macady had gotten a good look at the man's face. Macady would have said so if she'd recognized her cousin, wouldn't she? He hated the niggling doubt that wouldn't go away.

Aaron had already discovered Slade flew all over the West. He'd made at least three trips to Mexico since the first of the year. But that didn't mean anything; the ring might not mean anything either.

As Aaron drove to his brother's house to pick up Kelsey, he thought about what he'd learned from Sylvia. He could run a check on Sean Jaramillo and Stuart Johnson. He already knew Steve Jennings was employed here in town by Delgado Realty Company. He frowned, remembering Steve and the young girl in the tight shorts.

He'd make a few phone calls and start the ball rolling before he took Kelsey out to Hazel's store. Funny, he'd been looking forward to taking Kelsey visiting until Macady said she wouldn't be there. Now he wasn't sure he wanted to go. No, that wasn't right. He did want to take Kelsey to see the kitten.

Being a single father wasn't easy, but he savored every minute he found to spend with his daughter; it was just that Macady had a knack for making everything around her a little more real, a little more vibrant.

CHAPTER SIX

"Uh-oh." Aaron frowned as he pulled into Matt's driveway and parked behind a white LTD with Colorado license plates. Helen was here again. Even though he felt sorry for Helen—losing her only child had been painful—he wouldn't put up with her hints that he was somehow responsible for Alicia's death. Nor would he tolerate his mother-in-law's attempts to run him down before Kelsey. He refused to let her make him feel guilty for taking Kelsey so far away from her. He wouldn't pick a fight; he'd really like for Kelsey to have the benefit of two sets of grandparents in her life, but he wouldn't back off from his vow to raise Kelsey himself.

Denise met him at the door with apology written all over her face. "She just got here," she whispered, "and I've put my foot in it already. Kelsey and Jackie were playing next door with the Alverez kids and Rita fed them lunch. They came home with tacos in their hands and sauce dripping off their elbows. To make matters worse, the Alverez's had a load of top soil delivered earlier this morning and the kids have been playing in it. Kelsey looked a sight and Helen threw a fit."

"It's okay." Aaron tried to soothe Denise.

"Another fifteen minutes and they would have all been under the sprinklers in the back yard."

"Was Helen rude to you?"

Denise didn't answer directly, just shrugged her shoulders. "She's giving Kelsey a bath."

Aaron groaned. Unlike her mother, Kelsey had an aversion to

bathing. Alicia had spent hours soaking in warm bubble baths, but Kelsey fought bath time every night. Swimming pools and sprinklers were fun, but bathing was something she had no use for.

Aaron shrugged his shoulders helplessly and moved on into the living room.

"There you are!" Helen Randall sailed into the room, making it perfectly clear she'd tolerate no nonsense. "I won't put up with this any longer. I always knew you were irresponsible, but I won't stand by and see my granddaughter neglected."

"Hold on, Helen. Kelsey isn't neglected and you know it." Aaron spoke calmly even though he felt like shouting. What right did she have to accuse him of neglecting his daughter?

"When I arrived, she was filthy and eating some dirty mess those Mexicans next door gave her ..."

"That's enough!" Aaron cut her off sharply. "Children—real children, that is—get dirty. And you'd better think twice before you insult Rita Alverez. I'd trust her cooking over yours or almost anyone else's you can name any day. She and her family are good people, and I'm glad she lets her children play with Kelsey."

"Aaron!" Helen's lips tightened, revealing a white ring around her mouth. "Alicia would be heartbroken to see her daughter in this place and being raised like an animal. That woman who should have been watching Kelsey was insolent and rude to me."

"That woman is my sister-in-law, Denise, and if she was the least bit short with you, you must have really provoked her." Aaron knew Denise didn't start fights. Matt's wife was quiet, easily flustered, and a little shy. She went out of her way to avoid unpleasant confrontations and was probably in her bedroom right now crying her eyes out because unpleasant words had been exchanged.

"You never have shown any regard for my feelings, but then you never cared about Alicia's feelings either, did you?"

"I cared." Aaron saw Kelsey slip quietly into the room. Her bottom lip protruded and her eyes were red. She wore a pale pink ruffled dress with a matching organdy bow in her hair. Her outfit was obviously new, right down to the dainty sandals on her feet. "If I'd cared less, I wouldn't have stuck around to take your abuse for five years."

"That's right, blame everything on me; poor Alicia isn't here to blame anymore. You let her down. You couldn't support her. You expected her to live in squalor and you made her life miserable every time I gave her a few dollars. You stayed away for days on end, then blamed her for your shortcomings."

Aaron gritted his teeth. His objections to Alicia accepting money from her mother had been a constant source of conflict between them. Helen was the most short-sighted, selfish person he'd ever met. It was hard to believe that back in their ward in Colorado, she was considered a pillar. She taught beautiful, well-prepared lessons in Relief Society and was the first to rush to a neighbor with a hot loaf of bread at a hint of trouble. Her tunnel vision only came into effect where her child was concerned.

Aaron could see Kelsey's white face and wished he could protect her from hearing her grandmother's accusations. His and Alicia's marital problems were in the past, and they never had been Helen's business—except that Alicia had made them her mother's business.

Alicia hadn't been able to toast a slice of bread without asking her mother's advice. Alicia and Helen had seen each other daily, and still they had telephoned each other three or four times as well. Helen had known two weeks before he had that Alicia was pregnant, and when Kelsey arrived, it was Helen who held Alicia's hand through the delivery. Kelsey was four hours old before it even occurred to Alicia to call Aaron's dispatcher and let him know he was a father. Aaron's heart twisted at the remembered sense of betrayal he'd felt that day.

"Look, Helen, this isn't getting us anywhere. You can cling to your narrow prejudices and distorted views all you want, but I don't want Kelsey subjected to them. I never run down Alicia or you to her, and I expect the same courtesy from you. If you can't accept I'm Kelsey's father and stop trying to undermine me in her eyes, then your visits with her will have to end."

"I won't have it! Kelsey is Alicia's baby, and I won't stand by and see her life ruined the way you ruined hers. You won't be happy until you kill her, too!"

"I didn't kill Alicia."

"If you hadn't made her so unhappy she had to run away in the middle of the night on an icy road, she'd still be alive."

"I think you have to accept your share of the blame. If you hadn't trained her to run home to Mommy every time she didn't get her way, she wouldn't have been on the road that night." Memories of that last argument with his wife assailed him. He'd told Alicia he wanted to accept an offer of a better job in Twin Falls, and she'd insisted she wouldn't leave her mother. If he could get her away from Helen's dictatorial control, he'd thought their marriage still might have a chance. Alicia had refused to consider moving to Idaho. He'd lost his temper and told her she'd better get used to the idea, and she'd stormed out of the house.

A strangled sob behind him filled him with remorse. He'd known Kelsey was in the room and should have refused to be baited. He started toward her, but Helen got there first.

"Come to Grandma, baby," she crooned. "Daddy's being very bad to shout and scare my little Precious."

"Go away!" Kelsey slapped at her grandmother's hands.

"Now, honey, Grandma just wants to give you a little hug. Then we can go shopping for some pretty new clothes. Just Grandma and Kelsey. Won't that be fun?"

"Can't Daddy come?" Kelsey eyed her grandmother suspiciously.

"Of course not, dear. Men don't like to shop. He can watch a ballgame or something while we're gone."

Aaron clenched his fists. Kelsey's grandmother had driven a long way to see her, and in spite of his dislike for her, he didn't want to deprive her of a visit with Kelsey, but it was the first afternoon he'd had off since the day he and Macady were trapped on the desert. He didn't want to give up his time with his daughter.

Kelsey peered at him over her grandmother's shoulder. Tears gave her eyes an added sparkle. "Daddy, you promised we could go see Sandy."

That was all the encouragement Aaron needed to do what he wanted to do anyway. "We will, punkin, but maybe you ought to go change your clothes first." He smiled at her. "Sandy might not know you in that get-up."

With a squeal, Kelsey pulled herself free and started down the hall at a run.

"Come back here, young lady," Helen ordered in no uncertain terms.

Kelsey hesitated, then looked at her father uncertainly.

"Skip changing your clothes and come on." Aaron moved to his daughter's side and scooped her up in his arms before turning back to Helen. "Kelsey and I have been planning for a week to visit some friends this afternoon. There's a little yellow kitten waiting for her and we don't intend to disappoint it. If you had let us know you were coming, perhaps we could have made different plans." He headed for the door with Kelsey in his arms.

"I've driven a long way to see my granddaughter. How can you just walk out and leave me?" Helen's voice quavered and Aaron knew he was supposed to feel guilty. He turned and realized he'd made a mistake. Helen sniffed and touched a handkerchief to her eyes.

"No, you can't stay here. Denise would never forgive me if I left you here with her."

"Don't cry, Grandma." Kelsey pleaded. "You can come with us. You'll love Sandy."

"I know when I'm not wanted," Helen sniffed. "I'll go back to the motel until you return."

"Okay," Aaron sighed. "You know where our house is. We'll be back around six. If you change your mind about joining us, we'll be at Jackson's Point, just off the freeway."

Macady could see someone leaning against her car as she

walked across the parking lot, and she slowed her steps. The sun bore down on the back of the man waiting there, casting his face in shadow. An unpleasant memory of a man with a rifle surfaced. She considered returning to the news office to find a colleague to accompany her to her car. Heat radiated from the hot asphalt beneath her feet, and the late afternoon glare reminded her it was broad daylight.

A car door slammed, and somewhere nearby, a radio played. People were moving along the sidewalk that bordered the parking lot on two sides. This was Twin Falls, Idaho, not New York; if she screamed, someone would come. Slowly, she walked on.

She'd left the office a few minutes early hoping she could be home before Aaron and Kelsey left Jackson's Point. Surely no one would try to mug her in a busy parking lot at five o'clock in the afternoon with dozens of people around.

"Hello, Macady." She jumped, then stifled a giggle when she recognized Slade's voice. He moved toward her and she could see his face clearly.

"Hi, Slade. Need a ride home?" She attempted to hide her previous nervousness which she chalked up to the residual effect of her ordeal in the desert.

"No, I have my Ranger. I'd like to talk to you a minute though."

"Sure." She sneaked a peak at her watch. Aaron had probably already taken Kelsey back home anyway.

"Are you in a hurry? Maybe you've got a hot date." He'd seen her glance at her watch. He smiled, but the smile didn't reach his eyes.

"No. No date. Aaron was going to take his daughter out to the store to visit the kittens this afternoon, and I thought it might be fun to play with Kelsey a few minutes before they leave. She's a cute kid." She squinted her eyes against the bright light and looked up at her cousin. Something was troubling him, and suddenly Macady felt a touch of unnamed fear. "Is something wrong?" she questioned.

Slade raked one hand through his hair and tightened his mouth before speaking. "'Cady, darn it! I feel like a busybody fool asking you this, but are you seeing Aaron Westerman?"

"You mean, am I dating Aaron?" Slade nodded his head. "I can't believe you asked me that. I thought we settled this issue when I was sixteen and you and your brothers thought it was your right to check up on my boyfriends. I haven't forgotten how you scared poor Bobby Olsen into standing me up!"

"I know. Now don't get mad. I didn't mean to upset you, but this is important. I couldn't live with myself if I said nothing and you ended up getting hurt." He shifted uneasily and his nervousness spread to her.

"How could dating Aaron hurt me?" Slade's words made no sense. Slade and Aaron had been close since before she was born—why would her cousin have reservations about her seeing his old friend? Especially when Aaron obviously had all the qualities her cousins considered important—being a returned missionary as well as a college graduate with a good job.

"Could we sit in your car a minute? There's something you need to know before you get involved with Westerman." Slade took her arm and urged her toward her car. She probably should tell Slade she had no intention of "getting involved" with Aaron or any other man, but she was curious now.

Macady unlocked the car door and slid inside to release the lock on the passenger side. Slade sat and waited while she started the engine and fiddled with the air conditioning without saying anything. She found herself almost holding her breath. She felt a tightness in her chest and a queasiness in her stomach. Macady didn't want to hear anything bad about Aaron, but she couldn't drop it either. She didn't want to know, but she couldn't not know.

"Okay, Slade, what is this all about?" She heard the knuckles on his fingers crack, then he clasped one knee between his hands.

"This isn't easy for me either," he began slowly. "Aaron was my best friend for a long time, but I knew Aaron's wife, too. Fool that I am, I introduced them. He treated her pretty badly."

"He abused her?" Macady was incredulous.

"I don't think he ever hit her or anything like that, but he was cruel in other ways. He tried to cut her off from her family. He wouldn't let her have any money of her own, and he insisted she had to be completely dependent on him."

"That doesn't sound like Aaron," Macady protested.

"It's true." Slade's features were hard and unforgiving. "She left him when they were living in West Yellowstone. She would have filed for a divorce if she hadn't discovered she was pregnant. Aaron followed her back to Colorado and made her a lot of promises, so she decided to give him another chance. She soon regretted it. He insisted on living as far from her mother as possible. He stayed out all night and went away for weekends whenever it suited him. He spent a lot of time with another woman, even took her to their house when Alicia wasn't there."

Macady was quiet for several minutes trying to absorb all her cousin had said. Something wasn't right. "Slade," she asked softly, "how do you know so much about Aaron's marriage?"

"It wasn't what you're thinking, Macady," he answered harshly. "Alicia wasn't unfaithful to Aaron, and I don't date married women. But, she was my friend. She was hurt and lonely. Sometimes we talked."

Macady heard more than Slade's words. Her father had only meant to "talk" with Carol and offer her counsel. She wanted to believe Slade when he said he and Alicia hadn't had an affair, but she knew with deep certainty that her cousin had been in love with Aaron's wife. Might that have colored his perception?

"Did you go to Colorado for these friendly talks that weren't dates?" She hadn't meant to sound sarcastic, but her suspicions were quickly placing Slade in the same role her father and former fiance had played.

"I fly to Boulder on a regular basis. Alicia's mother owns a franchise at the airport and Alicia used to run errands for her. We ran into each other quite often and we talked. Satisfied?"

64

"I don't know." Macady felt uncomfortable with the whole conversation. It smacked of gossip and prying into something that was none of her business.

Slade raised one hand and slammed a fist into the dashboard. "Macady, I watched one woman I cared about change from a happy, carefree girl to a hurt and unhappy wife because her husband neglected her and kept her virtually a prisoner miles out of town. He left her alone at night and threatened to quit his job and take their daughter to another state where she and her mother would never see the child again. Alicia was torn between being a dutiful daughter to her widowed mother and Aaron's unrealistic demands."

For just a moment, Macady felt sympathy for Aaron's wife, but the sympathy was quickly replaced by bitterness. If Alicia was unhappy or mistreated, she'd had others she could have turned to for help. Crying on her husband's best friend's shoulder was an act of betrayal. It was the kind of disloyalty that had led to the breakup of her parents' marriage.

"Meeting Alicia behind Aaron's back and encouraging her to confide in you concerning her marriage was morally wrong."

"I'll tell you what's morally wrong," Slade snapped back. "Aaron's friends in the sheriff's office hushed it up, but Alicia didn't just slip on an icy road. She killed herself!"

"Suicide?" Macady felt a shiver of shock. "How do you know?"

"Her mother told me she was deeply unhappy and regretted marrying Aaron. If she had been only leaving him, she would have taken Kelsey with her. She wouldn't have left her behind with him." Slade's voice softened to a gentle plea. "I love you, Macady. Don't expect me to stand by and do nothing while Aaron ruins your life too."

CHAPTER SEVEN

Macady cradled the telephone between her cheek and shoulder as she rang up four colossal size drinks and an equal number of hot dogs on the cash register. She listened intently while making change.

"Sandy is doing just fine, Kelsey." She listened again and smiled. "Yes, I'm sure she misses you, too. I'm sorry I didn't get home in time to see you last night. When are you coming to visit her again?" She listened to the girl explain that she didn't know when her daddy could take her to see the kitten, but she hoped it would be soon.

"I asked Grandma if she would take me today, but she said no." A forlorn note entered the child's voice. "She's mad at Daddy because I tore my new dress, and it got all dirty while I was playing with Sandy. I don't think she likes kitties. She called Sandy a dirty beast."

Macady hid her laughter, even while she wondered why Aaron had let Kelsey wear a new dress to visit her barn. Aloud she said, "Is your grandmother tending you today?"

"No, Daddy left me at Aunt Denise's house, but Grandma is coming to get me at one o'clock. We have to go shopping to buy me another new dress."

Macady felt a rush of excitement. She was going shopping this afternoon, too—with Aaron.

"M-m-m, that's almost three hours." She had a wild idea. "Kelsey, let me talk to your aunt for a minute, okay?" When Denise came on the line, Macady asked permission to pick up

Kelsey and take her back to the store for the morning.

"I'm sure it will be all right, but I'll call Aaron and see if he has any objections," Denise agreed.

Macady helped two tourists select souvenirs from the craft section while she waited for Denise to call back. She checked with her mother to be certain Hazel felt like working for the short time she'd be gone.

Minutes after Denise called to say Aaron had given his okay, Macady started for Twin Falls. Perhaps encouraging Kelsey wasn't the wisest thing to do. Slade wouldn't approve, especially after his warning to stay away from Aaron. She tried to block out her cousin's words. Aaron might have been the worst husband on earth, but it wasn't any of her concern. She wasn't looking for a husband.

Besides, it was Kelsey she planned to see. Something about the child haunted Macady. She tried to analyze the pull between herself and Kelsey, but she couldn't define it. It was all tied up with a hint of loneliness in the child's eyes, her eagerness to please that ran at cross purposes with a need to rebel, and a vulnerability that reminded Macady of her own insecurity when she'd lost a parent.

Spotting the street sign she'd been watching for, Macady pulled into a new subdivision. Twin Falls was growing rapidly, and she'd never been in this new section before. The houses, nice, but not fancy, were generally two and three bedroom starter homes. Almost every lot boasted a new lawn and spindly young trees. An abundance of tricycles and big wheels served as a caution against speeding. She recognized the gray brick rambler from Denise's description and pulled into the driveway.

Denise met her at the door. At least Macady assumed the harried looking young woman with tears streaming down her face was Denise. "You're Macady Jackson?" The other woman swiped her hands across her cheeks and urged Macady to come inside.

"Is something wrong? Can I help?" Feeling helpless and uncertain, Macady put out a hand toward the diminutive blonde.

Denise gulped and tried to speak, cleared her throat and tried again. "They look awful. I don't know what to do. Mrs. Randall will kill me. I only left them alone long enough to take a load of towels out of the drier."

"Is Kelsey hurt?" She gripped the other woman's arm and felt her own heartbeat accelerate with fear. "Where is she?"

"She's not hurt. Neither one is hurt, but ..."

"Neither one? Who was with Kelsey?" Had something terrible happened to Kelsey and Aaron? If Denise didn't hurry and tell her, she'd be tempted to shake it out of her.

"I—I'll show you." Denise fled down the short hall with Macady right on her heels. She opened a door and Macady gasped. Staring at her from a set of bunk beds were two little girls with wide, scared eyes—one with ragged tufts of red hair, the other with radically jagged deep brown locks. Long dark curls lay on the floor beside two fat red plaits. It didn't take much guesswork to know what had happened. Two children had found a pair of scissors and cut each other's hair.

"I assume the redhead is your daughter?" Macady turned to Denise.

"Yes, that's Jackie." Denise looked as though she might start crying again any minute.

"Are we really bad?" Kelsey whispered.

"I don't think cutting your hair was a good idea," Macady drawled and found herself fighting the urge to grin. "But that doesn't mean you're bad. I like short hair, myself." She ran her fingers through her own closely cropped hair. "But some people may think you should have asked your Daddy first, then had someone a little more experienced than Jackie do the cutting."

"Are you never going to let me see Sandy again?"

"Let's leave Sandy out of this. She didn't have anything to do with your haircut, so why should I punish her?"

"Are you going to spank us?" Jackie turned horrified eyes toward her mother.

"I probably should, but I won't." Denise shrugged her shoulders, looking defeated.

Both girls turned questioning eyes to Macady. She threw her hands in the air and laughed. "Hey, don't look at me. I don't do spankings. If you want spankings, you'll have to talk to your fathers."

"We don't want to be spanked," Kelsey spoke for both girls.

"Then why are we talking about spankings? Come on you two. I think the kitchen is the best place to finish this job." She coaxed the girls off their beds. "Denise, they won't look so bad once their hair is evened up and styled. If you would prefer to take them to a beautician, I can drive them. But if you like, I can trim their hair myself. I wasn't much older than Kelsey when I cut two of my cousins' hair. They looked a lot worse than these two do, but after that Aunt Lucille taught me how to cut hair properly and I became the family barber."

"I don't want to take them out looking like this. You do it." Denise sighed and bent over. When she straightened one long red braid dangled from each hand, and fresh tears were making their way down her cheeks. "I'm going to put these in a plastic bag and save them."

"Good idea," Macady waved the girls ahead of her down the hall. "Maybe you ought to save one of Kelsey's curls for Aaron, too."

Since Denise felt so badly about her daughter's butchered hair, Macady trimmed it first. Only the braids had been severed, so Macady gave her a sleek mid-cheek bob and Denise seemed pleased with the result. Jackie stared for long minutes into the hand mirror her mother had given her before a slow grin spread across her face. Kelsey took the mirror and looked at her own image and started to cry.

"Okay, you're next." Macady swung Kelsey onto the kitchen stool. Kelsey ducked her head and stared at the floor. Her little shoulders shook. "I'm not going to hurt you." Macady tried to encourage her.

"It didn't hurt a bit." Jackie added her own encouragement. "My braids are all gone and your 'Cady made me beautiful."

Jackie had no regrets about the loss of her long braids and seemed perfectly satisfied to the point of smugness with her changed appearance.

Macady caught Denise's eye, and for the first time that morning, Denise smiled.

"Grandma's going to be mad, isn't she?" Kelsey turned her worried face up to Macady.

"Listen, Kelsey," Macady spoke reassuringly as she ran a six-inch strand of hair through her fingers. Unfortunately the hair next to it was less than an inch long. "Your long curls were very pretty and your grandmother probably wanted you to keep them as long as possible. She'll be disappointed, but having short hair won't change who you are. You're the same little girl you were before, and your grandmother will still love you."

Fortunately Kelsey's dark chocolate hair was curly, otherwise Macady would never have been able to cover some of the more bare spots. She snipped one last lock and stood back to survey the overall effect. Then she handed the mirror to Kelsey. Like Jackie, Kelsey examined herself closely for several minutes before a wide grin replaced the worry on her face. "I look like you!" Her bright smile let everyone know she liked the idea of looking like Macady.

"You look like a pixie," Denise beamed her approval.

"She does, doesn't she?" Macady agreed. With her heart-shaped face and big wide eyes, the boyishly shaped style lent the little girl an elfin quality. Macady controlled an urge to hug the child.

The doorbell rang, and Jackie rushed from the room calling, "I'll get it! I'll get it!" Denise followed right behind her, and in less than a minute they trailed Helen Randall back into the kitchen.

"Where's my baby? That child said ... oh!" Her voice ended in a shriek. Furiously she turned on Macady. "What have you done to her? You had no right! You should be horse-whipped." Sobbing, she turned to Kelsey and swept her into a tight embrace.

"I'm here now, baby. I'll take you away from these wicked people."

Kelsey's face crumbled, and she began to cry. Helen started for the door with the sobbing child in her arms and almost ran into Denise who stood in the doorway with her arms braced against both sides. She looked terrified, but she stood her ground. "Put her down. You're upsetting her."

"I'm upsetting her? Look what you and that crazy woman have done to this poor child." Mrs. Randall jerked her head in Macady's direction. "Her long, beautiful hair is gone, thanks to your irresponsible actions. You should be arrested. Now get out of my way!"

"Mrs. Randall, I'm responsible for Kelsey and I can't allow you to ..."

"You're fired!"

Macady watched in open-mouthed awe as Mrs. Randall shouted at Denise. This woman was Kelsey's grandmother? Grandmother or not, she was certainly overstepping her authority to fire Denise! Denise was shaking, and Jackie was crying as hard as Kelsey now.

"I want to go see S-S-Sandy," Kelsey choked out the words as she turned beseeching eyes toward Macady. That did it! Macady had never been shy, and she was probably jumping into something that was none of her business, but she couldn't deny the plea behind Kelsey's words. She set down the scissors and marched right over to the startled woman and lifted Kelsey from her arms.

"Sorry, Mrs. Randall. Your time doesn't begin until one o'clock. Aaron said I could take her until then."

"Aaron! I might have known." Her eyes narrowed and she shrieked, "He told you to cut her hair just because it looked like Alicia's, and he knew it would hurt me."

The woman was so angry Macady feared she might have a stroke. Striving to hold onto her own temper and calm the distraught older woman, she spoke gently. "No, Mrs. Randall. Aaron

72

doesn't know anything about the haircut. The girls were playing and they cut each other's hair. I only repaired the damage."

"I think you should leave," Denise stammered. "D-Don't come back unless Aaron is with you."

"You can't keep that child from me!"

"We can!" Macady confirmed. "You are too emotionally distraught to care for a small child right now. Go lay down for awhile and think about what has happened. A haircut isn't worth this much turmoil. This evening you can visit Kelsey at her home and talk to Aaron about it. By that time you'll probably be able to laugh about the whole thing."

"Laugh!" Mrs. Randall looked from the tall brown-haired woman holding Kelsey to the tiny blonde patting the back of the other little girl who sobbed against her leg. A look of scorn crossed her face as she returned her gaze to Macady. "I know who you are. You're Sandy, the hussy who thinks she can take my Alicia's place. You can have Aaron, but you won't get Alicia's baby!" She brushed past Denise and slammed her way out of the house.

"Oh my ..." Denise sank onto the nearest chair. She and Macady exchanged stunned looks.

Kelsey wrapped her chubby arms around Macady and whispered, "Grandma thinks you're Sandy. Grandma's silly."

Silly wasn't the word Macady would have chosen, but she wasn't sure there was a polite word she could use. She was just glad the woman was gone. She glanced at her watch and realized she'd been away from the store nearly two hours. A sudden urgency to get back swept over her almost like a panic attack. She shouldn't have left her mother alone so long, but stronger than her concern for her mother even was her need to put some distance between herself and the unpleasant confrontation with Kelsey's grandmother.

"Denise, you've had a pretty traumatic morning," she spoke to the woman she now saw as a friend in need of a little assistance. "If it's all right with you, I'll take Jackie with me, too. You look like you could use a little rest, and it might be easier for both girls to put this behind them if they both get away for a little while."

"Yes, you're right. Thank you. Aaron gets off at four. It might be best if you keep both of them until then." Macady took the children's hands and led them out the door.

As Macady reached the five-way intersection, the light turned red. She stopped and looked back at the girls strapped in the back seat. She smiled and they both gave her answering grins.

Returning her eyes to the front, Macady stifled a gasp. Across the street she saw a man leave a garage and walk rapidly toward a truck parked on the street. She knew the man. He was the one who had fired at her two weeks ago. Her hands shook and a protective surge of adrenaline urged her to speed away with the children as fast as she could. Common sense warned her not to draw attention to herself. They were in no danger, she tried to tell herself. The man didn't even know she had seen him when he followed her to the gully where she and Aaron hid.

A horn sounded behind her, alerting her that the light had changed. She hesitated another moment as the man paused on the sidewalk to talk to a shorter, well dressed man standing beside the small green pickup truck. Both men glanced her way when the driver behind her hit his horn again. Her foot slammed against the gas pedal and her car shot forward.

Aaron had to be told. She watched anxiously for a telephone booth, but she was almost out of town before she spotted one at the Stinker Station. When she asked for Aaron, the dispatcher informed her he was out. Turning so she could keep an eye on the girls, she asked for Sheriff Blacker.

"Sheriff Blacker, here," a voice barked into the instrument and Macady jumped. Reminding herself to remain calm, she told him about the man she'd seen. Blacker listened, then told her to go on home, and he'd have Aaron stop by when he got back.

CHAPTER EIGHT

Several cars were in the parking lot of the store, so Macady hurried the girls inside even though they wanted to go straight to the barn. Hazel was perched on a stool behind the cash register. She looked tired and a wave of guilt swept over Macady.

"I'm sorry I was gone so long, Mom. Go lie down, and I'll take care of things here." She hurried her mother down the hall to the family's living quarters and perched the girls on stools behind the counter with coloring books.

Almost an hour passed before business slowed down enough to allow her to take her small charges to the barn. She opened the barn door and the kittens came running. After allowing the girls to play for a little while, she returned them to the house for lunch.

Kelsey and Jackie began lunch with a lot of giggles, but ended up nearly asleep. Hazel volunteered to read to them after the meal, and they were both asleep before she got halfway through the first story.

Each time the door opened to the store, Macady glanced up expecting to see Aaron, but the afternoon wore on. Though she kept busy selling snacks and crafts, her mind was on the young deputy. Would the information she had help put the sniper behind bars? She wondered, too, how Aaron would react to his daughter's haircut. Better than his mother-in-law, she hoped.

"You're deep in thought." She looked up to see her mother enter the store and make her way to a stool behind the counter.

"Mom, I'm not sure I did the right thing." She related all that had happened at Denise's house. "Mrs. Randall is Kelsey's grand-mother and Aaron knew she planned to take Kelsey shopping this afternoon. I probably stepped way out of line by bringing her here instead."

"You did what you thought was best for Kelsey." Hazel gave serious attention to her daughter's concern. "Are you worried that Aaron will be upset with you?"

"A little bit, I guess. Oh, I don't care if he's angry because I took matters into my own hands, but what if he reacts the way Mrs. Randall did when he sees Kelsey's hair?"

"I don't think he will," Hazel spoke confidently. "He doesn't appear to be the kind of person who overreacts."

"I wish he'd get here."

"You're worried about him going after the man you saw."

She couldn't deny it, but she didn't have to admit how deep her concern ran. "I just wish he'd come before the girls wake from their nap, so I can break the news to him before he sees her."

"Sees who?" Macady felt a shiver run down her spine as Aaron's voice interrupted the conversation with her mother. He stood in the doorway looking tired and dusty. His uniform had lost its sharp creases and dust dulled the shine on his boots. A damp ring above his ears where his hat had been attested to hours in the sun. Even tired and dirty, he had the power to make Macady's pulse beat faster.

"Macady, take Aaron for a walk. Go sit in the shade of the barn and talk. I'll see that you're not interrupted for awhile," Hazel volunteered.

"Thanks, Mom."

"What's this all about?" Aaron asked as Macady steered him out the door. "Sheriff said you saw the man who shot at you. I checked out the garage at the address you gave Blacker, but the mechanic didn't recall seeing anyone with that description. He said a lot of people stop there to use the phone or restrooms, but he doesn't pay much attention to them."

"I should have gotten a license plate number or something."

"There's no telling if the truck you saw was his."

"Was the mechanic the only person you talked to?"

"No, I spoke with the cashier, but she didn't come in until noon, so she didn't know anything. The owner said he spent the morning in his office catching up on paperwork and working out a new toxic waste hauling contract. He didn't see anything."

"That man was in Twin Falls four hours ago. He could be anywhere now." She rested her arms on the top pole of the corral and gazed into the distance where Tasha grazed. "If you'd been able to come right over ..." Her voice trailed off.

"I was clear over on the other side of the county when Blacker called." Aaron defended himself. He couldn't quite keep his exasperation out of his voice. Alicia had questioned him every time he hadn't come as quickly as she'd demanded. "I've been hunting high and low for that man. I thought sure he'd left the state by now."

"I'm sorry," Macady suddenly apologized. "It's been a traumatic day. Seeing him was so unexpected. All the fear I felt when he was shooting at me came rushing back, and I was already on edge."

"Why were you on edge?" He, too, leaned folded arms against the top rail and watched as Tasha trotted toward Macady. He stood still, enjoying the picture she made as she touched her cheek to the mare's long face. He felt the tension drain away.

She sighed and turned to face him. "Kelsey and Jackie cut each other's hair this morning."

"Oh, no!" He slapped his hand to his forehead. "This is going to cause trouble."

"It already has." She told him about her confrontation with Helen. "I'm sorry it happened, but please don't blame Denise or Kelsey. Denise wasn't careless. The scissors the girls used were the blunt-tipped ones they use for their art projects, and children that age have no concept of the consequences of an action like that."

"Enough!" Aaron stopped her rush of words. "I'm not surprised at your defense of the two little stinkers. I remember very well what Jeremiah and David looked like a few years back when another little girl got through cutting their hair." He grinned wickedly as her cheeks turned pink.

"Macady, you don't have to defend either one of them to me. I love Kelsey, but I'm not blind to the fact that she's four years old and four-year-olds aren't long on studying out their actions in advance. And don't worry about Denise. I wouldn't leave my daughter with her if I didn't trust her judgement. I'm perfectly aware children get into mischief even when they're closely watched."

"Daddy!"

"Uncle Aaron!"

Aaron turned to see two small figures flying toward him. He scarcely had time to take in their changed appearances before they reached him. Stooping down, he scooped them both up in his arms. After hugs were exchanged, he leaned back to carefully examine one child, then the other. He closed one eye and squinted. "What happened to you two?" he asked. "Did you take your naps on the lawn and let your hair get run over by a lawnmower while you were asleep?"

Jackie giggled. Kelsey, looking very serious, shook her head. "Jackie and me cutted it."

"I don't believe it. I bet Sandy ate your hair."

"No, Daddy." Kelsey giggled. "Sandy doesn't eat hair!"

"Are you sure?"

"Daddy, you're teasing."

"Yup." He set them both on the ground and ran his fingers through the short silky strands left on their heads. "Think how much money we're going to save now. I won't have to buy half as much shampoo."

Both little girls giggled, appreciating his silly banter. Kelsey's attention drifted to Macady and Tasha. As though drawn by a magnet, his daughter moved toward them. Without taking her eyes off the animal, she insinuated herself between Macady and the pole fence. Her face looked like Christmas morning.

Macady looked down and grinned. "Would you like to pet Tasha?"

Kelsey nodded and Macady picked her up and stood her on the second rail. With one arm around the little girl's waist, Macady took one of the child's hands and showed her how to stroke the mare's neck. Aaron felt a lump form in his throat as he looked at the two heads of closely cropped curls come together as the woman and girl bent over the horse, one set of curls only slightly darker than the other. They crooned the same unintelligible words in the horse's ear. Anyone would think they were mother and daughter. The thought came unbidden—mother and daughter. It was a picture he wouldn't get out of his mind soon.

"Can we go see the kittens now?" Jackie asked. Macady turned her head slowly. She'd been so involved with Kelsey and Tasha, she'd almost forgotten Aaron and Jackie.

"Sure." She swung Kelsey down from the fence. "Run along with Jackie," she urged as the child stared longingly back at the horse. "Someday, when your daddy thinks you're ready, I'll take you for a ride on Tasha."

"Tomorrow?"

"No, not tomorrow," Aaron laughed. "But one day soon."

Kelsey flashed them both big smiles before racing with Jackie toward the barn door. Macady watched until she was out of sight before asking bluntly, "Who's Sandy?"

"Sandy?" Aaron looked puzzled. "I thought that was what Kelsey named that kitten she claims."

"I don't mean the kitten. When Kelsey named the kitten, she told me she was going to call her Sandy because you told her everyone should have a Sandy in their life. Then today your mother-in-law called me Sandy and made some nasty accusations. I just want to know what I'm being accused of."

Aaron's lip twitched. "You're not going to like this."

"Go ahead."

"Sandy was my grandmother's old one-eyed, lame dog."

"A dog?" Macady repeated incredulously.

"Yes," Aaron grinned. "Before my brother Matt was born, my mother had a difficult pregnancy and had to stay in bed for a couple of months. My parents sent me to stay with my grandmother in Salt Lake. I didn't know any other kids and I'd never been away from home before, so I was pretty lonesome. Old Sandy followed me everywhere, licked away my tears, and became my best friend. She got me through the longest, most difficult summer of my childhood."

Macady felt her lips twitch. "Your mother-in-law seems to think Sandy is an old flame of yours."

"She would," Aaron shook his head. "When Alicia died, Kelsey was lost and lonely. It scared me to see her become quiet and withdrawn. As much as I wanted to come back here and accept a job with Sheriff Blacker, I wanted even more to take Kelsey away from her grandmother's grief and anger. I told her about Sandy because I hoped she would understand that sadness doesn't have to last forever. I wanted her to find a friend and understand that even though she missed her mother, she could be happy again."

"She and Jackie seem to be good friends."

"They are, but one things puzzles me." Laughter lurked in the back of his eyes. "Kelsey never stops talking about her Sandy, so it's not surprising her grandmother picked up on the name. But who did you think Sandy might be?"

She didn't answer. No way was she going to tell Aaron that Slade had told her things that made her question his integrity. And she certainly wouldn't tell him she'd been just a bit jealous.

"What about that shopping trip you promised?" Macady hurried to change the subject.

"I'm ready when you are," Aaron laughed as he went in search of Kelsey and Jackie.

"How about this one?" Aaron plopped a ten-gallon Texas cowpoke hat atop Macady's head. Kelsey giggled and after one look in the mirror, Macady dissolved in laughter too.

"I think not." She removed the tall hat and set it back on its stand. "This is more my style." She reached for a traditional gray felt Stetson. She placed it on her head and turned toward the mirror to straighten the brim. As she turned her head, her eyes met Aaron's in the mirror. He winked and she watched a flush cover her cheeks. Good grief, she couldn't remember the last time such a simple gesture from a man had made her blush—or feel so warm and happy inside.

"Is this the one you want?" Aaron touched the lightly rolled brim.

"Yes, I'll take it, but I can pay for it myself." Aaron really didn't owe her a hat. Someone did, but not Aaron.

"I told you, don't argue." He lifted the hat from her hands.

"I want a hat, too, Daddy." Kelsey brushed her fingers across the soft felt of the hat Macady had chosen.

Aaron laughed. "I'm not surprised. Okay, punkin, let's go over to the children's department and find a hat for you."

"Aaron, while you do that, I'm going to look at boots. I saw a pair in the window as we came in that I'd like to try on."

"Sure, we'll meet you at the front door when we're through." Aaron held the gray hat in one hand and his daughter's hand in the other as he walked away. Macady followed them with her eyes and felt a sad little ache as they left her behind. Shaking off the momentary melancholy, she moved with purposeful strides toward the boot department at the front of the store.

Six pairs of boots later, she stood before a mirror twisting one way, then the other to get the full effect of the low-heeled, hand-stitched roper boots. A familiar face in the glass caught her attention. She turned toward the window in time to see Sylvia Ashcraft step out of the cafe across the street. Beside her was a tall man in jeans and a green polo shirt. He stood with his back to the street and ran his fingers through his hair, then nodded his head sharply. Sylvia clutched his arm, appearing to speak with some agitation.

Macady was startled. Was that Slade? But his hair wasn't that short, was it? Perhaps Slade had gotten a haircut since the last time she had seen him. And yet, the way he hunched his shoulders as he talked stirred an uneasy memory in the back of her mind. Guiltily, Macady wondered if she might be spying on a reunion between Sylvia and Slade—a reunion that didn't appear to be going well.

Although she turned her attention back to the boots on her feet, her mind continued to dwell on the couple across the street. She'd never snooped into her cousins' personal lives and she wasn't going to start now. If Slade wanted to see Sylvia again that was his business. Still there was something about the couple that nagged at her subconscious. Something that didn't seem quite right.

"Macady, look at my hat!" Kelsey ran toward her with a tiny, white, western hat perched on her curls. Leather thongs, laced through a wooden bead and drawn tight beneath the little girl's chin, held it in place.

"Wow! You look terrific!" Macady inspected the beaded band that circled the crown of the hat and voiced her approval.

Kelsey preened and Aaron whispered, "Let's get out of here before she decides she needs boots, too!"

Macady laughed as she accepted the wrapped boot box from the clerk and the three of them walked outside. Aaron reached for her package to add to the one he carried, and Macady held Kelsey's hand on the short walk to her car. Aaron stowed the packages inside for her and stepped back to the curb.

"Thank you for the hat." She felt self-conscious trying to express her appreciation.

"It was my pleasure." Aaron's voice, a little huskier than usual, touched a cord along her spine.

"I'd better be going." Still she hesitated before sliding behind the wheel.

"Take care." Aaron touched the brim of his hat before closing her door for her.

The interior of Macady's car felt like an oven, and she rolled down a window as she started the engine. Once the air conditioner kicked in she'd have to close it, but for a few minutes it would keep the stifling air from suffocating her. She pulled onto the street and accelerated slowly, her mind on the man and child she'd spent the afternoon with. They were both taking on an alarming importance in her life. Perhaps she should write her friend in Portland again about that job.

A block beyond the plaza she spotted a familiar truck and pulled up beside it. The lone occupant leaned out of the open window and called a greeting to her.

"Hi, Zack! What are you doing with Slade's truck? Is yours giving you trouble again?"

"No." Zack didn't sound too pleased with the situation. "I thought that since Slade and I both had to come into town, there was no reason to drive both trucks. His errands are taking longer than mine, so now I'm stuck cooling my heels until he gets back."

"Leave him a note and come with me," Macady invited. "I'm on my way home."

A horn sounded behind her reminding her she was double parked. She looked for a parking spot, but didn't see one.

"Swing around the block and come back for me," Zack shouted as he motioned for her to go on.

Macady touched the gas pedal with her foot and glanced apologetically in her rearview mirror. At the corner she turned right, then realized she'd have to go two blocks to avoid a one-way street running the wrong way. At the light she tapped her fingers impatiently against the steering wheel while she waited for it to change. When the light turned green, Macady stepped on the gas and returned to where Slade's truck was parked. The truck was just pulling away leaving Zack standing on the curb. She caught a quick glimpse of a husky arm waving at her from the window before Slade's dark green Ranger turned the corner and disappeared from sight. She reached across the seat to release the door lock and Zack jumped in.

"Thanks! Slade's in a hurry to get to the airport, so I told him to go ahead. I said I'd catch a ride with you."

Macady frowned as she concentrated on her driving. They'd gone several miles before Zack interrupted her thoughts.

"What's the matter, kid? You look like something's eating you."

She hesitated before confiding in Zack. "It's Slade. After the fit I threw when you two decided to check out my boyfriends a few years ago, I feel stupid to be worrying about him and Sylvia."

"Sylvia Ashcraft?"

She nodded her head.

"What makes you think he's seeing her again? And why do you care? I thought you always got along pretty well with her."

"I like Sylvia, but the Church doesn't mean anything to her anymore. Slade's vulnerable right now, and I wouldn't want to see him involved with someone who might hurt him. He hasn't gotten over ..." She stopped, knowing she'd said too much.

"Who?"

"I can't say anymore."

Zack was so quiet, Macady took her eyes off the road to look his way. He appeared deep in thought and she could see it wasn't happy thoughts he was thinking. She focused her eyes back on the road and turned onto Addison without speaking.

Outside of town, she asked softly, "What gives, Zack? You haven't said a word for two miles."

He sighed audibly. "Sylvia called Slade a couple of nights ago. He's been a bear ever since."

"I saw them together a little while ago. I got the feeling they were neither one very happy."

"Slade hasn't been happy for a long time." Zack spoke from tight lips. "He and Aaron and I used to be awfully close. There were no secrets between us, but he doesn't confide in me anymore. He's never talked about what happened between him and Sylvia. I always figured her brother had something to do with their breakup. Sid was always kind of strange. He enjoyed play-ing the big shot and ran with a pretty rough crowd. He never did like Slade, probably because Slade was one of the few people he couldn't bully.

"After Slade and Sylvia broke up, she used to call once in a while, but he wouldn't speak to her. When she called the other night, I got the impression she wanted him to meet her, and he refused."

It was Macady's turn to be quiet. She felt hurt and sad deep inside. She loved her cousins and she'd always looked up to Zack and Slade. She'd be the first to recognize that Slade's relationship with Sylvia or Alicia or anyone else was none of her business, but still she felt she'd been let down in some way. She pictured Slade with Sylvia as she'd seen them an hour ago and hoped with all her heart that he would walk away from a relationship that would bring him more pain and disillusionment.

"'Cady, the folks are planning a big cookout Saturday night." Zack's voice intruded on her thoughts. "You're coming, aren't you?"

"Probably. Mom doesn't plan to go, but I promised Uncle Carson I would be there."

"Will you do me a favor?" Macady stole a glance at Zack; his usually cheerful face looked serious. Faint white lines appeared at the edge of his mouth.

"If I can," Macady hedged.

"Don't mention Sylvia to Slade. Please."

"Why not?"

"Something's eating Slade. He's been moody and depressed for quite awhile. We haven't been as close since I got married, but I'm trying to change that. I invited him to go to the temple in Boise with me next Thursday, and I've been hoping ... and doing a lot of praying ... that if just the two of us get away together, maybe he'll open up and let me help him with whatever is wrong in his life."

"And you're afraid that if I say anything about Sylvia, he'll be angry and defensive, back out of your arrangement, and take off on one of his trips?"

"Something like that."

"I hadn't planned to say anything anyway." Macady didn't want to hurt Slade or damage her relationship with him. She harbored a suspicion there had been more than casual friendship between Slade and Aaron's wife, and though that possibility appalled her, she could understand that her cousin was genuinely grieving. Confronting him would only cause more pain.

CHAPTER NINE

Shadows from the poplar trees across the west side of Uncle Carson's backyard stretched almost to the opposite fence when Macady carried a platter of hamburger patties to her uncle. He studied them for several minutes, then beamed his approval. Macady hid her smile. The big bear of a man prided himself on his outdoor cooking skills. He frequently boasted of the great meals he cooked single-handedly on his grill or in dutch ovens for his family and friends.

She'd been about twelve when she'd noticed that Aunt Lucille spent all day making salads, baking beans, forming hamburger patties, slicing onions, mixing punch, baking cakes, wrapping corn in foil, and dragging out picnic utensils, while Uncle Carson tended the grill and reaped all the praise. At least, a couple of the boys usually mowed the lawn and hauled out the lawn furniture.

She took a deep breath of the clean, dry air before returning to the house to begin carrying out salads. This was what she needed, a few hours relaxing with her family. Tonight she wouldn't worry about finding a permanent job, her mother's health, or her experience in the desert, or even give a thought to a certain brown-haired deputy and his pixie daughter.

A two-year-old darted between her legs and made a dash for the open door. She corralled him with one hand while balancing a heavy bowl on the other.

"Gotcha!" The little boy giggled.

"Here," Lucille took the bowl from her. "You and Mary round up all of the kids and take them outside. Just keep them away from Carson's cooking."

"Want to help Grandpa!" the toddler announced.

"Forget it, Travis! Grandpa doesn't need your brand of help." Macady swung him over her shoulder and went in search of Zack's wife, Mary.

Soon the two young women had five little boys engrossed in playing games. The sixth wasn't interested. At three months he was content to sit in his infant seat and snooze. Several distant cousins and a few neighbor children joined their group. Macady started them on a simple game of Button, Button.

The older children waited for Mary to turn her back before trying to slide the button to the next child. One child craftily slipped the button under Travis's hand and closed his fat little fist tightly around it.

"I got it! Me!" The two-year-old struggled to his feet and danced in glee. He opened his hand to show everyone the prize. The other children groaned.

"He's too little to play."

"Travis is a baby."

"Pass it to Macady," a five-year-old ordered. But Travis balked at passing the button on.

Macady laughed and pulled him into her arms for a hug.

"I want to play." Macady swung around to face Kelsey. Standing behind his daughter was Aaron looking relaxed in pale blue faded jeans and an open-collar sport shirt. She hadn't expected Aaron to come—or Kelsey. She concentrated on Kelsey and a welcoming smile lit her face.

"Sure, you can play." She slid over to make room for her.

"How about me?"

Macady's attention focused on Aaron's dancing eyes, and she forgot to breathe for several long seconds. Her brain felt scrambled. As from a long distance, she heard herself say, "Sure, there's space on the other side of Travis."

"No way," Mary cut in. "He can take my place in the middle and we'll see how good the eyes of the law are. Besides my feet are killing me, and it's my turn to sit down."

Aaron wasn't sure why he'd accepted Zack's invitation. He'd been fairly certain Macady would be here. The Jacksons were a close-knit family and they did things together. Macady obviously hadn't been expecting him; she'd been surprised to see him, and after that first look, had avoided meeting his eyes. Had he misread the message of welcome and warmth in that first unguarded moment? Why was he looking for messages in her eyes, anyway?

He was attracted to Macady; he had to admit that, but instead of finding excuses to hang around her, he ought to be running for his life. His physical reaction to her warned him friendship alone was out of the question, and since he had moral objections to an affair, that left him with only two options: stay away from her, or marry her. He wanted nothing to do with marriage, especially to someone as attached to her family as Macady. He'd already made that mistake once. Staying away was his best option. Having made that decision didn't cheer him as it ought.

When Carson bellowed, "Come and get it," Aaron took advantage of the confusion to put some distance between himself and Macady. While he filled Kelsey's plate and his own, he was aware of Macady fussing with Zack's kids. The littlest one, Travis, stuck to her like glue. Irritated with the tug of jealousy he felt gnawing at him, he turned back to Kelsey.

"Let's sit over there." Kelsey started toward Macady and the three little boys sharing her table.

"Wait a minute." He grabbed the back of Kelsey's suspenders. "I think she's saving that space for the boys' mommy and daddy. There's plenty of room over here." He led her to another table on the opposite side of the patio. He thought for a few minutes that Kelsey might rebel, but when Web and his wife joined them with their baby, she seemed content to play with the baby.

Ben joined them a few minutes later, and a wave of nostalgia swept over him as he listened to the lanky teenager tease Kelsey. He thought of how he and Zack and Slade used to tease Macady. His eyes traveled involuntarily to the table where Macady sat.

Daniel and Melissa with their two children had joined her with Zack's family. He watched Macady cut a hamburger in half and divide it between the two younger boys. She laughed at something someone said and the sound tinkled like crystal in Aaron's ears. He swallowed and turned away. He couldn't explain the sudden longing he felt to be part of Macady's group.

An old station wagon bumped down the lane and Aaron watched gangly teenagers and children of every age tumble out and race for the still heavily laden food table. Lucille hurried forward to hug the stout woman who trailed in their wake, and Aaron recognized the women were sisters. Thoughtfully, he swept the crowd with his eyes and realized that of the fifty or sixty people present, most were related in one way or another, and more kept coming. He and Kelsey, Bishop Eames' family, and the three pretty girls sitting with Will, Jeremiah, and David were the only non-relatives as far as he could tell. He'd been included in a lot of Jackson family parties when he was younger, but with Slade's present attitude toward him, he was surprised he'd been invited to this one. Perhaps he was the reason Slade wasn't present. More likely, Slade was off on one of his trips.

Coming up the lane was a blue van. He watched it come to a stop beside the other vehicles. When tall, lean Spence Jackson stepped out followed by a boy who looked to be about eight, Aaron choked on a forkful of salad. This really was a family party if Spence was here.

He recognized Carol Morris—now Carol Jackson—when she came around the side of the van with two more little boys in tow. She was still pretty in a wide-eyed, fragile way. Spence was showing quite a bit of gray in his hair, but Carol's blonde hair looked no different than it had when he'd known her as a popular upperclassman.

Well, that made the gathering complete. Other than Slade and Hazel, every Jackson relative he knew was present. He'd be out of his mind to get any more involved with Macady. The Jackson boys had been great friends while they were growing up, but he couldn't imagine taking on the whole bunch for in-laws. The one in-law he'd acquired when he married Alicia was more than he could tolerate. No way would he take on a tribe the size of the Jackson clan. He turned his head, looking for Macady's reaction to her father's appearance. Her place at the table was empty.

An uneasy premonition climbed Aaron's spine. He hadn't heard her mention her father once in the times they'd been together. Her laughter sounded from inside the house and instinctively he rose to his feet.

"Is that all right with you, Aaron?" He jerked his attention back to his table mates. Ben was looking at him expectantly.

"Sorry. I guess I missed the question."

"That's okay." Ben repeated his question. "I just wanted to know if it would be okay if I took Kelsey down to the barn to see my new colt. I'll watch her really close."

"Sure. Go ahead. Kelsey, stay with Ben and mind him," Aaron cautioned his daughter as his attention reverted back to the young woman standing in the doorway with a plate of cake in her hands. Aaron knew from the look on her face that Macady hadn't known Spence was coming, and seeing him wasn't a pleasant surprise. Her face paled, and her lips tightened to a firm line. Her step faltered, and he expected to see the cake land in Lucille's flower bed, but Macady caught her balance and walked straight ahead to the first table where she deposited her plate before turning about and disappearing into the darkness beyond the patio lights.

Without conscious thought, Aaron followed her. He caught occasional glimpses of her pale blue shirt that appeared white in the faint light coming from a few far off stars. Her long legs carried her rapidly across the lawn and into the windbreak trees. Aaron stepped up his pace. He didn't want to catch up to her, but something inside him couldn't bear for her to be alone and hurting.

More than thirty years ago, Carson had planted a row of poplars on the west side of his house and gradually extended the trees for half a mile. Each year he'd added more trees: a row of jack pine, another of blue spruce, a mixture of fruit trees, and after digging a new well and building a stock pond at the far end of the trees, he'd added willows. Aaron found Macady sitting on the wide cement rim of the spillway, her face in the shadow of the willows. One hand dangled in the water that rushed madly from the well pipe to the pond, and her hunched shoulders spoke of deep sorrow. He saw a tremor wrack her shoulders and he stepped forward.

"Are you all right?" A strong urge to take her in his arms swept through him. Uncertain whether she would welcome the gesture, he bridled the impulse.

"Yes." He had to strain to hear her faint response. Sliding his fingertips into his back pockets, he moved a few steps closer. She didn't look up, and with studied nonchalance, he took a few more steps until he could settle himself on the cement beside her. He swung his feet in rhythmic thumps against the low wall and viewed her tear-streaked profile with compassion as she struggled to cut off the tears and act strong and unconcerned.

"I'm not much good in the advice department, but I'm a good listener." He spoke to her stiff back. He waited a few minutes then threw tact aside. "Seems Carson threw you a curve tonight. I take it, he didn't mention your father and his new family were going to show up."

"N-no, he didn't."

"Spence doesn't live that far away, just over in Burley, so you must see him fairly often."

"I don't see him. Ever. And I don't want to talk about him."

Aaron felt something twist in his heart. There was so much bitterness and misery behind her words. After eight years, her parent's divorce still had the power to shatter her world. He wanted to comfort and help her, to let her know she didn't hurt alone. He reached out to wrap his arms around her shoulders and draw her head back against his chest. She didn't resist, but leaned quietly against him. A sense of peace slowly swept over him. It felt right to hold Macady in his arms.

"Why couldn't he stay dead?"

"What!" Aaron wasn't sure he'd heard the softly spoken question right.

"I know he was never really dead." Her voice held a haunting sadness. "I pretended he'd died. That way I didn't have to face the truth. I didn't have to face knowing that my father was a weak, immoral adulterer."

"Macady ..."

"It's true. He told me himself, and I knew I had to pretend he was dead, or I would die from the weight of all the hate I felt."

"It's been eight years. Surely it's time to let it go," Aaron tried to soothe her.

"I can't. You don't know what it's like to spend all your life believing you're the center of someone's life, then suddenly learn you don't matter at all. Daddy used to talk a lot about being a family forever. We were really close—I thought. And we used to have long talks about keeping myself morally clean and temple worthy. I grew up believing in chastity, temple marriage, and the sanctity of the home. Then he betrayed us. Not just my mother, but me too. The day he decided to sleep with Carol was the day he decided he didn't want me any more than he wanted Mom to be with him through eternity."

Slowly Aaron rocked her back and forth, offering her comfort—the comfort for a child who believed herself scorned and denied. A silent prayer grew in his heart and he longed for a way to help her see that, although her father had made a serious mistake, he could still love her. A picture of Spence with his other family flashed through his mind and he ached for Macady. Seeing those little boys hanging on her father's arm must have been a bitter pill for Macady to swallow.

"Adultery, infidelity, cheating: they're such ugly words and they leave ugly wounds. Mom really loved him. Sometimes I think she still does, and that makes me angry. As long as she loves him, she won't even look for someone else. So she'll spend the rest of her life alone, and it just isn't fair. What right did he have to tear our lives apart? Mom kept her vows, but she's the one who is left out and lonely, while he's easily replaced us. Dad's the one who sinned, but he still has a complete family while Mom and I are alone."

"I know it doesn't seem fair." He ran his thumb across her cheeks to wipe away her tears.

"I'm sorry. I'm usually not such a baby. I hadn't cried for years until after we returned from the desert, and now I can't seem to stop. In my head, I know Daddy's unfaithfulness was not my fault, and I've gone way past being embarrassed because my friends know what he did, but I still feel ashamed. Why should I feel shame for what he did?"

"You don't have any cause to feel ashamed, but I understand better than you think, how much you hurt. I know what it means to give someone your heart and trust and have your expectations betrayed." He heard Macady's soft gasp. He wasn't sure why he'd told her that. His disappointment with his marriage was something he never discussed with anyone.

"Are you saying Alicia was unfaithful?" Macady turned to face him fully, and he wondered at the harshness behind her whisper.

"Not in the sense you probably mean." He'd never tried before to put the loss and betrayal he'd felt into words. "I don't believe Alicia was ever physically unfaithful to me, but there's another kind of infidelity that destroys a marriage as surely as adultery can. I've asked myself many times if my expectations were too high, and I've wondered if my interpretation of the scriptural injunction for married people to cleave only to each other was too rigid. But every time Alicia turned to her mother instead of me, I felt betrayed."

"Mrs. Randall indicated she and her daughter were close."

Macady's words reminded him that she had born the brunt of his mother-in-law's anger a few days ago. She deserved an apology, but he knew she'd never get one from Helen.

"I'm sorry she gave you a bad time. Usually she's cordial to strangers, but she's not adjusting well to Alicia's death. Her morbid absorption in Alicia and her obsession with comparing Kelsey and Alicia is driving me crazy. She left this morning to go back to Colorado, and I can't say I was sorry to see her go."

"It must be terrible to lose someone you love like that." There was sympathy in her voice and Aaron wasn't certain whether it was for him or for Helen. He didn't deserve her sympathy. He hadn't wanted Alicia to die, but he never once regretted that their marriage was over. He wasn't sure why he wanted Macady to understand that.

"You mentioned you thought Helen and Alicia were close. Close is a weak word to describe the bond between those two. They adored each other. They lived only for each other. I'm not sure whether Alicia's father minded while he was alive, but I did.

"I know Helen is hurting. Without Alicia, she has nothing left. From what I know of her marriage to Sterling, it was pretty empty. I suppose that explains why she made her daughter the focus of her life. Her possessive jealousy kept our marriage from attaining any real substance, and as time went on I realized that wasn't the kind of marriage I wanted.

"Alicia confided everything in her mother, and Helen picked our furniture, decided the color scheme for our bedroom, and not once did Alicia ask for my advice or opinion. If I volunteered an opinion, she looked right through me and said, 'But Mother said ...' She wasn't interested in sharing my day-to-day experiences and hers were so thoroughly discussed with her mother, she had nothing left to tell me. If I ever tried to call her from work, she was either on the phone with Helen or at her house. All she needed me for was to provide a paycheck and father the children she wanted."

Aaron stopped speaking, stunned at the bitterness he'd just expressed. He set Macady away from him and rose to his feet. How could he possibly comfort Macady or offer her advice when he felt so much bitterness and anger himself? And guilt. Surely it was wrong to accuse Alicia of cheating him when she was dead and could do nothing to rectify the past or defend her actions.

This time it was Macady who reached out to offer comfort. "Aaron?" She reached out and took his hand. "I'm sorry." She had nothing to apologize for, but her simple words carried a measure of peace to his heart.

"I need to get back to Kelsey. Are you coming?" He tugged gently on her hand. She withdrew it from his grasp.

"No. You go ahead. I'll be along in a little while."

He'd almost reached the deep shadows of the spruce trees when she spoke again. "Thanks for coming after me, and for not telling me I have to forgive him. I know what I have to do. I've already given myself all the sermons I need about forgiveness and how I'm hurting myself more than he is, and I know all about negative emotions retarding spiritual growth. But I'm not ready. Sometimes I wonder if I ever will be." She sounded so lost and sad, he wanted to go to her and assure her all would be well—but how could he assure her when his own heart echoed her desolation?

"Aaron," She spoke once more. He turned back to face her dark silhouette. "I can't handle going back to the party or seeing Daddy tonight."

"I understand." He walked away, with every step telling him he was going the wrong way. It was already too late to think he could just stay away from Macady. Somehow she'd laid claim to a corner of his heart, and he knew with a dreadful certainty that soon she'd claim it all.

CHAPTER TEN

When Aaron reached the edge of the lawn, he looked around for Kelsey and Ben. He couldn't see them, so he made his way to the barn. As crazy as Kelsey had been over Macady's horse, Ben had probably not been able to drag her away from the new colt. The door was open and a faint light burned at the far end. He walked toward it and paused when he heard voices coming from a stall midway down the long corridor. He recognized Spence Jackson's voice raised in anger.

"It was a fool stunt to pull. You saw what happened. The minute I arrived, Macady turned white as a ghost and took off for the trees. I've hurt her enough, and I won't stand still for you trying to trick her into seeing me."

"You're her father. It's time you remind her of that fact," Carson growled. "Macady will be leaving soon, and you'll have lost your chance."

"She wants nothing to do with me. In eight years she has never once let me even wish her Merry Christmas. If the only thing I can do for her is leave her alone, that's what I'll do."

"You're a fool, Spencer Jackson, even if you are my own brother. How you could give up a fine woman like Hazel and turn your back on Macady, I don't know. You've got a lot to answer for, and I just hope Carol's worth it."

"Carol has a lot of fine qualities," Spence's voice sounded tired and discouraged, "but it would be a lie to say I don't miss Hazel at times. I never appreciated her strength when we were married. Too often I felt threatened by her self-confidence and business instincts. Instead I envied you having a wife who thrived on running your home, and who was content to leave you in charge. At first it was flattering to have a pretty young wife who adored me and hung on every word I said, but I've learned it gets mighty lonely when you have to make all the decisions by yourself."

"Are you saying you're tired of Carol now?" Carson sounded about ready to explode. Aaron told himself he should move on. He had no business eavesdropping on a private conversation, but his feet stayed where they were.

"Don't get in a huff. I'm not saying any such thing. I do love Carol and our children. What I am saying is, I'm not any happier with Carol than I was with Hazel. I wasn't unhappy before, and life was a lot simpler. But now I have a lot of regrets, and the biggest one is that I lost Macady. Hazel forgave me. I think she always understood me better than I understood myself, but Macady may never get over what I did to her."

"That's what I'm afraid of. She took your leaving awfully hard. Thought she might be coming out of it when she got engaged to some fellow she met at school last year. But she caught him cheating, and now she blames every man she meets for what you and that guy did. That's why I've been trying to get the two of you together. She needs to know you never stopped loving her."

"No, I never stopped loving her. I never could."

Slowly Aaron retraced his steps, his mind troubled by the conversation he'd overheard following so quickly on the heels of his discovery that he held deep feelings for Macady. Carson said Macady was incapable of trusting any man. He'd lived with a woman who didn't trust him and knew that was a factor in destroying their marriage. Alicia had made some ugly accusations, most likely prompted by her mother because his work entailed odd hours. She'd hinted that he and Linda Otero, his field partner, did more than work together. Her lack of trust had angered him, and he didn't like to think he was sliding into another relationship with the same dark holes that had torn his first marriage apart.

Spence had been in the wrong, yet Aaron couldn't help feeling a tug of compassion for him. He wondered what Macady would say if he told her that her father was hurting as badly as she because of their estrangement.

He found Ben sitting with Kelsey, who had fallen asleep, on the porch swing. He slipped his arms under his daughter and lifted her to his shoulder. He walked back toward the light, carrying the sleeping child snuggled trustingly in his arms and wondered how Spence could have made that choice eight years ago that very likely terminated his relationship with his daughter forever.

Macady returned quietly to her car without meeting anyone and drove the short distance home. She parked in back of the store near the family entrance and stared at the dark shape of the only home she'd ever known. She'd loved growing up in that house, and even after her father had left, she had felt sheltered and comforted there. Tonight the house failed to stir the same sense of homecoming it always had before. Somewhere deep inside, she was changing and she wasn't sure she wanted to change. Stifling a longing for the simpler days of her childhood, she climbed out of the car.

Slowly she circled the house, checking windows and the front door, making certain everything was secure for the night. She'd taken over the chore for her mother when she'd returned home. She stepped into the circle of light from the overhead security lamp at the back door and paused at the sight of one of the kittens, lying there unmoving. She knew without taking another step that it was dead. Her throat ached and a helpless protest rose to her lips.

She wondered how the kitten had died and how it had gotten out of the barn. Slowly she bent toward the kitten and that was when she noticed the paper. With trembling fingers, she unfolded the sheet of notepaper. Shaky letters were scrawled across the page. *Mind your own business or else! You saw nothing!* Macady glanced from the paper to the kitten and bile rose in her throat. She fumbled to unlock the door and stumbled across the door ledge. She had to call Aaron. She needed to hear his voice.

"Please let him still be at Uncle Carson's," she breathed the words aloud while she waited for someone to pick up the phone.

"Hello." She recognized Ben's voice.

"Is Aaron still there?" Her voice ended with a quaver.

"Hold on! I think I can catch him!" Ben shouted and Macady winced as the phone clattered against a solid surface. She bit her lip and paced in short tight circles while she waited.

"Are you all right?" Macady looked up to see her mother standing in the doorway, tightening the sash on her housecoat.

"I'm okay, but something awful happened tonight. When I ... Aaron?" Macady broke off to speak into the telephone. "Aaron, can you come over here?" He sounded out of breath as if he'd been running. She listened a minute, then spoke again. "No, we're fine, but something has happened I thought you should know about ..." She told him about the kitten and the note, then paused. "Yes, we'll see you in a few minutes. Come around to the back. The front door is locked and the alarm set."

"Did I hear you say someone deliberately killed one of the kittens?" Hazel demanded to know. Macady nodded her head.

"Why?" she whispered. "Why would someone kill a helpless kitten?" There was a catch in Hazel's voice. "Some people have no respect for life, human or animal. Some people have shut God so completely out of their lives that they have no respect for any of his creations."

Macady peered out the window, watching for Aaron's headlights to appear.

"I didn't hear a thing. How could someone come here and do that without me hearing them?" Hazel sank onto a kitchen chair. "What about the kitten? Was it the one Kelsey claims?"

"No, it wasn't Sandy," Macady answered quickly, then added more slowly, "Maybe I ought to move it before Aaron gets here. Kelsey is with him."

"I'll go sit with her when they get here and make certain she doesn't see the kitten," Hazel volunteered. "What about the other kittens and Patches? Are they all right?"

Macady's eyes widened in fear. She hadn't thought to check on the other cats—or Tasha. She ran for the door just as headlights cut through the darkness and Aaron's truck slid to a gravel spitting stop beside the back door. She didn't slow down, but continued her dash for the barn. Aaron caught up to her as she swung the heavy door open.

"Don't go in there!" Aaron grasped her arm.

"I have to." She tried to free herself from his grip.

"Not until I check it out." Suddenly she was in his arms, shaking with tears and gasping as she tried to speak.

"I-I have to check on the other cats ... and ... and Tasha."

"Are there lights in the barn, or do I need to get a flashlight?"

"The light switch is just inside the door."

"Okay, stay right here until I call you." Aaron moved her gently away from him.

"I'm coming with you."

"No, don't argue with me this time."

Time telescoped seconds into hours until a light came on and she heard Aaron call her name. She rushed past him to Tasha's stall. She flung open the door and Tasha nickered in welcome. Macady flung her arms around the mare's neck and sobbed. Slowly she became aware Aaron was patiently standing behind her. She turned to see him with an armful of cats.

"Patches!" Macady murmured as she stroked the big cat. She dashed away her tears with the back of her hand. Her eyes met Aaron's and, though he made no move to touch her, she felt the same comforting warmth she'd felt earlier when he'd held her.

"Perhaps you'd better show me the other kitten and the note." He spoke softly, but there was an edge of steel behind his words which gave Macady courage. She reached into her pocket and handed him the paper she'd stuffed there earlier. While he read it she watched his face carefully. His expression never changed.

"Do you think it was the man who shot at me?" She finally asked.

"I don't know. This was most likely just some sick joke and whoever did it won't be back. On the other hand, as long as there's any remote chance some drug king knows you can identify him, we need to play it safe. Let's go talk to your mother and I need to call Blacker. Together we'll think of something."

While Aaron was on the phone with the sheriff, Macady carried Kelsey into the house, then encouraged her mother to go back to bed.

"Blacker doesn't think the dead kitten or the note have anything to do with our drug smugglers," Aaron turned from the phone. "He's convinced you were victimized by pranksters, most likely local high school kids who didn't mean to kill the kitten."

"What do you think?" Hazel asked for his opinion.

"I'm not sure." He spoke carefully. "It might have been kids, but my gut reaction is that the threat is real. At any rate, I don't think you should take chances. Moving out for a few days would be a good idea."

Macady watched her mother shake her head and smiled. Aaron didn't know her mother well if he thought he could convince her to leave her store. The store had originally been in her husband's family, but she'd been the one to make it a success and had incorporated into it a market for locally produced crafts.

"Look, Hazel," Aaron argued. "It needn't be for very long, and if you stayed with Carson, you could easily come back here every day to open your store."

"No, Aaron, I'm staying right here. Macady can go if she wishes."

Aaron turned to Macady and she shook her head. She wouldn't leave her mother alone, but first thing tomorrow morning she'd move her horse and the cats to the Jackson ranch.

Aaron sighed and rose to his feet. "I'll make certain everything is locked up before I go."

"I'll go with you," Macady volunteered.

Aaron didn't speak much as he walked around the house and store, checking the locks on the doors and windows. The barn didn't really have a lock, just a heavy bar that prevented wind or stock from sweeping open the door.

They returned to the house to find Hazel had retired, leaving only the kitchen light and a dim hall light glowing. Macady led the way into the living room where light from the kitchen dimly illuminated Kelsey as she lay curled beneath an afghan. Together they stood looking down at the sleeping child, and Macady experienced a strange sense of déjà vu as though she and Aaron had stood together at some other time watching their child sleep. It didn't seem strange at all when he moved closer and placed his arms around her. She met him halfway, his lips touched hers, and it felt incredibly right.

"Good night, Macady." He spoke the words softly into her mouth and she shivered as the warm puffs of air touched her sensitized lips. He stepped away and reached for his small daughter. Macady followed them to the door and stood listening as Aaron's truck drove away. Slowly she sank to the floor and sat with her arms wrapped around her knees. "Oh, Father," she breathed softly. "What is happening to me? I'm afraid I'm falling in love with Aaron Westerman."

CHAPTER ELEVEN

Aaron flopped over and pounded a fist against the top of his alarm clock. The ringing sounded again and he sat upright, groping for the telephone. "Yeah," he managed to mumble into the instrument.

"Westerman, get over to Magic Valley Regional. Paramedics just hauled in a coke-snorter who's blabbing his head off. Nothing he says will be admissible in court, but it could be a lead," Blacker's voice thundered in his ear. He opened one eye wide enough to check the clock. It wasn't four yet. He'd have to bundle up Kelsey and get her to Matt and Denise. He hated to disturb their sleep, but he didn't have much choice.

"I'll be there in twenty minutes, as soon as I drop my daughter off at my brother's house." He disconnected and immediately hit the direct dial button to alert Matt he was on his way with Kelsey, then slammed down the phone and reached for his pants. Kelsey mumbled and snuggled into his arms when he picked her up. She didn't awaken even when he strapped her into the safety restraint in his truck. Matt met him at the door and Aaron transferred the sleeping child to his brother's arms.

Barely twenty minutes had passed when he stepped through the sliding glass emergency doors of the hospital and hurried to the desk. A nurse pointed down the hall.

"'Bout time," Blacker growled as Aaron joined him beside a gurney in a partitioned alcove. A young man, who appeared to be about thirty, was strapped to it. Aaron winced as he looked at the cuts and scrapes on the man's face. One eye was swollen nearly shut and a dot of blood escaped from a split lip to run down his chin. A monitor tracked the patient's pulse and respiration. His heartbeat was erratic. In spite of his battered condition, the guy's styled blond hair and manicured nails told Aaron this wasn't some drifter or street junkie.

He leaned over the bed rail and spoke softly to the man. Brendon Wilcox, Aaron had been informed, was the name on the driver's license in the man's wallet. He'd been picked up wandering down Addison Avenue east of town. Aaron asked questions and received long rambling answers that had little to do with the questions asked. One minute Brendon was excited and talkative, the next melancholy and tearful. He reached forward and Aaron felt the clamminess of damp skin and found himself disconcerted by dilated eyes peering wildly into his.

Patiently Aaron tried to direct the panting, almost incoherent ramblings of the man toward the party he had attended that evening, but Brendon couldn't recall where he'd gone or who he'd been with. He'd had a disagreement with someone and wanted to leave, but the other man had tried to stop him. Brendon had gone outside and been followed by a truck.

"Blue, maybe green, not white like the California car. Pretty little truck with shiny wheels. Big man grabbed my shirt. Paid eighty-five dollars for that shirt. He shouldn't have touched it. The other one told him not to hit me any more. He was a good man. Gave me a drink. Vodka isn't made out of potatoes. Somebody said it was. Russians make vodka." He spoke in short fluttery breaths and his agitation increased. A few minutes later a doctor asked the sheriff and Aaron to leave.

Together they walked out to the hall and followed the corridor to a deserted waiting room. Aaron leaned his forehead against a heavy glass pane and stared into the dark. Gradually the darkness began to lift and faint streaks of pink and gold touched the sky. He'd seen his share of drunks and O.D.'s, but each one had the power to rip his heart to shreds. Perhaps he was too soft-hearted to be a law officer. He'd never understand men like the one he'd left down the hall: professional men who were apparently educated, dressed well, and had youth on their side, who spent a fortune on so-called recreational drugs. Where was the recreation in floating right out of your mind into lala land? They were no better off than the street junkies who shot up a few hours of oblivion in some dirty alley. At least the addicts had an excuse.

"The Jackson woman said the man who had shot at her was heading for a green truck when she spotted him in town. Do you think there's a possibility she saw the same guy our friend back there did?" The sheriff jerked his head in the direction of Brendon's room.

"It's possible." Aaron felt emotionally drained, but his mind went on to another point. "I think he told us a second vehicle was involved, a white car with California plates."

"I read it that way, too, but look around. Every other car these days has California plates and a lot of them are white."

And there are a lot of green trucks out there, too, Aaron reminded himself. Slade drove a green truck, a Ranger with bright chrome hubcaps.

"Go on home," Blacker dismissed him. "I'll have Laura add these bits to the computer. You look like you could use some sleep."

"Thanks."

Aaron climbed into his truck and sat hunched over the wheel. After several long minutes he pounded the steering wheel with his fist. Why this obsession with cocaine? There was a twisted kind of logic to street drugs. Despair, crime, and poverty bred a life devoid of dreams, and those without hope sold their souls to gain oblivion. But what about the Brendon Wilcoxes of this world who threw away promising futures for the sake of being "in" or trendy? How could they close their eyes to the fact that the scum that dealt death in the worst city ghettos were the same people profiting from their fun and games?

Grimly he started the truck engine and left the parking lot

behind. The drug itself wasn't the only instrument of death the drug runners were pedaling. They would kill to protect their dirty secret, as he well knew. He and Macady could have easily died in the desert, and in spite of Sheriff Blacker's assurance that the strange happenings at Jackson's Point last night had no connection with the case, Aaron wasn't so sure.

Going home and crawling back in bed was out of the question. He was too keyed up to sleep, and it didn't make sense to disturb Kelsey then take her back to his brother's house again in a few hours. What he really needed was breakfast and to check on Macady. He wouldn't have left her the previous night if he hadn't felt reasonably certain whoever left the threatening note would sit back and wait for a reaction before striking again. After eating and checking on Macady, he'd follow up on three old classmates. If one of them was the owner of a certain lost class ring, he'd have the clue he needed.

Three pickup trucks were parked beside Macady's little sports car when he pulled behind the store. Fear stabbed his chest and he flung open the door ready to do battle before he noticed one truck belonged to Zack and the battered king cab was clearly old Carson's. Ben walked from the barn carrying a box, which he placed on the passenger seat of the king cab and, hearing the howls coming from inside it, Aaron figured Patches wasn't too happy about her imminent change of address.

"Morning, Aaron." He looked toward the corral where Zack leaned against a post. He returned the greeting, but his eyes were on Macady who stood with her back to him, adjusting the straps of Tasha's bridle. His eyes stayed on her red plaid shirt and tight denim jeans as he walked toward the corral. He noticed her new boots and remembered the pair she'd abandoned. It pleased him to see her new gray Stetson on her head. A fickle morning breeze teased the short dark curls peeking beneath the hat, drawing attention to the smooth curve of her cheek. No woman had a right to be as beautiful as Macady in plain work clothes.

She turned and flashed him a quick smile when he reached the fence, then turned back to her horse. Aaron folded his arms across the top rail and watched her.

"You should have called us last night," Zack's words were intended for his ears alone.

"There was a deputy keeping an eye on the house all night."

"I know. Will and Jeremiah noticed his car when they went out to tend water at four, so I figured I better come on over and see what was going on."

"Hazel refused to call Carson or go to him last night. Has she changed her mind this morning?" Aaron asked, though he suspected he already knew the answer.

Zack shook his head. "She won't leave, and Macady won't go without her. No use fighting them about it, though. I expect you've already discovered they're a couple of mighty stubborn women. Ben and Jeremiah brought their gear. They'll just move in here for awhile." Zack spoke matter-of-factly.

"Are you planning to ride that horse over to the ranch by yourself?" Aaron raised his voice.

"Not you, too!" Aaron didn't miss the exasperation in her voice. "Don't worry, I won't be alone. Zack will follow me over, then he'll bring me back. My dear cousins have arranged for around-the-clock babysitting service!"

Aaron exchanged a smile with Zack. Macady had put her fears of the previous night behind her and was chaffing at their well-intentioned efforts to protect her. Macady wasn't a woman to take any curb on her independence lightly.

Macady gathered the reins in one hand and swung into the saddle. Tasha tossed her head and pranced sideways a couple of steps before settling down. Macady nudged her against the fence where the two men stood. Her eyes sparkled as they traveled up and down Aaron's rumpled uniform. He felt a slow flush climb up the back of his neck.

"Have you been up all night or have you just had a rough morning already?" she teased.

"Do you care?" He hadn't meant to sound so serious, and her

face sobered. Before she could say anything more, he told her about his early morning call. "It seemed a waste of time to go back to bed without running out here first."

"You could have saved yourself a trip and just called." She looked down at him from the horse's back. Her words indicated his arrival meant little to her, but something he saw in the back of her eyes told him another story.

Aaron smiled. "But I wanted to see your face when I asked you to have dinner with me tonight." He couldn't believe he'd just asked Macady Jackson to go out with him. And right in front of Zack. He cast a sideways glance at Macady's cousin. The grin on Zack's face was a little too knowing.

"I have to go to Sun Valley late this afternoon. I just thought it might pass the time more quickly for me and help you forget last night if you came along." Well, he did need to go to Sun Valley to meet with Stuart Johnson and having Macady along would make their meeting appear more natural.

Macady bit her bottom lip and turned away. She wouldn't go. He anticipated her refusal. Perhaps if he took Kelsey along. He almost didn't hear her softly spoken response.

"All right. What time?"

"Five okay?" He tried to cover his sudden elation behind a cool facade, but he was sure his cracked voice gave away his nervousness. Get a grip, he chastised himself. He was behaving like an adolescent anticipating his first date.

When he got back to the office, he found a stack of paperwork waiting and a couple of phone messages from DEA. With a sigh, he sat down and reached for the first sheet. The words ran together and he wasn't certain whether he was reading a report or a piece of junk mail. He wasn't going to get anything done until he followed up on all the possible owners of that class ring the sheriff had found. He'd let thoughts of Macady and memories of old friendships slow his search long enough.

With one hand, he dragged the telephone closer, then used his PC to locate the number for the San Diego police department. He drummed the fingers of one hand on the desk as he waited for the call to go through. His mind went back ten years to the Sean Jaramillo he'd known then—senior class president, a brilliant strategist on the football field, and a bit of a goof-off in class.

After being routed to four different departments, he finally reached a young woman in records who had a soft Hispanic drawl and agreed to see what she could find.

After a call to the California Bar Association, Aaron turned his attention to Stuart Johnson. Stuart had been well-liked in school. An old girlfriend had dropped Aaron when Stuart asked her out, but Aaron hadn't held it against the other boy. They'd played softball and basketball together on the ward team. They didn't win many games, but all the girls came out to watch Stuart play. A quick check of Motor Vehicles showed a couple of DUI's several years back and a more recent speeding ticket. Stuart always had driven too fast, and Aaron had known back when they were kids that even though Stuart went to church, even showed up once in awhile for seminary, that he wasn't adverse to attending keg parties in the hills with some of his other friends.

Sylvia had said Stuart was divorced and Aaron had requested a background check. The report should be on his desk by now. Quickly he thumbed through the papers and found what he was looking for. He scanned the columns quickly and frowned. The DUI's coincided with his first divorce. A second brief marriage had terminated six months ago. No children. He lived considerably beyond his income and was in debt up to his ears. If he was picking up extra cash on the side, he certainly wasn't using it to pay his bills.

"Aaron?" A young officer stood in the doorway. "A call just came in. Some kid is stranded on a ledge along the canyon not far from Balanced Rock. Paramedics are on their way. You'll have to go."

Aaron stood. "Let's go." He headed out the door, knowing everything he might need was already stowed in the department truck. He'd learned to rappel during his forest service training and had worked on technique both at Yellowstone and in Colorado. In Colorado he'd added an Emergency Medical Technician course, and since returning to Idaho he represented the Sheriff's Department in search and rescue operations whenever needed.

Thirty minutes later he stood at the top of the sheer canyon wall, assessing the situation. A volunteer fire unit had responded to the call and a squad car had arrived right behind his truck. One paramedic had already gone over the edge and another one was monitoring his descent while making preparations to provide medical assistance. In minutes the paramedic at the accident scene called for backup.

"Patient is conscious and in a great deal of pain. Appears to have a fractured femur, possible broken ribs, probable collar bone. Experiencing shock. Send basket down right after Westerman." The walkie-talkie in the other paramedic's hand spit static. Aaron didn't wait for him to respond. He buckled his safety harness in place, wrapped one leg around the strong nylon rope, and slid over the canyon rim. Brinkerman monitored his line.

There wasn't enough room on the narrow ledge for both men to stand beside the injured youth. Aaron found a foothold about twelve inches lower than the ledge. He glanced down once and breathed a prayer of gratitude that the ledge had interrupted the boy's fall.

"Hi!" Aaron spoke to the boy who appeared to be about sixteen. He introduced himself in an attempt to soothe the young man's fear and distract him while the paramedic started an I.V. and prepared him to be transferred to the metal basket. "What's your name?"

"Ryan Adams." The name was whispered. Ryan's eyes were wide and he stared apprehensively at the basket his rescuers were preparing to strap him into.

"We've never dropped a patient yet." Aaron tried to reassure him. He helped slide a back board under Ryan's body, then took the neck support from the other man's hands and fastened it in place. Together they transferred the fall victim to the basket and secured him.

"Mr. Westerman?" The boys' voice shook and his eyes glittered with moisture. "Are you a Mormon?"

"Yes."

"I don't know if I have the right to ask, but will you administer to me? I know I shouldn't have come with them. I've never done anything like this before." His face contorted in pain, and Aaron gripped the boy's hand.

"Take him up slowly." The paramedic spoke into his walkie-talkie.

"Wait!" There was panic in the boy's voice.

"It'll be all right. I've been praying ever since I got the call, and I have consecrated oil in my truck. As soon as we get you to the top, I'll find another elder and you'll get your blessing." He smiled encouragingly at the frightened boy. "I'll be right beside you all the way up. We both will." He nodded toward the paramedic.

A subdued group of teenagers waited at the top. They clustered around their friend, blaming themselves for his fall, until Aaron ordered them back. He stepped inside the ambulance with one of the firemen he knew held the priesthood to keep his promise to the boy. Then while the ambulance began its thirty minute run to Magic Valley Regional, the two deputies retrieved equipment, briefly interviewed the remaining teenagers, and turned them over to the juvenile authorities.

"You ever do anything that stupid?" Deputy Brinkerman shook his head as he asked the question once the two deputies were alone again.

"Probably." Aaron smiled wryly. "I never messed with drugs or drank, but I did other stupid things. You most likely did, too. Even good kids who are generally pretty responsible forget the good sense they were born with sometimes and do their share of showing off and taking chances. There's so much talk about drugs these days and kids are curious. Those young people aren't drunks or addicts. They tasted a few swallows of beer and shared a joint. Their high came from the excitement of doing something forbidden. They felt fine and it never occurred to any of them when they ran across the rocks along the rim that they were in less than full control. If one of them hadn't been hurt, they'd probably remember today as a day they had a lot of fun and the next time they went looking for a good time it would be easier to include drugs or booze."

Aaron closed his eyes and feigned sleep while Brinkerman drove. He thought about the young man who had wanted a blessing. He admired his faith and wondered if his own was as strong. Elements of his life seemed as reckless as the actions of those young people, running and leaping across boulders at the edge of an abyss. His parents had had a good marriage and his brother, Matt, seemed happy with Denise, but his own experience had left him equating marriage with a drop off a sheer cliff. Wasn't his preoccupation with Macady Jackson a lot like leaping across those boulders? It was time he exercised some faith and had a good talk with his Heavenly Father. He needed to know whether pursuing Macady would plunge him over a cliff—or if she might be the rescue team.

By the time he reached the office, it was late afternoon and he debated whether or not he had time to stop at Steve Jennings' office. Jennings sold real estate and Aaron had to drive right by his business to get home. He glanced at his watch and decided to give it a try.

He picked up the phone to speak to the dispatcher. "Berniece, I'm leaving. I'm picking up some papers at the sheriff's office in Sun Valley, then I'll have dinner at the King Sol before starting back."

"Pretty ritzy," Berniece chuckled. "You must be seeing someone special."

"Business." He grinned back, though she couldn't see him.

"Business, my foot!" Berniece snorted. "If you're eating at the King Sol, you've got yourself a hot date!"

Hot date? He wasn't sure taking Macady to dinner constituted a hot date, but he did look forward to spending the evening with her. It had been a long time since he'd last taken a woman to dinner. He started to whistle, then stopped abruptly as a twinge of guilt hit him. He wondered if he had the right to feel happy about taking a woman other than Alicia out.

"Westerman! Aaron!" He'd almost reached the door when another deputy called him back. "I almost forgot. A message came for you."

Aaron's heart dropped. Macady was canceling. He turned around and his feet moved much slower as he walked toward the message the deputy extended toward him. He didn't want to read it. He stared at the paper for several seconds before he realized he held a faxed letter. It wasn't from Macady. It was from a Ms. Mendoza in San Diego. Briefly she informed him Señor Jaramillo had been in court all day on the day in question and the following day as well and that a more detailed report would follow.

"Thanks, Anderson!" He folded the paper and stuck it in his pocket, his earlier good humor restored. He could almost certainly remove Sean from his list of suspects. He'd always liked Sean and he was glad he appeared to be in the clear. He avoided admitting that some of his good mood was due to the restored prospect of seeing Macady in an hour.

CHAPTER TWELVE

"It's beautiful here." Macady turned her eyes to the heavy beams framing floor to ceiling windows that let in a panoramic view of the mountains. A lingering touch of lavender and gold highlighted the purple peaks as day slipped into night. She leaned back against her chair and surveyed the room. Rich creamy linen graced the tables, and china and crystal glistened in the candlelight. From their table overlooking the patio, they had an unobstructed view of the mountains.

Along one side of the interior, trees and potted plants formed romantic alcoves. Macady sighed as she imagined sharing one of those secluded tables with Aaron. She shook her head to clear the image. Actually she was glad Aaron's friend had reserved a table with a view.

Macady's perusal of her surroundings stopped. There was something familiar about the couple in the last alcove. Could it be that Slade and Sylvia were here? In the dim candlelight, she couldn't be certain. A man wearing a light-colored sports jacket stopped at the table in the alcove, then took the seat next to the woman. He seemed vaguely familiar, too. No, she was being silly. Slade's shoulders were broader and the woman's hair was too dark to be Sylvia. Macady opened her mouth to tell Aaron of the couple's uncanny resemblance to her cousin and his former girlfriend, then changed her mind. She didn't want to talk about Slade. Even thinking about him reminded her of his accusations and she didn't want unpleasant thoughts to mar the evening.

Candlelight flickered like tiny stars in Macady's eyes and

Aaron focused his attention on the soft glow of her cheeks and the dark sweep of her hair. He ignored the lingering sunset to watch his dinner companion. The view from the window wasn't the only beauty this night.

"When is your friend arriving?" Macady's softly voiced question brought him back to the real reason he was here. After bumping into Sylvia Ashcraft and learning Stuart Johnson worked for the King Sol Hotel, he'd called and spoken briefly with Stuart. He'd told him he had been out of Idaho for nearly ten years and now that he was back and had to make a business trip to Sun Valley, he looked forward to renewing an old friendship. He'd invited Stuart to meet him for lunch. Stuart had responded with enthusiasm, changed their meeting to dinner at the King Sol, and urged him to bring a companion for the evening.

"Stuart said eight o'clock, and it's a little after that, now. I expect he'll be along any minute." As he spoke, his eyes moved across the room to where the maitre d' was greeting a striking couple. The woman was as tall as Macady, with the help of spindly high heels. Her bright red dress, made out of some kind of shiny material sprinkled with sequins, was short—at both ends. Her near-white hair tumbled in a carefully calculated riot of curls across her bare shoulders and down her back. Her face was that of a hauntingly beautiful, pouting child. Beside her stood his old friend, Stuart, still tall and lean with dark wavy hair and a dimple in one cheek.

"Aaron, isn't that Kiffanie Carter?" Macady's voice sparkled with excitement. Aaron followed her eyes to the woman Stuart was leading toward them and stifled an urge to dive under the table. What was a plain county deputy like himself supposed to say to a glamorous recording star? No wonder Stuart had been so anxious for them to have dinner together. During their school days, Stuart had thrived on being a step ahead of the other guys in asking out the most popular girls in school. No doubt he was relishing showing off this latest conquest.

Aaron stood as the other couple reached the table. Stuart introduced Miss Carter with obvious enjoyment. Aaron turned to Macady to complete the introductions. Lightly he touched her hand as he spoke her name and Aaron felt an electric thrill of pride as he introduced her as his companion. Macady could hold her own with any company. She wore a pale mint green dress that buttoned down the front and had a wide lace-trimmed collar that disappeared where the buttons began. A fabric belt accentuated her narrow waist. He didn't know much about fashion, but he recognized beauty when he saw it, and each time he looked at Macady, he saw it. He wouldn't trade ten minutes with her for an hour with the glamorous Miss Carter. And he certainly wouldn't sacrifice a minute of the tomboy with wisps of hay in her hair and a kitten on her shoulder for the shimmering lady clinging to Stuart's arm.

When all four were seated, Stuart leaned forward to speak to Macady. "Aren't you Hazel and Spencer Jackson's daughter? I think maybe we already know each other."

Macady nodded her head.

Stuart smiled broadly. "I never forget a beautiful woman, even when that woman was last seen in ranch clothes and pigtails."

Macady blushed and Aaron found himself quietly resenting the attention Stuart was paying her. He was glad when the other man signaled for a waiter and they all became busy perusing the menu.

Stuart recounted a couple of stories from his and Aaron's school days while they waited to be served. As Stuart talked, the incidents became more humorous than Aaron remembered. He tried several times without success to bring the conversation around to Stuart's present activities. He didn't want to turn dinner into an interrogation, but he'd like to know where Stuart got the money to drive a flashy sports car, wear two hundred dollar ties, and escort a famous recording star. No wonder Stuart's credit limit was bursting at the seams and half his generous salary as assistant manager of the King Sol was garnished for settlements with his ex-wives, Aaron thought.

Midway through dinner, the waiter approached their table to let Stuart know there was a call for him at the front desk. He excused himself and Aaron noticed the way Miss Carter's eyes followed him across the floor. He suspected they were more than casual friends. If he read Miss Carter right, there was a great deal of warmth in her regard for his old friend.

When she turned her attention back to their table, she smiled at Macady and asked, "Do you live on a real ranch? Stuart mentioned a Jackson ranch."

"The ranch belongs to my uncle and his sons. My mother's house and store were once part of the ranch," Macady answered.

"Lucky you," the blonde sighed. "Owning a big western ranch has always been my dream."

"You could buy one, couldn't you? Your songs are always at the top of the charts. I would think you could afford anything you want," Aaron interjected.

"Someday I plan to buy one." Her big eyes were round and serious. "But, there isn't time now. My agent doesn't want me to risk any capital or let anything distract me from my career. He says I have to make all the money I can while the public is anxious to hear me. In a short time someone else will catch their attention and my bookings and contracts will slide."

"I've told you before, Kiffanie—fire the jerk." Stuart was back and rested one hand on the back of her chair. "Maybe you guys can help me persuade her. Her uncle is her agent and her business manager. She supports her whole family, and every time she wants something—even just a little time for herself—Uncle James starts in with the sob stories."

"Stuart—" Kiffanie protested.

"Honey, he's taking you for a ride."

"But they're my family. I can't …"

Aaron partially tuned them out. Not even being rich and famous was protection from a controlling family. His cynical side wondered if Stuart's interest in her family's stranglehold on her time and finances came from real concern for the vulnerable young star, or whether he saw her as the answer to his own financial problems.

The dinner ended pleasantly and the two couples lingered in the lobby afterward, bidding each other goodnight. Aaron smiled as the two young women exchanged addresses, and Macady extended an invitation to Kiffanie to visit her and tour her uncle's ranch. Stuart's arm circled the young singer's waist and Aaron slipped his own arm around Macady. It felt right and natural, and he left it there as the two of them walked out into the star-spangled night.

As they approached his truck, he sensed something wasn't right. The headlights were empty holes. Shards of glass glittered on the ground beside an iron pipe. The windshield was a mosaic of tiny bits of glass, and a hole the size of a baseball indicated a missile had passed through it. Every window was shattered.

Macady gasped and his arm tightened around her. Aaron scanned the parking lot for any sign of the vandal who had attacked his truck, but he and Macady were alone.

"We'll have to go back inside to call the sheriff." Aaron led the way.

Stuart and Kiffanie were still at the front desk. Stuart looked up and started toward them. "Change your mind about leaving?" He grinned. "If you're looking for a room, I'm sure I could find something."

Aaron felt Macady tense and he lost no time telling Stuart he only needed to borrow a phone to call the sheriff. When Stuart learned of the vandalism, his face turned dark and he barked orders at the desk clerk to call security. Two beefy young men appeared almost immediately.

Leaving Macady inside with Kiffanie, Aaron accompanied Stuart and the security men outside. The sheriff joined them a few minutes later. There were no clues and no witnesses. Aaron was well aware of the difficulty in tracing a random act of violence, but deep inside he wondered if the act had really been random. No other vehicle in the large parking lot had been damaged. Why his truck? Had the Twin Falls County Sheriff's office logo on the doors set it apart?

It was possible he was being warned just as someone had warned Macady. But who—other than the dispatcher back in Twin Falls, Macady's family, his own brother, and Stuart—knew he was in Sun Valley? Stuart had left the table once during dinner. He'd had ample time to order someone, maybe one of his security men, to do the job.

"Sorry for that crack about a room," Stuart spoke quietly before rejoining the women. "You haven't changed that much. I could find two rooms."

"Thanks," Aaron responded, "but I'd better find a way to get Macady home. The sheriff said he'd have a tow truck haul my truck to a garage where the glass can be replaced and everything else checked."

"Look, I feel responsible. We pride ourselves on providing a pleasing, worry-free environment here, a place to kick back and enjoy the finer things in life. For a guest's vehicle to be vandalized is unacceptable. Let me redeem our reputation a bit by loaning you my car. You can bring it back tomorrow when you pick up yours."

"I'm not holding you responsible." Aaron had reservations about accepting Stuart's generous offer.

"I insist." Stuart pulled his keys from his pocket and reached for Aaron's hand.

Aaron glanced down and felt a jolt go through his body. Stuart's hand grasped his own and numbly he accepted the keys, but his eyes were on the ring clearly displayed on Stuart's third finger. Stuart was wearing his high school ring.

Stuart noticed the direction of Aaron's attention. He laughed and touched the ring with a self-conscious gesture. "My high school years were good years. I guess I'm being a little sentimental to still wear my ring, but it brings back a lot of good memories."

"I still have mine," Aaron responded with a touch of emotion. He was glad Stuart was in the clear, and he felt ashamed of the suspicions he'd held largely on the basis of Stuart's lifestyle.

Aaron was quiet as he drove back to Twin Falls. Macady couldn't blame him for being preoccupied. He was driving a strange car and couldn't help being concerned about his own truck. She hoped county insurance would cover the repairs. She didn't ask him since he didn't seem inclined to talk. It was disappointing though. The evening had been so enjoyable, like a magic moment out of time, until the minute they'd seen Aaron's vandalized truck.

An ugly thought which persisted in hovering near the edge of every other thought in her head, prompted her to ask, "Do you think the person who broke the glass in your truck knew it was yours?"

Aaron groaned and turned his face partially toward her. "I was hoping that question wouldn't occur to you. I should have known you'd pick up on that possibility."

"Am I becoming paranoid? I keep having this feeling I'm being stalked."

The car swerved and Aaron quickly corrected it. "You mean you think someone is watching you and following you around?"

"No, that's too dramatic. I just meant I have an uneasy feeling that someone knows I can identify the man who shot at me, and I'm being warned to forget what I saw."

"Are you saying that vandalizing my truck was another warning for you?"

"Maybe." She chewed on her bottom lip for a minute before going on. "If someone found out I was out on the desert that day, I think there's a good possibility they know you were, too."

Nearly fifteen minutes passed before Aaron spoke again. "There's no way to know for sure how many people know you were shot at. Your family knows, so do Matt and Denise, and quite a few people at the sheriff's office, as well as several Drug Enforcement agents. We can't be certain one of them didn't tell someone else. But how many people knew we would be at the King Sol tonight?"

"Ben was in the kitchen when you called me. I don't know why he'd mention it to anyone else, but he might have."

"I told the dispatcher at work, and of course, I had to tell Denise where I'd be."

"We might have been followed."

"Yes, I thought of that."

"But you don't believe it."

Aaron shook his head. "I keep trying to remember if I saw anyone at all tonight who looked familiar, but frankly, I paid little attention to the other people around us." He smiled warmly across the narrow width of the car. Macady looked startled, then dropped her eyes to her lap. He wondered if he'd embarrassed her.

"Once I thought I saw Slade and Sylvia," Macady spoke as though reluctant to mention her cousin, "but after a moment I realized it couldn't possibly be them."

Aaron recoiled. Had Macady been mistaken or had Slade been in Sun Valley tonight?

A little after ten the next morning, Aaron turned onto the street where Steve Jennings worked. He parked the department truck on the street under a huge elm. The street was still mostly residential, but a few businesses like the realtors' office were gradually taking over.

A receptionist greeted him as he walked through the door. "I'll be with you in just a moment," she whispered, then turned her attention to the telephone she cradled against her shoulder. She glanced back at his uniform and was immediately flustered.

"No hurry." Aaron sat down and picked up a magazine, but he didn't read it. He glanced around the paneled room, noting how the old house had been completely remodeled inside to accommodate a business. Behind the receptionist's desk, a hall led to four closed doors. From where he sat, he could read the names on two of the doors. The first name plate read Lois

Delgado; the second office belonged to Steve. Curious, Aaron stood up and crossed the room to a water cooler.

He filled a little paper cup and let the cold water trickle down his throat before casually turning back toward the desk. He had a good view of the other side of the hall. The first office belonged to Garret Delgado and the second to Brendon Wilcox! He swallowed hard and his pulse raced. This might be the connection he was seeking.

"Sir!"

Aaron realized the receptionist had tried more than once to get his attention. "Yes." He stepped to the desk. "I'd like to see Steve Jennings, please."

"I'm sorry, Mr. Jennings isn't in today. Could Mrs. Delgado help you?"

"No, I need to see Mr. Jennings." He almost asked for Wilcox, then decided he wasn't ready to talk to him. The man had been released from the hospital just this morning and probably wasn't back to work yet anyway. "Will Jennings be in tomorrow?"

"It's hard to say," the woman smiled sadly. "His wife is ill and he tries to be with her as much as possible. That makes his office hours quite unpredictable."

Aaron thanked the woman and left. He'd known from Sylvia's remarks and his previous checking that Steve's wife had leukemia. He also knew the medical bills were horrendous, but between insurance and assistance from his father-in-law, Steve wasn't facing bankruptcy. He'd also learned Steve was finance clerk in his ward, and that he took his four small children to church nearly every week. He was well liked and had a lot of friends.

Aaron thought of the night he'd seen Steve talking and laughing with a young woman and trying to persuade her to let him take her home. Then there was the association with Wilcox. Wilcox had implied a friend was involved. Could that friend be Steve Jennings? There was something distasteful about suspecting a man Aaron knew was a member of the Church and a father of young children, but he'd learned long ago that members succumbed to temptation, too, and far more frequently than he'd like to believe.

CHAPTER THIRTEEN

For a week, Macady tolerated having one or more of her cousins accompany her everywhere she went, hanging around the store, and even donning running shoes to accompany her on her early morning runs. They took turns driving her to work and squiring her around the various businesses as she consulted with managers and owners concerning their advertising needs. By the end of the week, being constantly chaperoned was eating at her nerves.

Slade showed up at seven Saturday morning to accompany her on her daily run and snapped at her because she wasn't ready to go the minute he walked through the door.

"I always run an hour later on Saturday," she informed him and refused to hurry.

"Not this Saturday." He picked up her running shoes from where she'd dropped them beside the sofa and tossed them toward her. "I have an appointment at the airport at eight."

"You don't have to run with me. I'm only going as far as your house and back. I'll be fine."

"Zack said you wanted to do some shopping today, so I'll take you to town with me. If you plan to run this morning, you'll have to do it now."

"Nothing's open at eight," she argued as she tied her shoe laces.

"By the time I'm through at the airport, every store in town will be open and I'll help you shop." He shoved her none too gently out the door.

"I don't want to sit around the airport for two hours, and I don't need your help shopping for a bridal shower gift." Annoyance shortened her breath, and she had to strain to keep up with the blistering pace Slade set.

"I don't care what you want," Slade roared. "Stop acting like a pig-headed brat and do what you're told."

Macady stopped. She stood still and glared at Slade. "I'm not going with you. You can go by yourself." She turned on her heel and ran back to the house.

She stormed into the kitchen and slammed the door behind her. Hazel jumped, and Jeremiah and Ben both looked up with spoons suspended in midair as she stormed across the room and down the hall. The bathroom door crashed shut behind her.

Twenty minutes later, she emerged from the bathroom wearing denim shorts and an old T-shirt. A towel was wound around her head like a turban.

"Took you long enough," Slade growled. She raised her chin and pointedly ignored him. "Get in the truck."

"No! I told you, I'm not going."

"Yes you are." He reached for her and, when she dodged his hand, he picked her up like a sack of flour and headed for the door.

She kicked and screamed for Ben and Jeremiah to help her. They both stood back with shock and amazement written all over their faces.

"Slade, this isn't necessary," Hazel protested. "If Macady doesn't want to go to town, you can't force her."

Slade turned to face Hazel and nearly banged Macady's head into the side of the door. She renewed her efforts to escape, all of which, Slade ignored.

"I'm sorry, Aunt Hazel, but I don't have any choice. Someone has to keep the little fool safe. A message was left on Westerman's answering machine last night threatening to harm his girl if he doesn't back off from the drug case he's on."

"What!" Macady screamed. "Someone threatened Kelsey?"

"No! You, you idiot. Someone threatened you!"

"Put me down! I've got to call Aaron." She pushed against Slade's hard chest to no avail. He continued walking toward his truck, shoved her inside, and swung in after her. He gunned the engine and Macady slumped against the seat. To continue fighting would be a waste of strength. She was as tall as most men, but no match against one Slade's size. She'd wait until they reached the airport, then find a way to escape and call Aaron.

Macady seethed as the miles passed. Something didn't add up. Aaron had leveled with her on everything that had happened. That was one of the things she liked about him—his openness and the way he respected her ability to think for herself. Why wouldn't he warn her if there had been a threat against her? Slade was wrong. The threat was against Kelsey.

A trickle of water ran down the side of her face, and she faced a horrifying reality. She was on her way to Twin Falls, barefoot, and with her wet hair wrapped in a towel.

"Do you really plan to take me shopping like this?" she asked snidely. Slade only shrugged his shoulders, infuriating her more.

"Why the caveman tactics?" she taunted. "Have you ever known me to be the least bit suicidal? Do you really have so little respect for my intelligence that you couldn't have told me straight out that a threat had been made?"

"I warned you about Westerman, but you ignored my advice and went right on seeing him. You're too stubborn to reason with."

"Sort of the pot calling the kettle black," Macady resorted to an old cliché. "I learned eight years ago not to trust a man who was trying to justify an affair."

"I told you I didn't have an affair with Alicia."

"Oh, but you did," Macady let her contempt show. "You can't excuse yourself by denying that you physically committed adultery. Infidelity isn't all physical. You encouraged her discontent, met behind Aaron's back, and listened to confidences that she should have shared with her husband and no one else." Again

Slade shrugged his shoulders, but she could tell she'd touched a tender spot on his conscience.

When they pulled into the airport, Macady jerked the towel off her head and fluffed her curls. She didn't relish being seen looking like a wild woman with uncombed hair, no makeup, a faded T-shirt and no shoes.

Slade parked behind the last hangar. A white Piper Seneca with a bright blue stripe and the courier company logo stood in the open mouth of the shed-like structure and Macady recognized it as one of the two planes her cousin frequently flew. He opened the cab door and looked at her expectantly.

"Are you getting out or do I have to drag you out?"

She shot him a belligerent glare before sliding off the seat. She winced as her feet landed in loose pea gravel, but when Slade reached for her arm, she shrugged off his assistance. Inside the cluttered office at the back of the hangar, she balanced on one foot, then the other, to brush away the tiny rocks clinging to the bottoms of her feet. She looked around. No one else was in the office.

Slade stepped to a desk and began sorting through a pile of messages. He looked up once as though listening, then went back to sorting papers.

Macady glanced at her watch and noticed it was a quarter to eight. "Nothing like being early," she remarked sarcastically. "If I'd only known this was a command performance, I could have put on some shoes and combed my hair."

Her cousin looked up and a pained expression crossed his face. "There's a comb in the restroom. Help yourself." He pointed to a short hall and his voice was almost gentle.

Macady walked from the room. The hall was only about four feet long with a door on each side and the restroom at the other end. From the hall, one door opened into the hangar and one into a storage closet.

Macady scowled as she shut the restroom door behind herself. The room held a sink and a toilet and barely allowed enough room to close the door. It didn't even have a window. She walked to the sink and splashed water on her face to clear her head. She picked up a comb from the side of the basin and decided to wash it before using it.

Standing before the small square mirror, she dragged the comb through her hair. No matter what she did, her hair looked awful. She needed her blower and a brush. Oh well, what did she care? It wasn't her choice to be here. She shook her head in disbelief. Her cousins had always been domineering and bossy, but she couldn't believe Slade was so worried about her safety that he'd pull a stunt like this morning's circus. Guiltily she acknowledged she'd given him a hard time. She probably should go back into the office and sit quietly until Slade's meeting ended. When he cooled down, he'd realize she couldn't go shopping looking like this.

But what about Kelsey? Macady wouldn't be able to sit still until she talked to Aaron and knew his daughter was safe. Besides, she hadn't spent a lifetime making certain her cousins understood that just because she was the only female in the bunch, she didn't have to take any guff from them to throw away her independence now.

She eased the door open. If she were really quiet, she might be able to slip into the hangar and from there make her way to the next hangar. A woman's voice caught her attention.

"Did you have any trouble persuading her to come with you?"

"She didn't come willingly." Slade didn't sound happy and Macady stifled a gasp as she realized they were talking about her.

"Did you tell her mother where you're taking her?" The woman's voice was low and muffled.

"No. I decided you were right; the fewer people who know about the cabin, the better. I don't even plan to tell her until we're in the air."

Macady's hand went to her mouth. Slade really had kidnapped her!

"She's going to hate me, but she'll be safe. Did you bring some clothes and things for her? Poor kid, she doesn't even have a pair of shoes."

"I packed a bag. It's in my car."

Slade's expression of concern didn't placate Macady. No way was she going to let him fly her to some isolated cabin where she'd worry herself sick about Kelsey—and Aaron. Besides, there was a principle involved—she didn't allow anyone, even with the best of intentions, to run her life! But how was she going to get away?

From the other room, Macady heard the telephone ring and when Slade answered it, she took a deep breath and eased the bathroom door open wider. This might be all the distraction she was going to get. Her bare feet made no sound as she slipped out the door and through the opening into the hangar. Frantically her eyes searched the cavernous space for a place to hide. To her right were a couple of steel drums, the kind used by mechanics for disposing of used oil. Hiding behind them would be too obvious. The Cessna 172 didn't offer any place to hide. She'd have to risk running across the hangar.

She dashed across the open space and into the sunshine. Ahead of her was the Piper Seneca, but she couldn't fly it and she couldn't hide in it. Slade would look for her there. That would only solve his problem of how to get her inside the plane. She should take his truck. That would serve him right! Except that she remembered seeing him pocket the keys.

She crept around the edge of the huge shed until she saw a late model Subaru parked beside Slade's truck. It was probably locked, and unfortunately both vehicles were in plain view of the office window. Going in that direction wouldn't work anyway. There was too much open space, visible from all of the buildings between herself and the canal bridge. Of course, if she were in any real danger, she'd head straight for the main terminal, but she had no desire to embarrass herself or Slade just because he happened to be a pig-headed chauvinist! She'd have to give up hoping she could drive away.

Slade and his friend would discover any minute she was no longer in the restroom. Her eyes narrowed as she contemplated the pea gravel. She turned her head toward the runway and her shoulders sagged. Both were out of the question. The only direction left open to her was the weedy ditch bordering the field and she had to cross twenty feet of open ground to get to it. She was in for a long walk and she'd better get started.

Tiny rocks and the weeds made a whispering sound as she scurried across them. Terrified she would be seen or heard, she ignored the sharp pricks to her feet. In seconds, she parted the weeds and dived into the shallow ditch. She lay still in a couple of inches of mud and water, panting to catch her breath, and listened for sounds of pursuit. She didn't have long to wait.

"Macady!" She heard Slade call her name as he rounded the side of the hangar. He sounded angry. If he caught her, he wouldn't hurt her. He would just pick her up and strap her in his plane. She was no physical match for him, but there was no way she was going to meekly let him hide her away somewhere. She held her breath and watched him through the shield of weeds as he hurried around the building and disappeared again from sight. Slowly she crawled forward. It wouldn't take him long to extend his search to the ditch.

Mud soaked through her clothes and the plants tickled her legs as she crawled. Up ahead, a culvert connected the ditch to the canal. When she reached that point, she'd have to stand and dash across the bridge. Anyone seeing her would probably call the men in white coats to come get her.

Macady paused and slowly parted the foliage. She wanted to be certain Slade wasn't anywhere in sight before she left the ditch.

She raised her head and looked straight into the face of a stranger, a very young stranger. Wide, brown eyes met hers and a hand snaked out to cover her mouth.

"The señor, he look for you? He beat you?" Sympathy reflected in the boy's eyes. He looked about ten years old, but he might be small for his age. He glanced around, then removed his hand from her mouth. "Sorry," he apologized in a whisper. "I help you."

"Thank you," Macady mouthed. She wasn't being honest to let the boy think she was married and hiding to escape a beating from her husband, but his halting English made her wonder if he'd understand if she tried to explain. Unfortunately, her Spanish was far worse than his English. Besides, she was curious what kind of help he had in mind.

"Come." He motioned with his hand for her to follow him as he crawled through the weeds away from the ditch. He headed straight for the highway. A few feet from the road, he stopped, holding himself motionless as he watched the traffic. A large truck lumbered into view. Suddenly he leaped to his feet, calling softly for her to run.

Once again sharp stones cut into her bare feet, but they didn't stop her as she sprinted across the bridge, using the truck to shield her from the eyes of anyone watching from the airport. She lunged for the tall grass on the other side and rolled with her arms folded in front of her face for protection. When she came to a stop, she lay still, feeling the whoosh of wind as a diesel rig swept by. Gathering her courage, she moved her arms and turned her head to discover she lay nose-to-nose with her would-be rescuer. White teeth flashed an "all's well" signal across his round face.

She grinned back. The scamp was enjoying this.

A barbed-wire fence separated the highway from a field of corn, and a bus provided the cover for them to roll under the wire and disappear among the tall stalks. The boy was completely hidden by the tall plants, but Macady had to crouch low to keep her head below the silky tassels.

When they reached the other end of the field, the boy rushed toward a pile of rusty brown metal, which turned out to be the sorriest looking bicycle Macady had ever seen. He barely managed to get a chubby leg over the bar before he was urging her to climb on the back. Dubiously she seated herself and clasped her arms around his waist. She lifted her feet and wondered what to do with her long legs as he started pumping. The bicycle wobbled and weaved as they followed a narrow lane set between a double row of poplars.

The front tire hit a rock and the young driver struggled to keep the bike upright. He lost, spilling them both in the dust. Macady saw the worry in her young gallant's eyes and smiled reassuringly at him. He scrambled to his feet and, using both hands, dusted off the seat of his pants.

Macady glanced down at her own grimy clothes and started to giggle. She couldn't help it. The ragged, dirty, little boy beside her looked dressed for church compared to her appearance. Dried caked mud clung to her clothes and knees. A plaster-cast of mud stuck to her feet and over all lay a thick layer of dust. This had to be the most absurd morning of her life!

"Come, señora." The boy reached for her hand and she clasped his warm brown fingers. Again she didn't correct his assumption of her marital status. Together they continued up the lane, pushing the decrepit bike between them.

At the end of the lane stood a modest frame house, in evident need of repair. At least a half dozen small, barefoot children ran around the open area and crawled over an ancient pickup truck that could best be described as a match for the boy's bicycle. When the children spotted her and her companion, they shrieked with excitement and ran toward them. A short, round woman followed them.

As Macady's young friend dashed toward the woman, he spoke so rapidly she couldn't understand a word he said. The woman's response came just as fast. The two chattered excitedly with a great deal of arm waving. They both smiled broadly as the boy turned back to Macady.

"Mama will drive." He pointed grandly toward the truck.

Macady's heart sank. She doubted the thing would even start, and if it did how safe would it be to ride in something that looked like the only thing holding it together was rust! The woman spoke again and Macady could tell the boy would like to argue with his mother, but decided against it. Resignedly he started shooing the children toward the porch. Obviously he was the designated babysitter.

Macady started to follow the woman to the pickup, then stopped. "I don't even know your name," she called to the boy.

Straightening to his full height, he introduced himself. "I am Emelio Rolando de la Cruz."

"Gracias, Emilio Rolando de la Cruz." She smiled and his eyes sparkled as he grinned back.

"Vaya con Dios, mi amiga."

The starter scraped gratingly for what seemed a long time before the truck shuddered and the engine roared to life. The gears protested loudly as Mrs. de la Cruz ground the black knob into the desired position. The children shouted and waved and the truck moved slowly down the lane.

When they reached a road, Mrs. de la Cruz looked at Macady expectantly, and she pointed to the left. With another clash of gears and no attempt by the driver to check for traffic in either direction, the truck lumbered onto the street. Brakes squealed and Macady shut her eyes. She had to get out of this truck as quickly as possible, but where could she go? She couldn't allow Mrs. de la Cruz to drive her all the way to Jackson's Point. If they made it in one piece, it would be more than a miracle.

She needed to talk to Aaron, but she didn't know where he lived, and she wasn't about to show up at the sheriff's office looking like a war refugee. Besides, Kelsey needed her. She didn't know how she knew Kelsey needed her, but the feeling had persisted all morning.

She'd go to Denise's house! Carefully she began plotting a backroads approach. Considering her driver's aim-and-shoot driving style, she preferred skipping the busier streets.

Ten minutes later, she stood in Matt and Denise's driveway waving to Mrs. de la Cruz. The cheerful woman waved back, smiled broadly, revealing a gap where a front tooth should be, ground the gears, and shot back down the street. Macady hurried up the walk to ring the doorbell.

"Macady?" Denise stood in the doorway eyeing her hesitantly. "My goodness, it is you. What happened? Are you hurt? Come in, let me help you."

"I'm fine." Seeing Denise's dubious expression, Macady repeated, "I really am fine. I may have a few scratches on my feet, but other than that I'm just dirty. What about Kelsey? Is she safe?"

"Kelsey? She's fine. Why wouldn't she be?" Denise looked puzzled. "Come on inside," she urged.

Macady stepped inside, but refused a chair. "I was told someone called Aaron and threatened his girl if he didn't back off from a case he's working on."

Denise's face paled. "He didn't say ... He would have ... I'm going to call him right now."

A child's scream came from the back yard. Macady's eyes met Denise's for only a fraction of a second, then both women raced for the back door. Macady got there first. She flung open the screen door and raced toward a group of children huddled near a swing set. The children moved back to let her past, and she knelt on the grass beside a sobbing little girl.

It was Jackie, not Kelsey, holding her arm and howling with pain.

"What happened?" Denise knelt beside her daughter. When Jackie didn't answer but continued to cry, she turned to Kelsey who stood by with round scared eyes.

"It was my turn, but Monica said it was her turn. Jackie wouldn't stop. I told her to get off the swing, but she didn't. I caught the rope to make her stop and Monica tried to get the swing first." Kelsey dissolved into tears.

"I fell and my arm hurts," Jackie wailed.

Macady looked around at the other children. Several were crying sympathetically for their friend. "Run home," she told them. "We'll take care of Jackie."

"Are you going to tell Monica's mother?" one little boy asked.

"I'm sure Monica will tell her mother herself," Macady answered. She didn't like the implication that Monica was somehow at fault. It sounded to her like all three little girls had been squabbling over the swing, and if anyone was to blame they shared the blame equally.

"I think her arm should be x-rayed," Denise spoke. "I need to get her to the clinic." She sat on the grass with her daughter on her lap. Jackie's red hair gleamed against her mother's white blouse where the child lay her head. Macady, who knelt beside her, instinctively reached for Kelsey to hug her reassuringly.

Macady helped Denise to her feet and offered to carry Jackie, but Denise shook her head, reluctant to release her hold on the little girl. In the house Denise called Matt, then suggested Macady use the bathroom to clean up, and she loaned her a pair of Matt's sweats. Kelsey followed Macady around the house, refusing to leave her side even while she changed her clothes.

Matt arrived before Macady finished dressing. She walked into the living room to see him anxiously patting Denise's shoulder and urging both his wife and daughter not to cry.

"Don't worry about Kelsey. I'll watch her while you and Denise take Jackie to the clinic," Macady assured Matt.

Looking harassed, he swept one hand through his hair, then reached in his pocket for his keys. He pulled Denise's car key off his ring and handed it to Macady.

"Thanks," he told her. "I didn't see your car out front and there's no reason for you to be stuck here until we get back."

CHAPTER FOURTEEN

Aaron stomped into the office and headed for his desk, ignoring everyone on his way. The whole trip to Castleford had been a waste of time. The farmer who had called to complain of a small plane taking off and landing late at night from an old access road on the far end of his beet field didn't exist.

He'd talked to every farmer for thirty miles around the location he'd been given. They not only denied making the call, but implied he was a few bricks short of a full load if he thought an airplane could land anywhere near the fields so recently brought under cultivation. That's what made him so angry. He knew that part of the county was nothing but lava rocks and brush, much too rough for a landing field in the areas that hadn't already been claimed for growing crops. He should have suspected the call was phony.

"Westerman!" A thick hand came down on his shoulder. "When was the last time you had the brakes checked on that truck you drive?"

He looked up into the livid face of Deputy Rodriguez and felt his stomach lurch. "I had everything checked after that window-smashing incident. Why? Did you have a problem?" He'd switched trucks with the other deputy this morning because his truck needed gas. He'd been in a hurry and hadn't wanted to waste even five minutes getting it filled.

"You bet your sweet life I had a problem! Somebody cut a fence out by Kimberly, so I went out to take a look. Went around a corner and saw a tractor and mower coming, so I hit the brakes and nothing happened. I couldn't stop and the tractor was taking up the whole road. The truck went right through the fence and ended up to its axle in a newly watered bean field."

Aaron had a sudden picture of himself driving across Lily's Grade that morning. He should have been driving the truck assigned to him through the narrow cut slashed across the canyon wall. But he'd been driving Rodriguez' truck on a wild goose chase, while Rodriguez ...

"You have any idea how embarrassing that is to have a farmer pull you out of his field with a tractor?"

"Did you look at the brakes?" Aaron asked quietly.

"Huh?"

"I said—"

"I know what you said." He jerked Aaron out of his chair and stormed out of the office without loosening his grip. In the parking lot where the farmer had left Aaron's truck, the two men gave each other a grim look and went to work.

Rodriguez pointed to the brake line and Aaron felt a cold sweat break out on the back of his neck. It had been cut. Someone had planned for his brakes to fail, someone who knew he'd be crossing Lily's Grade.

"You better write a really detailed report," Aaron advised the other deputy. "And get a mechanic to go over every inch of this truck."

"Hey, you write the report," Rodriguez objected.

"I wasn't there. Besides, I have some calls of my own to make."

Rodriguez swore in both English and Spanish all the way back to the court house.

Aaron walked to his desk and punched in the numbers for Matt's phone. He let it ring ten times, then set it down and picked up his hat. Before he'd taken a step, he slammed the hat back down and grabbed the phone once more. His fingers knew the number. When had he memorized Macady Jackson's telephone number?

Hazel answered.

"Could I speak to Macady?" he asked. There was a long pause.

"Macady isn't here. Actually, I'm getting a little worried about her," she told him. "She and Slade had an argument this morning and he picked her up and carried her to his truck which made her angrier. He said you'd received a threatening call, and that she was in some kind of danger. You know how protective he's always been toward her—and how angry she gets when he carries his 'big brother' complex too far."

Aaron felt the blood drain from his face. What if the niggling suspicions he'd had about Slade were correct?

"Do you know where they were going?"

"No. Macady said she had some shopping to do, but she doesn't have her purse with her. I don't think she even had shoes on. She'd just gotten out of the shower and Slade brushed aside her objections and took off with her."

Aaron bit his tongue to keep from uttering the expletive that hovered in his head. He ended the call with a promise to find Macady, then sat still staring at his rolodex for several long minutes before bounding to his feet again. He stopped long enough to let Rodriguez know he needed to borrow his truck again and to let Berniece in dispatch know he was looking for Slade Jackson. She promised to ask the other officers to keep an eye out.

"Don't apprehend," he warned. "Tell them to just radio his location to me."

Aaron headed for the airport. It was the only place he could think of to look for Slade. He came upon the turnoff to the airport a little too fast. His tires skidded as he cornered, leaving him scrambling to avoid hitting a familiar-looking truck leaving the airport. For just a moment he thought he'd found Slade, but neither of the two men glaring at him through the windshield was Macady's cousin. A barrel bounced off the back of the truck, but Aaron kept going. In the back of his mind, he recalled seeing a barrel like that somewhere recently. He shrugged his shoulders. All barrels looked pretty much alike. The mishap was his fault.

He should stop to help the guy retrieve his load, but he kept going.

At the airport he questioned everyone from pilots to mechanics, but no one remembered seeing Slade all day. He finally reached the last hangar and entered a cramped office. The young woman who sat behind the desk told him Slade flew for the courier service that operated out of that office, and that he'd been scheduled to fly to Colorado that day, but he'd had a personal emergency and one of the partners had gone instead.

Aaron walked through the hangar on his way back to his truck. A two-seater Cessna 172 was the only plane in the hangar with space for three more. A mechanic worked over what looked like engine parts spread across a drop cloth. Behind him were two large metal tool boxes on wheels and a couple of hazardous waste barrels for used oil. A shelf held several cardboard boxes addressed to the Bureau of Land Management in Rawlings, Wyoming.

He stopped to speak to the mechanic, but the man shook his head when asked if he'd seen either Slade or Macady.

When Aaron reached his truck, he sat with his head bowed, trying to think of a place Slade might have taken Macady. Even if Slade were mixed up in the drug mess, he couldn't believe he'd hurt Macady. In some ways, the big man was as tender-hearted as she was, and his only female cousin had always been his soft spot. But where had he taken her and why? Aaron closed his eyes and prayed.

The radio interrupted the silence and Aaron heard Berniece ask him to respond. He identified himself and listened as she told him another deputy had spotted Slade's truck headed toward the Jackson ranch and that the driver appeared to be the sole occupant of the vehicle.

"I'm headed out there," he told the dispatcher as he hurried to start the engine, back out, and aim for the airport exit. Traffic seemed especially slow and he was tempted to turn on his lights and siren to clear a path. Instead, he pounded on the steering wheel and muttered under his breath until he passed beyond the city limits where he could pick up speed.

It took less than fifteen minutes once he left Twin Falls to reach the ranch. He skidded around the corner and pulled to a stop in front of the house. The green Ranger parked next to the fence belonged to Slade. The driver-side door hung open and the engine was running. He could see Slade standing on the porch talking to his mother, Lucille. They both appeared agitated.

Aaron leaped from his truck and ran toward the pair on the porch. "Where is she?" he demanded as he rushed toward Slade.

They both answered at the same time. "Macady has disappeared." "None of your business."

"I'm making it my business," Aaron snapped looking straight at Slade. "You can answer me now, or I can haul you downtown to answer my questions. Where did you take her?"

"Don't be absurd! You couldn't haul me anywhere." Slade shouted back.

"You're bigger, but if you don't cooperate I can charge you with resisting arrest, obstructing justice, or a number of other charges."

"Slade! Aaron! This isn't helping Macady. We've got to find her," Lucille cut in.

"It's your fault she's in this mess," Slade accused Aaron. "You got her shot at, then hung around turning her into bait. You won't protect her. You didn't even tell her or her family the people you're chasing were coming after her."

"I'm not the one who jerked her out of her own home and placed her in jeopardy. You seem to know a lot more about this so-called threat than I do. Why is that?"

"Don't play dumb with me. I know about the telephone call you got this morning threatening Macady."

"I don't know anything about any telephone call, but you better start explaining where Macady is right this minute."

Slade stepped menacingly toward Aaron.

"Slade!" Lucille chided.

"Where is Macady?" Aaron grasped Slade's shirt as if he would shake an answer out of him. Instead Slade doubled up his fist and sent a blow to Aaron's midsection. Aaron staggered back against the porch rail. His eyes narrowed, and the next blow was his. Startled, Slade wiped blood from his mouth. Then like a bellowing bull, charged straight into Aaron and the two men tumbled together into Lucille's flower bed.

It wasn't the scent of flowers that stilled Aaron's temper. Slade froze momentarily, too, sniffing the air. Then as both men surged to their feet, they heard Ben shouting, "The barn's on fire! Kelsey and Macady are inside!"

He was on his feet and running, vaguely aware that other feet ran beside him. From half-way across the yard, he caught a strong whiff of smoke. Glancing up, he spotted a delicate curl of flames eating its way across the eaves on the north side of the barn. Smoke billowed from behind the structure.

"The doors are padlocked!" Ben shouted.

"They can't be," Slade roared. "We've never put keyed locks on the barn."

"Macady!" Aaron called as he ran.

Fear ran like ice through Aaron's veins. The two people he cared most about were inside. He had to get them out. He knew the double doors were heavy solid core panels and he could see the shiny new lock securing them in place. He tore around to the back door. The smoke was heavier, but from ten feet away he could see that door was secured by a padlock, too.

He hammered on the door and called Macady's name. He threw his shoulder against the panels and pushed. A weight slammed beside him, and he became aware Slade had joined his effort to break down the door. Their combined efforts weren't enough.

"The window," Aaron gasped. "I might be able to get through it." The barn had one small narrow window over the front doors. Like old times, he and Slade worked together as a team. The bigger man cupped his hands, and Aaron gained the boost he needed to reach the window. He smashed out the small panes and shouted, "Macady! Kelsey!" He held his breath and listened.

A faint cry reached his ears, followed by a wracking cough. He directed his eyes downward and saw two bodies lying on the floor in front of the door. He couldn't tell which one had answered, but it didn't matter. He had to get them away from the door. Then he could use the truck as a battering ram to break it down.

He unsnapped his gun and used it to knock out the rest of the glass and remove the wooden supports between the small panes. Then taking off his belt, he passed it and the gun to Ben who stood beside his brother.

Aaron stuck his head through the window and coughed as the thick smoke swirled around him. He could see flames creeping across the heavy roof beam that ran the length of the barn. As soon as it burned through, the roof would collapse. As far as he could tell, the horse stalls all appeared to be empty and there were no sounds of panicked horses.

A heavy roll of smoke shifted, and he saw the two figures still lying face down on the floor beneath him. Neither had moved. Sweat rolled down his face, and he wiped it away with the back of his arm. Time was running out.

"Kelsey! Macady!" He screamed into the swirling cloud as he tried to force his shoulders to follow his head through the narrow opening.

"Daddy!" A small voice reached his ears.

"I'm coming, honey." Relief washed through him at the sound of the child's voice even as fear reached a fever pitch. Why didn't Macady answer? He withdrew his head and shouted at the group gathered beneath him. "I'm going to force my way in. I'll hand Kelsey through the window, but I won't be able to get Macady out that way." He coughed as smoke bit his lungs and shouted one last instruction, "Slade, get my truck, and as soon as Kelsey is clear, give me a minute to move Macady out of the way, then ram these doors." The heavy reinforced bumper on the sheriff's department truck was Macady's only chance of rescue.

He got one shoulder through and twisted. Ben grabbed his legs and pushed. Pain slashed through his shoulder and undercut his ribs, but he felt the window frame give, and he was through. He'd fall on his head now if he wasn't careful. He turned to his side and clung to the window frame as he drew his legs through the opening. He let go and dropped ten feet to the floor. He leaned forward and gasped for breath. The thick clouds of smoke swirling around him brought on a paroxysm of coughing. His nose ran and tears streamed from his eyes. He dropped to his knees and crawled toward Macady and Kelsey.

Kelsey saw him coming and started toward him, making soft mewling noises in the back of her throat. He clasped her to him and felt tears sting his eyes. He blinked them away and looked toward Macady. He wanted to go to her—he needed to go to her, but both of them stood a better chance of survival if he got Kelsey out as fast as possible.

He staggered backward and prayed he hadn't been overly optimistic about his chances of getting back up to the window with Kelsey. A shower of sparks filtered through the roiling gloom and a movement caught his eye. Patches leaped to the top of a stall box with a kitten in her mouth. Another kitten crawled and scratched its way behind her. Patches had her eye on the small square of light leading to safety. All right, Aaron thought. The box stall could support his weight, too. He scrambled up its side. If the supporting post held a few minutes longer, he could boost Kelsey through the window.

"Sandy," Kelsey whimpered. She'd seen the cats. Without slackening his pace, he scooped up the kitten and handed it to Kelsey. She buried her face in its fur and Aaron hoped it would help to keep the smoke out of her lungs. A sound reached his ears and he glanced back at Macady. She hadn't moved. He tried not to think about her and looked toward the window instead. A head leaned through the opening and Aaron saw a blanket hanging from Ben's hand. Patches saw it, too, and leaped from the stall toward it. Her claws sank deeply into the fabric. Aaron heard Ben let out a yell, then pull frantically at the blanket. Ben's head disappeared for just a moment, then he was back.

"Drop the blanket." The instructions he tried to call to Ben ended in another coughing spasm. Kelsey coughed and shuddered, then went limp. There was no more time. He braced his feet under the top panel of the stall and swung his daughter toward the window. Ben was ready and grasped her around the waist. Slowly Aaron released his hold and watched with his heart in his mouth as she disappeared through the opening and out of his sight.

He nearly fell in his haste to return to Macady. As he sank to his knees, he felt grateful the air was a little better near the floor. With one hand, he grabbed the blanket Ben had dropped. There was no time to check for a pulse or injuries. Slade would be coming through that door any second and he had to get Macady out of the way. He dropped the blanket over her and rolled her into it. As fast as his straining lungs would allow, he dragged her toward the closest horse stall.

A loud crack reached his ears, and he turned his head back toward the double doors. Then he glanced behind him to see a heavy beam drop to the floor, sending a shower of sparks flying every direction when it shattered against the concrete. The stalls would burn. He didn't want to be trapped in one.

Speculatively he looked toward the roof again. It wouldn't hold much longer. He prayed that his truck wouldn't bring it down on their heads the minute Slade rammed the doors. He crouched on the floor and slid his hand inside the blanket to touch Macady's cheek. He felt something wet and sticky. His hand froze, then he frantically sought a pulse in the side of her neck. A faint pulsing beat met his questing fingers and thick choking emotion blocked his throat. She was alive, and he loved her. He closed his eyes that were already streaming with tears from the thick smoke and pleaded with God to let her go on living, to give him a chance to tell her he loved her.

Another sharp crack sounded over the roar of flames. A shower of sparks filtered through the smoke to land on the blanket. Aaron brushed them away before they could catch flame. A shudder swept the building as Aaron watched the doors splinter and the nose of Rodriguez's truck ease its way inside. He dragged at the blanket. From deep inside, a hidden reserve of strength gave him the power to stagger toward the vehicle with his burden.

Then the truck was gone, and he was no longer struggling alone. A dozen hands reached to help. Zack lifted the blanket into his arms, and Slade and Daniel wrapped their arms around Aaron and walked him out of the building, through a cascade of water falling from hoses and buckets everywhere he looked.

Sounds like rifle shots erupted behind him, but he didn't look back to see timbers crashing to the floor. He never took his eyes from the blanket-wrapped bundle in Zack's arms. When Zack laid Macady gently on the lawn, it was Aaron who knelt beside her to pull the blanket away from her face. She groaned softly, and he thought it was about the most wonderful sound he'd ever heard.

"Macady! 'Cady, can you hear me?" He stroked her cheek and off in the distance he heard the wail of a siren. An ugly bruise covered her temple and he clenched his fists as he wondered how she'd gotten it. Her eye lids fluttered and she looked him straight in the eye. The corners of her mouth turned up in a faint smile for just a moment before her eyes closed again. Aaron closed his eyes, too, and clenched his bottom lip between his teeth. Breathing deeply, he struggled to hold back the emotion that threatened to swamp him.

When he opened his eyes, he saw Hazel watching him. She sat on the grass only a few feet away, with Lucille hovering at her shoulder. Shiny tracks down her cheeks revealed the depth of her own emotional turmoil. Nestled in her lap was Kelsey.

"Is she all right?" he mouthed quietly.

"Yes, I believe so. But I expect she'll have to spend the night in the hospital."

He dropped his gaze to Macady. "They both will. And I'll be

right there with them," he added softly.

"I will, too," Hazel echoed.

"They better have a mighty big holding pen for relatives at that hospital 'cause we're all staying." Carson stood at Macady's head with his legs braced apart and his massive arms folded across his chest. Aaron felt a flicker of wicked amusement. No one in his right mind would tell Carson he couldn't stay. He felt himself sliding toward the ground. It would be all right if he slept. No one could get past Carson and his boys to get to Macady. Maybe the Jacksons wouldn't make such bad in-laws after all. His hand settled over Macady's as his head touched the grass, then he knew no more.

CHAPTER FIFTEEN

"You think it was deliberately set, don't you?" Matt's voice was grim.

"Yes!" Aaron didn't elaborate, but he couldn't close his eyes without seeing new padlocks on the doors. Someone had tried to silence Macady permanently—someone who didn't care that a four-year-old child might have died, too. Slade? No, Slade might be involved and there was something peculiar about him forcing Macady to accompany him yesterday morning, but he'd been genuinely terrified for his cousin and had done everything possible to save her life. As soon as he could leave the hospital, he'd hunt up Slade. One way or the other, he'd find out who locked Kelsey and Macady in that barn.

Aaron reached for his gun belt and winced as he buckled it in place. His abdomen was tender and his shoulder ached. Whether crawling through the too-small barn window or his fight with Slade was responsible for his aches and bruises, he wasn't sure. With his tongue, he touched a deep groove running across his bottom lip and grimaced. He could definitely blame Slade for his split lip.

"You ought to take the day off and get some rest." Matt frowned disapprovingly at him as he finished readying himself to leave the hospital room where he'd spent the night.

"Can't," Aaron picked up his hat and twirled it between his fingers. "Thanks for bringing my clothes. Tell Jackie I'm sorry about her arm and that I'll bring Kelsey by to see her cast as soon as possible."

Matt walked with him as far as Kelsey's door then said good-bye.

"Hi, punkin." Aaron walked across the room and leaned over the bed rail to give his daughter a hug.

"Daddy!" A bright smile spread across Kelsey's face. "You didn't get burned up!"

"No, honey. Just like you, I breathed too much smoke and the doctor made me sleep here last night, but he says I'm fine now."

"I'm glad." She hugged him fiercely.

"Me, too." He returned her fierce hug and swallowed a thick lump in his throat. He didn't want to even think about the nightmare fear he'd faced when he thought he might lose her. His marriage hadn't been all it should have been, but his daughter was one good thing that had come from it. He loved her more than life.

"Kelsey, can you tell me what happened?"

The little girl nodded her head and launched into her story. "We went to Ben's barn to see the kittens and Patches jumped up and her tail went this way, then that way." Kelsey demonstrated with her arm. "Macady sniffed, then she took my hand and we ran to the door, but it wouldn't open. She said we'd go out the back door, but it wouldn't open either, and there was too much smoke, so we went back to the other door."

"Did you see anyone at the barn?"

"Yes," she nodded her head. "Ben talked to us. Macady told him not to tell anybody we were in the barn. She said it was a secret."

"There wasn't anyone else in the barn?"

"No, just Macady and me and the kitties. I was scared, Daddy, and the smoke made me cough and my throat hurt. Macady told me to lay on the floor 'cause there wasn't so much smoke on the floor. Then she got a ladder. It took a long time and it wasn't a very good ladder. It already got burned."

"A ladder! I didn't see a ladder."

"Macady said she was going to break the window then come back down to get me 'cause I'm little enough to go through it.

She said she'd yell real loud and Ben would come get me."

"Why didn't she do that?" He lifted Kelsey to his lap and stroked her hair.

"The ladder falled down and Macady falled down too." Tears streamed down his daughter's cheeks. "She wouldn't wake up, and I was scared. I didn't want her to get burned up."

"She didn't get burned up, honey, but she's going to have to stay in the hospital a few days, and she's going to have a big headache when she wakes up." Aaron swallowed again. Macady had fallen to the concrete floor while trying to save Kelsey. He had no way of knowing whether she'd slipped or if the damaged ladder had given way.

"Sandy runned away. I wanted to catch her, but Macady said her mama would take care of her. She did, didn't she, Daddy?"

"Yes, Patches took care of Sandy."

"I wish I had a mommy to take care of me." Aaron swallowed against the thickness in his throat. Kelsey was quiet for several minutes and Aaron laid her back against the pillow. Her round, solemn eyes looked into his and she whispered, "Macady taked good care of me."

For just a moment Aaron couldn't speak, then he told her, "I'm going to go see her now. You rest, and I'll be back this afternoon to see you again."

"Daddy?" Aaron had almost reached the door when her small voice stopped him.

"Yes?" He looked back at the figure in the bed.

"Macady told me a boy came to the store, and he didn't have a mommy and daddy so she let him 'dopt one of Patches' kittens like I 'dopted Sandy, but could I 'dopt Macady too 'cause I don't have a mommy and Macady doesn't have a little girl? I'd like Macady to be my mommy."

Aaron walked back to Kelsey's bedside and looked down at her earnest face. His lips twitched. "I think I'd like that, too. But we'll have to wait until Macady's all better before we ask her if she'll let us adopt her."

"I hope she'll say yes." Kelsey beamed and Aaron wondered if he had raised her hopes recklessly. He'd suspected for weeks that he was falling in love with Macady, and yesterday's events had left him with no doubt about his feelings for her. He didn't doubt she liked him, but might she love him? She'd been hurt twice and she didn't have much confidence in men. He couldn't blame her if she found it impossible to trust a man who worked odd hours and often couldn't even tell her where he'd be.

Macady was sleeping when he reached her room. He stepped past Web Jackson who lounged in a chair outside the door and Aaron approached her bed. Hazel sat beside her and he suspected she'd been there all night. He nodded toward her but didn't speak. He stood beside Macady's bed and watched her. She breathed heavily as though a great effort were required. He understood she'd suffered greater smoke damage than either Kelsey or he had. She'd been in the smoke longer. Then too, she'd been closer to the actual fire when she'd gone after the ladder.

She had a mild concussion, as well, the doctor had said, and though she hadn't been burned, she'd suffered minor abrasions to her feet. He'd like to know how that had happened. He jammed his hat on his head. Macady wouldn't be talking for a while, and that left only one person who could do the explaining. It was time to find Slade.

On his way out of the hospital, he stopped at the gift shop to order flowers sent up to Macady's room and a bouquet of balloons for Kelsey. He remembered Jackie's broken arm and arranged for balloons to be delivered to her, too.

Several deputies greeted him as he walked through the sheriff's office door.

"I thought you were taking the day off," Anderson called as he passed his desk.

"You don't look good," Rodriguez grunted.

He ignored them both and made his way to his desk. After easing his scraped and bruised body into his chair, he reached for the telephone. Driving out to the airport, then to the ranch if necessary, would be the best way to proceed, but the department was temporarily short on vehicles. His truck was still in the shop getting brake work done and Rodriguez's truck had joined it, needing new headlights and body work. A call to the mechanic brought a promise his truck would be ready by late afternoon.

Aaron called the courier service first and found himself talking to the same woman he'd talked to the day before. Slade wasn't scheduled to fly today, she told him, and offered to take a message. Aaron thanked her politely and hung up.

Next he called the ranch and learned Slade wasn't there either. Lucille questioned him about Macady and Kelsey and asked about his own condition. After assuring her they were all doing well, he asked if she knew where he could find Slade.

"He drove to Boise with Zack this morning. He didn't want to go, but Zack convinced him he could take his turn being with Macady tonight and that the younger boys could watch her through the day."

"Do you have any idea when they might get back?" Aaron made his voice sound casual. He didn't want to alarm Lucille.

"I'm not sure. It might be quite late."

Aaron set down the phone then sat with his forehead resting against his clasped fists. He didn't understand the anger he'd sensed in Slade yesterday. What had happened to cause Slade to turn on him? This whole mess didn't make sense. On one hand he had a life time of trust and respect for his friend. Slade's influence had played a major role in his own decision to go on a mission, and later Aaron had followed Slade to BYU.

On the other hand, even though Slade frequently flew to Boulder, the other man had avoided every invitation Aaron had extended to get together or come for dinner in all the years he and Alicia had lived there. He'd gone on avoiding him after Aaron returned to Idaho. And he'd been behaving strangely ever since Aaron and Macady had been trapped in the desert. Then there was the ring. Who did it belong to and how had it gotten to the spot where someone had waited to ambush him that night?

He couldn't reach Slade, but he couldn't just sit here. He had to do something. There was still Steve Jennings. Once more he reached for the telephone. It didn't take long to learn Jennings was still out. His wife's condition was critical and it was uncertain when he would return to the office. Aaron ran his fingers through his hair in frustration. He needed some answers.

For the next hour he poured over the papers that had accumulated on his desk. Concentrating on reports wasn't easy when his mind insisted on returning over and over to Macady and Kelsey. He forced himself to pick up a paper. A sheriff in the panhandle had contacted the department. He'd traced a cocaine shipment to Twin Falls, then hit a blank wall. Nearby Cassia county and the Boise city police were demanding information on the investigation. Both areas were flooded with powder and crack of the same quality as that found in Twin Falls and both departments were convinced the junk was coming in through Twin Falls.

The DEA had several leads that indicated the stuff was leaving Twin Falls by truck, and they had an agent staked out watching the suspected freight company. The discovery of that hidden airfield had merely slowed the flow for a couple of weeks. Evidently the drug traffickers had found another route into the county.

Aaron's stomach growled and he glanced at his watch. It was well past lunch time. He could pick up a sandwich close by, but he'd rather return to the hospital. He'd promised Kelsey he'd be back. And Macady might be awake by now.

Macady couldn't get her eyes open. She couldn't lift her eyelids for some reason. She coughed and her lungs hurt. Something smelled terrible, like smoke and antiseptic. She tried once more to open her eyes, and this time she succeeded in lifting her lids enough to reveal a blinding streak of red light. She closed her eyes against the pain in her head.

When next she awoke, she was aware of being in bed with her

head on a pillow. It didn't take any great reasoning to know she was in a hospital room. There had been a fire. She remembered that. She lay still, remembering it all—the flames and the smoke, the horror of being unable to get a door open—and Kelsey. Kelsey! She had to know if Kelsey was safe. She called her name, and when there was no answer, she screamed the child's name. A harsh croaking sound reached her ears and she realized the sound came from her own throat.

"Macady. It's okay. You're safe now." She recognized the soothing voice of her mother. "Don't try to talk. Your throat is too sore."

Yes, her throat was sore. Her head ached and she couldn't see, but she had to know about Kelsey. Again she tried to speak, but she couldn't form the words.

"Kelsey is safe. She's here in the hospital, too, but she's in no danger." Her mother seemed to know what Macady needed to hear. Hazel's hand lightly stroked her own. "Aaron and your cousins got both of you out. Neither of you were burned, but you inhaled quite a bit of smoke. You have a bump on your head and that will have to be watched for a few days, but Kelsey will be released later today."

She felt so tired. She could sleep now she knew Kelsey was safe. Was she really safe? Maybe her mother just told her that Kelsey was unhurt so she wouldn't be upset and make a fuss. No, her mother didn't lie. She wouldn't.

Macady lay very still. Behind her closed eyelids she could tell the light was different. It was late afternoon, or maybe another day. Someone stood beside her bed, and it wasn't her mother. She strained to open her eyes and a narrow sliver of light showed her Aaron leaning toward her. His lips gently touched her cheek. A longing to reach out to him, to feel his arms around her swamped her senses. Slowly her fingers uncurled, and she lifted her hand until it touched the hand grasping the rail beside her bed.

He caught her hand between his and brought it to his mouth.

"I thought I'd lost you," he murmured. Was she imagining or did a tear touch her hand?

She wanted to speak, to ask about Kelsey, to tell Aaron she loved him. Love? When had she fallen in love with Aaron? She tried to turn her head to see his face better and a stabbing pain brought tears to her eyes. She felt a matching pain in her heart. She couldn't love Aaron. She couldn't love any man because some day he'd leave her just the way Daddy and Brian had.

No, not Aaron. Aaron was different. She could count on him. She found she wanted to believe in Aaron with all her heart. She did believe in him. She couldn't go to Portland and leave him and Kelsey.

Another face crossed her narrow range of vision. This one a nurse. She heard her tell Aaron she was adding a pain killer to the I.V. She didn't want a pain killer. She needed to stay awake so she could talk to Aaron. She needed to know about Kelsey and there was something she had to tell him. She had to tell him she lov ...

Leaving Macady's room, Aaron nodded acknowledgement to Jeremiah Jackson who now occupied the chair outside her door. He nodded back, but Aaron didn't pause to talk. He couldn't. Deep in his heart, he acknowledged gratitude for her family's diligence in watching over Macady. His long strides carried him quickly down the corridor and around the corner where he stopped and leaned brokenly against the wall. His shoulders shook, and for just a moment, he gave in to pain and frustration. Why had this happened to Macady? She'd been a feisty tomboy all her life, but she was sweet and gentle, too. She was strong in so many ways, but vulnerable. She didn't deserve the terrible things that had happened to her.

Mixed with the love and compassion in his heart was a sense of guilt. Intellectually he knew he wasn't to blame for the fire or for Macady being trapped inside the barn. Neither was it his fault someone had tried to shoot her earlier, but he couldn't help feeling guilty because she had been mistaken for him when she rode in the desert and because he hadn't found the people responsible for endangering her life.

Aaron rubbed the back of his sleeve across his eyes, took a deep breath, and stepped away from the wall. It was almost time to pick up Kelsey and take her home. His stomach growled and he glanced at his watch. There was just time enough to grab a sandwich in the cafeteria.

The cafeteria was almost deserted when Aaron walked in. He picked up a tray and stared morosely at the sandwiches behind a glass barrier. He didn't really want one, but he had to eat. He pointed indifferently and someone handed him a cellophane-wrapped packet.

He'd already stepped past a table with one lone occupant before the man's identity registered. Steve Jennings sat with his shoulders slumped over a piece of pie. He'd been there a while, judging from the puddle of melted ice cream surrounding the pie. Aaron had been trying for more than a week to catch up to Steve. This was his chance.

"Mind if I join you?" Without waiting for a response, he lowered himself to the seat across from his quarry.

"No, of course not. How are you?" Steve lifted his head, and Aaron could see his red-rimmed eyes and the white lines around his mouth. Aaron could see that the man was suffering. He watched Steve twist his fork between his thin fingers, but none of the pie made its way inside the gaunt figure.

"How's your wife?" Aaron felt a sudden kinship with the man across the table. His own feelings for Macady were close to the surface, and he could relate to the terrible strain the man was under.

"Barb isn't doing well. She needs a bone marrow transplant." He took a crumpled handkerchief from his pocket and wiped his eyes.

"What are the odds of finding a donor in time?" Aaron's heart twisted for his old friend. The procedure was risky and expensive. It could also be the reason a nice man might become involved in illegal drug trafficking.

"We've found an ideal donor; unfortunately she isn't willing. Barb's younger sister has been tested and she's a highly compatible candidate, but she's young, just eighteen, and scared. Barb's afraid if I push her, she'll run away again."

"Again?"

"Yes, you remember. You were there when I was talking to her over at K-Mart. She and I always got along pretty well, and Barb was worried about her, so I found her and tried to talk her into going home with me. She didn't go with me that night, but the next day she showed up at the house on her own. She's been with us ever since." He reached for the handkerchief again and Aaron watched him twist it between his fingers.

Aaron remembered seeing Steve with the young girl. He was ashamed of the suspicions he had entertained at the time. Steve hadn't been playing around. And he wasn't the owner of the ring locked in the sheriff's evidence room either. Steve had always been thin, bordering on emaciated. That ring would never have fit his bony finger. It belonged to a big man—a big man with large hands. A man with hands like Slade Jackson's. He closed his eyes and saw once more his old friend cupping those huge hands to form a stirrup to boost him toward the window of a burning barn.

CHAPTER SIXTEEN

The lights were dimmed and the air held a hushed note which told her the day had gone and night had taken its place. Macady didn't try to open her eyes beyond the narrow slit that had worked before. She knew she wasn't alone. The dim shape of a man stood beside her bed. He was larger than Aaron, but she didn't feel threatened. His voice startled her, made her want to turn away, but something anchored her head to the bed. She couldn't move.

"Macady, my little 'Cady." There was a world of sorrow in her father's barely voiced words. "I know that if you were awake, you wouldn't want me here. But I had to come. In spite of all I've done that hurt you so terribly, I'm your father, and I've never stopped loving you. I had to see you."

Go away, she wanted to scream, but the words were trapped inside her damaged throat. She couldn't escape her unwelcome visitor, nor could she order him to leave.

"Once we were so close," his voice, tinged with regret, continued. "I was there in the room with your mother when you came screaming into the world. My arms were the first arms to hold and rock you, and though I was there to witness the births of my other children, there has never been another moment in my life when I felt so strongly the link between heaven and earth as that moment when Dr. Davis placed you in my arms." His soft voice broke in the dimly lit room.

"I feel a father's rage that someone has hurt my little girl. You shouldn't be in this hospital, you shouldn't be hurting, and you shouldn't need a guard at your door to keep you safe. And you shouldn't be without a father's help and protection." Anger and frustration crept into his voice lending it strength before a harsh catch revealed the proximity of tears.

"I've failed you. Just as surely as I failed your mother—I failed you. It's too late for me to give you the secure transition from child to adult that should have been yours. It's too late to meet your boyfriends at the door and make certain they know to bring you home on time. I wasn't there when the man you'd promised to marry broke your heart. It's too late for so much we should have shared. But there's one thing I hope I'm not too late for. I hope I'm not too late in asking your forgiveness.

"For eight long years, I've begged God to forgive me. I've begged your mother's forgiveness and Carol's too, but I need yours as well. Please forgive me, Macady—not for my sake, but for yours. I know what it is to be separated from God, and I don't want that for you. The scriptures tell us that if we don't forgive, we will be cut off from God's blessings. Please don't make me responsible for denying you all those choice blessings that should be your birthright."

Macady squeezed her eyes tightly shut. She didn't want to hear her father's words. She wasn't ready to face the pain in his voice. She hushed the surge of love that tried to rise from the ashes of her wounded heart and closed her ears to his plea. If she recognized sorrow and repentance in his voice, then she would have to think of forgiving. She reached for her cloak of anger. It was her armor, her shield that protected her from feeling too much. No, she wouldn't listen. Too late, the painful words were already indelibly printed in her heart.

Aaron lifted Kelsey in his arms for the short walk from the garage to her bedroom. She clasped her arms tightly around his neck and leaned her face against his shoulder. He enjoyed every step of his walk down the hall.

"Okay, in you go." He pulled back her sheet and laid her against her pillow.

"I have to say my prayer first, Daddy." She chided him patiently for forgetting. "The nurse wouldn't let me get out of bed to say my prayer last night, and she pulled up the side of the bed so I was stuck inside like a baby in a crib. I didn't like it. But I prayed anyway. I kneeled on my pillow." She slipped out of bed and knelt beside it.

"Here, Daddy." She patted the spot beside her, indicating he should join her. The stiffness in his back and side reminded him he hadn't escaped the events of the day before unscathed. He bowed his head and experienced a sense of awe as his child prayed simply and naturally with a faith that astonished him.

"Bless Grandpa and Grandma Westerman in New Zealand so they can baptize lots of people. And bless Grandma Randall so she won't miss me too much. Bless Jackie so her arm will get better. Please bless Daddy, and bless Macady so she will want to be my mommy." Aaron felt a jolt go through him. He wanted Macady to join their family, too, but he had no intention of allowing Kelsey to rush her. At the same time curbing Kelsey when she went after something she wanted was no easy task.

"And bless Sandy," Kelsey's prayer went on, "so she can go home to her own barn 'cause Ben's barn got all burned up." She took a deep breath before ending her prayer. Aaron echoed her amen, then once more tucked her in bed. He bent over to kiss her good night.

"Daddy?"

"Yes?"

"Can I sleep in your room tonight?"

"Are you afraid?" His hand gently stroked her silky curls.

"A little bit," she admitted hesitantly as though it pained her to admit she wasn't totally fearless.

"I think you should stay in your own bed, honey. But I'll stay here in your room until you fall asleep." He moved to the rocking chair a few feet from the bed. "I'll leave both your door and mine open tonight, so if you need me, you can just call and I'll come."

"Okay, Daddy."

Aaron leaned back in the simple wooden rocker and closed his eyes. He could easily fall asleep. But the moment he began to relax, his thoughts turned to Macady. The doctor had assured him she would be fine, but that she would sleep a lot for the next couple of days. None of the cuts on her feet were serious and she hadn't suffered any permanent lung damage. He'd spoken to Hazel before he left the hospital and had obtained a promise from her that she would call to update him at ten. His head began to nod.

A muffled ringing awakened him. He raised his head and knew immediately that he'd added a stiff neck to his other aches and pains. He glanced at Kelsey and was pleased to see her sleeping peacefully. The ringing sounded again and he dashed across the hall to pick up the phone from his night stand.

Before he could finish saying hello, Helen Randall demanded to know why he'd taken so long to answer the phone and accused him of ignoring her call the previous night.

"I called an hour ago, and when you didn't answer, I called your brother. He said Kelsey had been released from the hospital and that you'd taken her home. Why was Kelsey in the hospital, and why wasn't I informed? I don't like this. If something has happened to that child ..."

"Kelsey's fine," Aaron interrupted. "She was playing in a barn with a friend when somehow a fire started. She wasn't burned, but she inhaled quite a bit of smoke, and the doctor kept her over night for observation."

"My poor baby. Let me talk to her."

"Not now, Helen. She's asleep."

"She won't mind being awakened to talk to me."

"Not tonight. She really needs to rest." Aaron tried to soften his refusal. "I'll let her call you in the morning."

Helen sniffed loudly. "You don't watch her closely enough. A barn is no place for a little girl to play. I've offered to take responsibility for her. You know I can give her a better home than the cheap, tacky house you live in. A child shouldn't be shuffled off to a babysitter every day. Besides, Alicia would want me to raise her child. You know that, but you refuse to follow her wishes. You won't be satisfied until I lose Kelsey, too."

"Helen, I've had a long day, I'm tired, and I don't have the patience to listen to your warped reasoning. You'll have to take my word that Kelsey is fine."

Helen was crying when she hung up the telephone. Aaron sat on the edge of the bed with the telephone in his hands, wondering what to do. Helen had been charming and welcoming when they'd first met. But later, after he and Alicia were married, he discovered she was bitterly disappointed in his choice of career. Alicia had mentioned he was studying law, and Helen assumed she meant law as in attorney, not law enforcement. Helen accused him of misleading Alicia.

That had only been the beginning. She'd demanded he buy the house next door to the Randall home. Instead, he'd accepted a job in Yellowstone. They'd been at odds ever since.

Right now he was too tired to worry about Helen and her demands or hurt feelings. He needed some sleep. Tomorrow he had an investigation to work on, and it was imperative that he get some answers.

Aaron twisted around to return the phone to his night stand. As he set it in place, he noticed the blinking light on his answering machine. He considered ignoring it. Helen had said she'd called earlier. But it might be important. He pointed his finger toward the play button and paused. A sudden sense of dread swept over him. Ignoring the uneasy premonition, he pressed the button. The first message was Helen, as was the second. Then another voice came on the line, and Aaron sat up straight. This voice was obviously disguised, making it impossible to know whether the voice belonged to a man or a woman.

"You're playing a dangerous game you can't win. You got lucky once, but next time I won't miss. Get off my back, stop asking questions, or your girl just might have a serious accident."

Cold chills ran down Aaron's back. Did the caller mean Kelsey or Macady? Which one was he threatening? Enough people knew he'd been seeing Macady that someone might easily refer to her as his girl. He hadn't been home to check his answering machine for messages since before he went to work early yesterday morning—since before the fire.

Had the fire been an attempt to force him to drop his investigation? Surely anyone smart enough to operate the drug ring he was pursuing would be smart enough to know he was just a deputy, and even if he withdrew from the investigation, the sheriff would assign someone else to take over. The drug people couldn't help knowing federal agencies were already involved as well. Why did they want him off the case? Unless they thought he knew more than he really did—or there was something he knew, but wasn't aware he knew—something another deputy might never discover.

A picture of the ring locked in the evidence room rose before his eyes. No, it wasn't enough. Blacker knew about the ring and could trace it as easily as Aaron could. There had to be something else.

Aaron stiffened. Slade had known about the threat on Aaron's answering machine. Both he and Hazel had mentioned it and its specific reference to his girl. But Slade couldn't have known, unless he'd been in Aaron's house—or he knew who was responsible for the message being there.

Aaron rolled over and blinked. His room was daylight bright. He cast one eye toward his alarm clock and sat straight up. Nine o'clock! He couldn't remember the last time he'd slept so late. He leaped out of bed and dashed across the hall.

Through the open door, he could see Kelsey curled face down against her pillow with one tiny fist brushing her cheek. Her quilt had slipped to the floor and the sheet was tangled around her feet. Her breath came in soft whispers, and Aaron thought his heart would burst with the love she evoked in him. No one could be allowed to hurt or threaten Kelsey in any way. Friend or not,

Slade would answer some questions today. Aaron turned abruptly toward the shower.

Throwing back his head and letting the force of the water pound his face and chest, Aaron's mind grappled with the message left on his answering machine. Blacker had agreed when Aaron had called him that there was no way to be certain whether the threat was meant for Kelsey or Macady. He'd promised to send an officer over to the hospital to keep an eye on Macady, which was probably unnecessary since Carson had already decided one of his sons would remain parked outside her door until she was well enough to go home. Kelsey was Aaron's main concern at the moment, though thoughts of Macady were never far away.

Perhaps he ought to send Kelsey to Helen until this was over. No, that wouldn't be a good idea. He couldn't count on his mother-in-law being able to protect her. Besides, if Helen ever got her hands on his daughter, he'd have a battle royale to get her back. He'd have to think of a really safe place to hide her.

"Daddy!" Kelsey's wail sounded through the closed door, followed by the pounding of small fists.

Aaron shut off the water and reached for a towel.

"Just a minute, honey," he yelled back.

"I have to go right now!" She sounded desperate. He grabbed his robe off the hook on the back of the door and twisted the door knob. Kelsey pushed the door open and rushed past him. Aaron grinned and retreated to his own room to dress.

On the way to the kitchen to start breakfast, he tapped on the bathroom door to remind Kelsey to hurry and heard sobs coming from behind the closed door.

"Kelsey! What's the matter?" He twisted the handle and stepped inside the small bathroom. "Are you sick?"

Kelsey stood huddled against the sink sobbing. He knelt beside her to pull her into his arms.

"I-I wetted my pants." She cried harder. "You took too long." Slowly Aaron became aware of dampness spreading across the knees of his uniform. He closed his eyes and counted to ten. He'd have to change.

"It's okay," he attempted to soothe her wounded pride. "Don't worry about it." He helped her clean up, then sent her to her room, wrapped in a towel, while he mopped up the bathroom and took care of her wet nightie and underpants.

Once he'd dressed again, he crossed the hall to see if she needed any help. He found her sitting in the middle of her unmade bed, still wrapped in the towel.

"Kelsey, I overslept. It's late, and we have to hurry. Why aren't you dressed?"

"I don't know what to wear."

Aaron groaned under his breath. Where was his usually independent daughter who insisted on dressing herself most mornings?

"Here." He rifled through her drawer and tossed her a clean pair of panties.

"They have puppies. I don't want puppies today." She flung the panties on the floor.

Aaron stopped himself from ordering her to pick them up. She was understandably upset over her close call with the fire, and she'd likely be upset further when he told her he was sending her away somewhere. He just hoped Matt could take some time off work to take his family and Kelsey some place where she'd be safe. It would be a good idea anyway for Matt to get his family away for awhile. That way, they couldn't become targets, too.

"All right, this pair has kittens." Aaron walked across the room and handed the panties to Kelsey. She thrust out her lip, but slowly pulled them on.

It took another ten minutes to convince her to wear her gray striped Osh Kosh overalls and a pink T-shirt. She dawdled over putting on her shoes, and Aaron left her to it. If he didn't get breakfast ready pretty soon, he might as well forget it and start on lunch.

He had to call Kelsey twice before she finally appeared at the breakfast table. As she reluctantly plopped herself down on her chair, her arm brushed her cereal bowl sending it crashing to the floor, splattering Fruit Loops and milk in every direction. Aaron grabbed for her glass, which teetered on the edge of the table. His fingers only succeeded in sending it after the cereal.

If he were a swearing man, this would be the moment. One look at Kelsey's face told him the disaster was far worse from her point of view. Silent tears ran down her cheeks, and she breathed in great gasping breaths.

Aaron stood. Ignoring the crunch of cereal beneath his shoes, he reached for Kelsey and lifted her in his arms to hold her against his shoulder. Rhythmically he patted her back while whispering reassurance in her ear. When her sobs settled to gentle hiccups, he lowered himself to a captain's chair and settled her on his lap.

"Okay," he turned her small body so he could see her face. "The kitchen is a mess, but we can clean it up. Nothing's broken, so it won't take long, but something was bugging you before everything got spilled. How about telling me what's wrong?"

"Nothing." Kelsey swiped a fist across her eyes.

"Nothing? Did you have a bad dream?"

"No. I didn't dream about anything."

"Then what's the matter?"

"I don't want to go to Jackie's house." She stuck out her bottom lip and glared defiantly at him. Aaron's heart sank. Kelsey had never objected before about being left with Jackie and Denise.

"But you have fun at Jackie's house."

"I want you to stay home and tend me."

"You know I can't," he tried to reason with her even though he knew reasoning with a four-year-old was an exercise in futility. "I have to go to work."

"If I had a mommy, she'd stay home and tend me." Aaron stared at his young daughter. Talk about emotional blackmail!

"Sometimes mommies have to go to work, too." Aaron returned her to the table and prepared another bowl of cereal for her.

"Your toast is soggy. I'll make you some more." He turned to the toaster.

Kelsey stirred the cereal in her bowl, turning the milk to a rainbow. She took a couple of bites of toast, then made faces in it by poking her finger through the soft center of the bread.

"Kelsey, eat your breakfast." Aaron tried to hurry her.

"I don't like Heavenly Father. He's mean."

"What?" Aaron rose to his knees from where he'd been crawling across the floor mopping up spilled milk and cereal.

"He took my Mommy." Her lower lip extruded belligerently.

Aaron groaned. He didn't know how to deal with this. He had to make arrangements for Kelsey's protection and check on Macady, then find Slade.

"Look, honey," He placed his hand on the arm of her chair, "your mommy died because her car slipped on the ice, and it ran into a big rock. She hurt an awful lot and the doctors couldn't make her stop hurting, so Heavenly Father let her go to Heaven where she wouldn't hurt any more. That wasn't mean."

"I know." She sighed. "Grandma says if I'm a really good girl, sometime a long time from now, when I'm an old lady, I can go to Heaven and be with Mommy, and Grandma will be there, too, and we'll be happy because we'll all three be together again."

Of course, that would be Helen's idea of heaven—just her, her daughter, and her granddaughter. No inconvenient husbands to mess up her picture.

Aaron remembered he'd promised Helen Kelsey would call her this morning. One more delay, but it couldn't be helped.

"Do you want to call Grandma Randall?" He reached for the telephone and began punching in the numbers.

"I guess so," Kelsey shrugged her shoulders. "But if Heavenly Father isn't mean, why won't he let me have a new mommy? I prayed last night and when I woke up Macady wasn't here."

Aaron listened to the phone ring two more times, then hung up. He'd try again later. He folded his arms and leaned against the wall, watching Kelsey. Finally he had some idea what was really bothering her.

"Just because your prayer wasn't answered over night doesn't mean it won't be answered some time."

"Tomorrow?" Kelsey's face brightened.

"No, not tomorrow. First Macady needs a few days to get better, then it might take a whole bunch more days for us to make her want to be part of our family."

"Oh," she paused. "Does Macady hurt really bad?"

Oh-oh! He knew where this conversation was headed. "Macady isn't going to die, punkin." He picked Kelsey up and carried her to the sink to wash her face. He'd planned to drop her off at Matt's house before driving to the hospital, but under the circumstances perhaps he ought to take her with him to visit Macady. He just hoped she wouldn't put Macady on the spot by inviting her to be her mommy! He'd like to do the proposing himself when Macady was ready, and he had a strong hunch she wasn't ready yet.

"Are you sure?" Kelsey scrunched up her face, revealing her worry.

"Let's go visit her."

"Me too?" She squealed in excitement.

"Yes, you too." He gave her a hug before setting her on her feet. Hand-in-hand, they left the house and climbed into Aaron's truck.

CHAPTER SEVENTEEN

Aaron checked his watch several times as he drove across town. He didn't have to report to work today, but he felt an urgency to get on with the investigation. Once and for all, he needed to settle the question of Slade's involvement. Slade had a chip on his shoulder where Aaron was concerned, but Aaron could not believe he personally had anything to do with either attempt on Macady's life. The Slade he knew would never endanger a child either. Yet, he'd seen pillars of the community, even seemingly fine upstanding members of the Church, commit terrible crimes before. His training wouldn't let him dismiss the ring, nor could he overlook the fact that Slade had abducted Macady. And he'd known about the message on Aaron's answering machine before Aaron did.

Aaron found a parking spot and locked the truck. Kelsey clung tightly to his hand as they made their way inside to the elevator. A nurse lifted her eyebrows as Aaron walked past with Kelsey, but no one attempted to stop them.

Deputy Rodriguez and Ben Jackson sat in front of Macady's door. After greeting Aaron, Rodriguez excused himself to go hunt up some lunch.

"Hello, squirt!" Ben grinned at Kelsey. The young man leaned back, tipping the chair on its back legs.

"Are you taking care of Sandy?" she whispered.

"I sure am."

"Good!" she pronounced before stepping past him to follow her father into Macady's room. An attack of shyness struck her, and she clasped Aaron's leg as he moved to Macady's side.

His heart picked up its pace the moment he saw Macady. Settling one hand on his daughter's shoulder, he kept his eyes on Macady's face. Her eyes were open, and a faint smile touched her lips in welcome as he walked toward her. He swallowed a lump in his throat and smiled broadly. Now wasn't the time to let her see how deeply touched he was by the sight of the heavy bruise on her temple, a bruise she'd received trying to protect Kelsey.

"Hi!" Kelsey stuck her head through the bed rails and spoke to Macady. Macady appeared startled, then a light appeared behind her eyes, and she smiled at the little girl. He felt a surge of joy knowing these two cared for each other.

"Hi, yourself," Macady whispered.

"You sound funny." Kelsey looked worried.

"I know."

"Are you going to talk funny all of the time?"

"No," Macady croaked. "My throat is getting better."

A wide smile lit Kelsey's face and she turned to look at her Dad. "She is getting better!"

"Don't talk," Aaron reached across the rail to pick up Macady's hand. "I spoke with your mother earlier; she said you weren't supposed to talk yet. So, I'm going to ask you a few questions, and I want you to just signal your answers. Do you feel up to answering?" He could see puzzlement in her eyes. She attempted to nod her head and he saw her wince.

"You don't need to speak or move your head. If the answer is yes, squeeze my hand twice; if no, just once. Okay?" Her hand tightened around his once, then twice.

"That's the way," he smiled and nearly forgot his questions as he gazed into her eyes.

"We know the fire was arson. Did you see who started it?"

Her thumbnail dug into his hand as she squeezed just once.

"Did you see anything unusual around the barn?" Again the answer was no.

"Slade took you somewhere that morning, and when you showed up at my brother's house hours later, Denise said you were muddy and limping. Did Slade hurt you?" Her eyes widened and she forgot to answer with her hand.

"No," she gasped.

"Where did he take you?" The question should have been worded so she could answer yes or no. He tried to reword it, but Macady spoke before he could.

"Airport." He barely understood the harsh sound coming from her throat.

"I'm sorry. I asked the wrong kind of question. I don't want you to strain your voice. Please go back to squeezing my hand." He paused a moment before continuing.

"Was anyone else at the airport while you were there with Slade?" Aaron didn't feel any pressure against his hand for what seemed a long time, then Macady pressed it twice very quickly. He felt rising excitement as he planned carefully how to ask his next question.

"Do you know the person or persons you saw with Slade?" Confusion clouded her eyes. She opened her mouth, but no words came out. Finally she pressed his hand, paused, then pressed it two more times in quick succession. Then she held up one finger.

Aaron was puzzled, then understanding dawned. "There was only one person there, but you don't know whether you knew the person or not?" She smiled and pressed twice.

She looked tired. The rest of his questions could wait until later. He'd let her rest, then see if she could write out her answers. Reluctantly he released her hand. He looked down at her and felt his heart constrict. Leaning further, his lips touched hers. Soon, he promised silently. Soon this nightmare will be over, and we'll be free to explore our relationship and I can begin to convince you that some men can be trusted, that you can trust me. I'll never betray you.

He still had reservations about acquiring another set of in-laws, but he felt increasingly reluctant to contemplate a future without Macady in it.

"I want to kiss Macady, too." Kelsey tugged at Aaron's pant leg.

"Okay, punkin." He picked her up and held her while she planted a kiss on Macady's cheek. A glint of moisture added a sheen to Macady's eyes, and Aaron suspected his eyes might be slightly damp, too.

"Time to go," he told Kelsey. "I'll be back later," he spoke to Macady and let his eyes say much more.

"I have to tell Ben good-bye." Kelsey marched to the door.

As Aaron and Kelsey spoke with Ben, Deputy Brinkerman stepped off the elevator. They exchanged greetings and Aaron learned the young deputy had been assigned to guard Macady.

"Send him home to get some sleep," Ben muttered to Aaron. "He sat up all night with Slade. He's tired and I don't need him. Besides Daniel will be here any minute."

"Slade was here all night?" Aaron turned to the deputy.

"Yes, he got here around midnight and insisted on staying even though he has to fly this morning." Brinkerman yawned.

"What time does he leave?" Aaron was already estimating how long it would take to get Kelsey to Matt's house, then reach the airport.

"He's gone." Brinkerman yawned again. "I took him to the airport myself and watched him take off less than thirty minutes ago. I've got to hand it to him, I couldn't do it. All I can think of is getting home to my bed."

Gone? Slade was gone? If he'd only gotten to the hospital sooner! Aaron fought to control his disappointment.

"How long does he plan to be gone?" He snapped the question at Ben.

Startled, Ben stammered, "Four days, but don't worry. There are still enough of us to keep an eye on Macady."

"Miss Jackson wasn't in any danger," Brinkerman defended himself. "Rodriguez stopped by. He stayed with Ben while I took Slade to the airport."

Aaron struggled with his frustration. There wasn't anything he could do about questioning Slade for a few days. He glanced down at his daughter and made up his mind to go see Matt. With his brother's help, he could at least see that Kelsey had the protection she needed.

It was evening when Aaron returned to the hospital once more. As soon as he appeared, Hazel decided to go to the cafeteria for dinner, leaving him alone with Macady.

"Are you feeling better?" he asked her.

"Yes," Macady whispered back. Her voice sounded much stronger than it had that morning. "My head still hurts a little, but my throat feels much better. I'm glad you brought Kelsey to see me this morning. It meant a lot to see with my own eyes that she's safe and well."

"She needed to see you. You mean a lot to her." Aaron felt a surge of gratitude that this woman he had begun to care deeply about returned his daughter's love.

Aaron smiled tenderly and Macady couldn't help wondering, if she asked, would Aaron say she meant something to him, too?

"She matters a great deal to me, too." Macady looked into Aaron's face. "I've never been more frightened in my life than when I thought she might die in that barn. I kept hoping Ben was still weeding the garden and would hear me call for help. When he didn't come, I tried to reach the window."

"I know." Aaron stroked her cheek, and she found herself wanting to turn her face to touch his hand with her lips.

"Ben did hear you and when he couldn't get the doors open, he came after Slade and me." Aaron's voice dropped and she sensed a tension behind his words as he asked, "Why did you leave Denise's car behind the haystack and go to the barn instead of the house?"

She squirmed, knowing her answer would sound foolish. She'd behaved childishly. "Kelsey wanted to see her kitten, but I was hiding from Slade."

"Why were you hiding?" he asked, though he wished he didn't have to.

Briefly she told him of going to the airport, of Slade's concern for her safety, then sneaking away when she learned he planned to take her to a cabin somewhere to hide her until the people threatening her were captured.

"I tried to tell him Kelsey was in danger, not me, but he wouldn't listen. I wanted to help you protect her, instead I nearly lost her." Tears ran down the back of her throat, causing her to choke.

Aaron sat on the edge of the bed and held her. "Don't cry. You're not to blame for what happened. Your insistence that she stay on the floor probably saved her life."

"You saved both of our lives."

"I had a lot of help."

Macady was quiet for a long time, enjoying the feel of Aaron's arms around her and his hand gently stroking her hair. Finally, she had to speak. "It's not over. They might come after Kelsey again."

"I know," Aaron continued to stroke her hair. "What you don't understand is that I don't know whether the threat was aimed at Kelsey—or at you."

"Me? But ..." She sat up a little straighter.

"The voice threatened my 'girl.' That could mean you or Kelsey."

"But ..."

"You are my girl, aren't you?" It was a quaint, old-fashioned term. She was of a generation that considered herself a woman, not a girl. Still, she didn't feel offended. Aaron was asking her if she felt a bond with him, and it was true, she did. His claim made her feel both proud and apprehensive.

Unable to speak, she nodded her head. Did she dare trust Aaron with her heart? She thought fleetingly of the letter from her friend in Portland still in the drawer beside her bed. Panic fluttered in her breast. Feeling the way she did about Aaron, he could hurt her far more than Brian had. He had the power to wound her as deeply, maybe deeper, than her father had. She watched him lower his head. He was going to kiss her and some-how she knew this kiss would be different from any other she'd ever received. With this kiss there would be no career in Portland. Slowly she lifted her lips to his.

Aaron left Macady's room with a lighter step than he'd felt for days. Though no words had been exchanged, he had reason to believe she cared about him. And in a few hours Kelsey would be on her way to a safe haven with Matt and Denise. Things were looking up.

He reached for the elevator button to take him to the lobby, then changed his mind. He'd stop at the cafeteria for a quick sup-per before going to Matt's house. He spotted Steve, sitting at the same table he'd occupied the first time Aaron had found him there.

"How's your wife?" Aaron slid into the chair opposite him.

"I think it's going to work out." Steve's smile revealed hope and relief. "Barb's sister has agreed to the surgery and we're all feeling pretty optimistic."

"That's great news!" Aaron clasped the other man's shoulder in a gesture of support.

Steve talked about what the surgery would entail while they ate, then he paused. "Something strange happened today ... you're a deputy and you might know if it's serious or just my imagination."

"Tell me about it." Aaron encouraged him to proceed.

"Well, there's this guy who works in my office. I think he's messing around with drugs, but I don't have any proof. Just after five, I went to the office to pick up some papers I could work on here. His car was parked behind the office with another car I didn't recognize—it was a white Subaru with California license plates. I used my key to go in the back way, and I heard them yelling the minute I walked inside."

"Heard who?" Aaron asked calmly, though he didn't feel the least bit calm inside. Since Steve worked with Brendon Wilcox, the overdose victim who had recently been released from the hospital, he might have some important information for Aaron.

"I didn't recognize the others, just the guy from my office. They were making so much noise, they didn't hear me come in. I hesitated a minute, wondering what I should do, and I recognized Brendon's voice when he mentioned your name."

"My name? Why would he mention me?"

"The guy doing most of the shouting accused him of shooting off his mouth to the law because they'd seen you at the office a couple of times. He tried to tell them that you and I are old friends, and you'd stopped by to see me, not him."

"I take it they didn't believe him?"

"No, I don't think they did. Then Brendon accused them of giving him junk. The other guy, the softer-spoken one, said they were really sorry about that, and they'd make it up to him by giving him a little something that would make everything right."

Aaron frowned. "What did you do then?"

"I left without going into my own office. Something kept telling me to get out of there, so I did. But I've been sort of uneasy about Brendon ever since."

Aaron thought it best to tell Steve straight out. "Brendon is dead. I learned about it when I checked in with the sheriff an hour ago. We won't know the full story until the coroner finishes the autopsy, but it looks like heart failure brought on by a cocaine overdose. His past history indicates he snorted cocaine and occasionally smoked pot, but whatever lethal mixture he took this time was injected. Bruises on the body suggest he might not have taken it voluntarily."

Steve turned pale, and his eyes behind thick lenses protruded in shock. "Dead? But ... he ... oh!" He leaned back against his chair and shook his head in denial.

"What can you tell me about the people you saw arguing with Wilcox?"

"Not much. I didn't actually see anyone. There were two voices besides Brendon's. One was deep and kind of crude, the other was softer and seemed more refined."

Aaron jotted a note in a small tablet, then asked, "Can you give me any other details? Try to visualize the car. Do you remember even a partial plate number? Concentrate on what you could see from the back door. Anything unusual."

"No... wait a minute. I saw a woman's leg." Steve suddenly sounded excited. "The door to Brendon's office was open, but the men must have been standing near his desk because I couldn't see them. Anyway, there's an armchair beside the door. I couldn't see who was sitting there, but I knew it was a woman because I could see this lady's leg bobbing up and down like its owner was impatient or angry. It was kind of distracting." Steve took a handkerchief from his pocket and wiped his face.

"Can you leave the hospital for a little while, Steve?" Aaron asked. "I know you want to stay near your wife, but I need you to go down to the station and make a formal statement."

"I guess so. Barb's sister is with her right now."

Aaron was glad Steve's sister-in-law had gained the courage to help her sister before it was too late. He'd resented Helen's interference in his marriage, yet the events of the past few days had reminded him of the value of family support. Not only had his view of the close-knit Jackson clan softened, but he could never repay his brother Matt and Denise's family for the steps they were taking to protect Kelsey.

Aaron glanced at his watch. He'd have to hurry in order to see Kelsey before she left. Matt had arranged with Denise's parents to go camping in their RV. The camper would be all stocked and ready to go by the time Matt, Denise, and the two kids reached Pocatello. Matt's father-in-law was a retired army colonel and would help guard Kelsey. By leaving at night, they hoped their departure wouldn't be noticed.

When Aaron reached Matt's house, he was surprised to find Matt and Denise alone.

"Where's Kelsey?" Aaron glanced around.

"Kelsey called Ben to ask about her cat and he told her he'd taken Sandy back to Jackson Point since he was staying there until Hazel and Macady get back home," Matt explained. "She insisted she had to see her cat, so he and one of his brothers offered to come get her. I thought if anyone was watching, seeing us leave separately might throw them off, and since Jackson Point is right on our way anyway, I let Kelsey and Jackie both go. Ben said Zack and Mary were there helping out, so I figured she'd have plenty of protection."

It made sense, but a vague uneasiness swept over Aaron. The change of plans bothered him. Perhaps he was being paranoid. Maybe what he was experiencing was disappointment that he wouldn't be able to see Kelsey tonight, and he didn't know how long it might be until it would be safe for her to return.

All the way home, Aaron fought the urge to turn around and drive out to the Jackson Point store. He knew he couldn't go there because if anyone was watching he'd lead them right to his daughter. Still the feeling Kelsey needed him persisted. Matt had promised to call as soon as they reached Pocatello and again when they got to Salmon. He'd have to be content with that promise.

CHAPTER EIGHTEEN

Aaron could hear his phone ringing as he unlocked his door. The answering machine clicked on, and after the recorded message he could hear Ben's frantic voice telling him to call ...

"Hello," he shouted. "This is Aaron Westerman."

"Aaron! We can't find Kelsey." Ben's voice broke off and another came on the line.

"Can you get right out here?" He recognized Zack's wife.

"Mary, what's going on?" He struggled to keep the panic out of his own voice and felt his heart pounding a frightening tempo.

"Kelsey's kitten got out and we think she went after it. Oh, Aaron, I'm so sorry. Everyone's out looking, and we've called the sheriff's office. She couldn't have gone very far, but it's dark out, and she's just gone through one terrifying experience." Her words ended with a little catch.

"How could she just disappear?" Fear tightened his throat, leaving him almost incapable of speech. "What happened?"

"She and Jackie fell asleep on Macady's bed with her kitten. There were several customers in the store and Zack had to leave because it was his turn to stay with Macady. After he left, an old woman came in with a flat tire. She was pretty upset when she found out the store doesn't have any car service, so Ben and David changed the tire for her. After she left, Ben found Sandy wandering around outside. I ran to check on Kelsey and she was gone."

"And Jackie?" He could barely whisper the words.

"Jackie was still asleep on the bed. Only Kelsey is gone."

Horror held Aaron in its grip for long minutes after he hung up the phone. Kelsey might have run out into the dark chasing her kitten and gotten lost, but he didn't believe it. Someone had taken her. He knew, deep in his soul, his baby wouldn't be found anywhere near Jackson Point.

He leaned his head against the kitchen wall and tried to shut out the ugly pictures forming in his mind. No! He slammed his fist into the wall. Plaster trickled to the floor and the pain in his hand reminded him he was wasting time.

He tore out of the house and jumped into his truck. All of his training and his years as a law officer were not enough to keep his foot from pressing the gas pedal to the floor. He turned the corner into the store's parking lot, sending gravel spewing against the official vehicles that had barely beaten him to Jackson Point.

Sheriff Blacker stood talking to Ben in front of the store. Two deputies with flashlights were poking around the barn, and he could see a police cruiser moving slowly along the lane leading to Carson's house. Before he could ask, Blacker shook his head and told him no trace of Kelsey had been found.

Matt and Denise arrived, and Matt strode to Aaron's side, clasping an arm around his shoulder. His face twisted in a grimace as he tried to speak.

"My fault. I shouldn't have let her out of my sight."

"I promised to watch her." Ben's voice shook.

"Don't blame yourselves. There's no time for that. We've got to concentrate on finding her." Aaron spoke through clenched teeth. He couldn't give in to emotion and his own guilt for not heeding the prompting he'd felt an hour ago to go to Jackson Point. Right now he had to think like a law officer. He had to know everything Matt and all the others had seen and done all day.

Slowly he took Ben through the whole day while Sheriff Blacker went inside to interview Mary.

"We were really busy," Ben explained. "Mary couldn't handle all of the customers, even with David helping her. I stayed in the back watching the little girls until they fell asleep, then I came out to help in the store."

"Go on." Aaron struggled to keep his voice calm.

"Some guy was giving Mary a bad time because there wasn't any beer in the drinks case. She told him Aunt Hazel doesn't stock beer. I think he had already had a few, and he was getting pretty loud and pushy, so I stepped in." Ben explained. "He backed right off. About the time he left, an old woman came in looking for a mechanic to change a tire. Mary told her to go back across the river to the Traveler's Oasis, but she said she couldn't go that far. She was so upset, I offered to change the tire for her and Mary sent David out to help me."

"Was she alone?"

"Yes."

"Do you remember what kind of car she drove?"

"Yeah, it was a light colored bug, you know an old VW. We don't see many of them anymore."

"Do you have any idea what kind of car your loud-mouthed drunk drove?"

"Full-sized pickup truck. I can't tell you the color or model."

"Did you notice any of the other vehicles parked in front of the store while you were changing the tire?" Ben was an observant young man, but he couldn't recall for certain how many cars had been there. Five or six. He wasn't sure.

"What can you tell me about the other cars?" Aaron pursued the question.

"Not much. My brothers and I used to play a license plates game, so I notice plates. There was a van from Kansas with a lot of kids in it and stuff strapped on top. A couple of pickups, different sizes, both with Idaho plates. One of the cars had an Alaska license plate, and I think there was a Utah and a Wisconsin. I couldn't see it real well, but I think the white car down at the end by the trees had blue plates—that would be California."

A white car with California plates. Aaron's blood ran cold. It could be just a coincidence, but a sick feeling in the pit of his stomach told him there was a good chance it wasn't.

An hour later all of the deputies in the area had reported in. No one had seen any sign of Kelsey. Sheriff Blacker informed Aaron he didn't care what the FBI did, they could wait twenty-four hours if they wanted to, but his office would treat Kelsey's disappearance as a kidnapping at once.

Aaron thanked the sheriff, then followed him back to Twin Falls to alert the state police and nearby counties and states. Every statement Matt and the Jacksons had made needed to be examined and evaluated. Experts would be called in to re-examine the voice tape from Aaron's answering machine and analyze the handwriting on the threatening note Macady had received. Blacker promised to send for an artist to develop a sketch of the man he and Macady had seen in the desert.

While Aaron worked, he forced himself to ignore the pictures that rose before his eyes of Kelsey, scared and crying or hurt. "Please, God," he found himself praying over and over, "Keep her safe, help me find her."

The sheriff left about three o'clock to get some rest and told Aaron to do the same, but he couldn't face returning to his empty house. Besides he couldn't go to bed as if nothing had happened.

Aaron awoke with a start and a stiff neck. He hadn't slept long, but a wave of guilt swept over him. How could he sleep when his daughter was missing? She was out there with desperate criminals who wouldn't hesitate to harm a child. A wave of agony tore through him. There wasn't any way to be sure she was still alive.

"Aaron?" He jerked to attention. He hadn't been aware of the man standing near his desk. He looked closer at the lean figure with faint touches of silver at his temples and recognized Bishop Derricott who had been sustained bishop of Aaron's ward a few months ago. Aaron hadn't had an opportunity to get to know him well. Slowly Aaron rose to his feet.

"Carson Jackson called me. He said you might need someone to talk to."

"You know—?"

"Yes, he told me what he knew and said you had insisted on your brother taking his family home and staying with them. He didn't think you should be alone. Your police chaplain told me a little more. Is there anything I can do? I've already contacted the priesthood quorums. They'll begin combing a five-mile radius from the store at daybreak. Bishop Eames from out that way will have his ward out, too."

"Thank you." Aaron found speaking difficult.

"What about your parents? Have you called them?" Bishop Derricott settled himself on one corner of Aaron's desk, and Aaron sat back down.

"Matt and I decided when Mom and Dad left that we wouldn't bother them with our problems. They've dreamed of this mission for a long time. I'd like them to be free to concentrate on the work they're doing."

"Ordinarily I'd agree with you, but in a few hours the media will be spreading the story world wide. Kidnappings frequently hit the international news. I don't think you should risk them hearing it from someone else."

Aaron's shoulders began to shake and Bishop Derricott got up and came around the desk to place his arms around him.

"Could we go somewhere and talk privately?"

Aaron straightened, nodded his head, and led the way to a small room off the main office area. He sat on one of the two chairs in the room and waved a hand at the other.

"Why Kelsey?" Aaron slammed a fist against the battered table separating the two chairs. "She's already lost her mother, and she nearly died a few days ago in a fire. Now this!"

"Why does any child suffer because of the greed and corruption of adults? It's easy to accept cause and effect, and preach the concept that evil happens because we each have our own agency to act for ourselves and some people choose to do evil, until evil touches our own lives. Then we want to limit agency to our own terms. Even knowing that the person who did this will be punished severely for committing a crime against one of God's innocent little ones is not comfort enough right now. I know that. You'll need to call on the deepest well of your faith, more than at any other time in your life, to carry you through this."

Aaron ran his hand down his face, letting his thumb and forefinger push away the tears threatening to spill from his eyes and he felt a closeness to this man he barely knew. "I know that, bishop. Don't think my faith is wavering. To tell the truth, it's the only thing holding me together right now."

"The faith and prayers of the ward are behind you, Aaron."

"I appreciate that. You asked if there was anything you could do. My father isn't here to ask. Would you give me a blessing?"

"I'd be honored."

After Bishop Derricott left, Aaron borrowed Sheriff Blacker's office to place a call to New Zealand. He found himself battling a lump in his throat when his mother's voice came on the line. When she started crying, his father took the phone. He listened without interruption as Aaron explained the situation, then in a choked voice cautioned him to stay close to God and listen carefully to the promptings of the Spirit.

"Your mother and I will be praying for Kelsey's safe return."

His mother came back on the line to ask him to call again when Kelsey was found. He was glad she said when not if.

After speaking with his parents, Aaron felt more hopeful that Kelsey would be found. He had to believe that. Then he remembered he should call Kelsey's other grandmother. Helen needed to be told for the same reasons his own parents had to be told. Heaving a sigh, he picked up the telephone again.

He let the phone ring until the answering machine picked up, then left a brief message. He glanced at his watch. Helen had most likely driven out to the airport to check on her shop. He'd try again after he saw Macady. He needed to see her. A fierce longing to be with her and share his pain and fear made him ache. Still he dreaded telling her. She wasn't Kelsey's mother, yet he sensed a depth of caring between the two that came very near a maternal bond. Knowing would hurt her; not knowing would inflict a deep wound once she learned he'd kept Kelsey's abduction from her.

Early morning traffic was sparse as he drove toward the hospital. He caught a glimpse of a white Subaru and his pulse accelerated until he saw the Idaho license plate. In the hospital parking lot, he pulled alongside a green Ranger. Macady had connected the man who shot at her with a green Ranger. Slade drove a green Ranger too. For that matter, so did several thousand other people. He must be losing his mind to imagine every vehicle that remotely resembled the two identified with the drug gang had something to do with Kelsey's disappearance.

David Jackson was sharing guard duty with Deputy Brinkerman when Aaron approached Macady's door.

"Any news?" Brinkerman asked kindly. Aaron shook his head.

"Does Macady know?" Aaron asked.

"No. We haven't told Hazel either," David responded, and there was pain and anger in his voice. Aaron remembered David's missionary farewell was only a little over a week away. The young man should be shopping for white shirts and conservative ties, not spending his last week at home guarding a hospital room.

Aaron opened the heavy door and stepped inside Macady's room. She was sitting cross-legged on the bed and had swapped her hospital gown for an over-sized T-shirt and sweat pants. She sent him a welcoming grin. Hazel glanced his way, too, with a smile. Her smile faded as did Macady's, as he walked toward them. His appearance alone was probably enough to scare them. He still wore the clothing he'd worn the day before, he hadn't shaved, and no doubt the long night and a bout of tears had left him with red eyes. He seated himself beside Macady and unconsciously picked up her hands. There was no way to soften the words. He had to say them straight out.

"Kelsey's gone. Someone took her from the store last night."

Macady's eyes grew round. He could see her struggle to assimilate his words. Denial was followed by sheer, brutal pain.

"No, no, no," she repeated the words like the keening,

anguished wail of a bereft mother.

Hazel rushed to her daughter's side, but Macady turned to bury her face against Aaron's chest, and Hazel embraced them both. Aaron felt strangely comforted. This was as it should be; Macady turning to him, and her mother wrapping her love and support around them both. If only Kelsey were here, this moment would be sweet beyond belief.

Finally Macady lifted her tear streaked face to his and demanded details. He told her all he knew.

She listened attentively, occasionally wiping away a tear. Now came the touchy part. He had to ask questions. He didn't want to hurt her further, but he needed answers.

"Macady, tell me everything you remember about the day of the fire, starting with your trip to the airport with Slade."

"Slade has always been overly protective of me. When he heard about the threat you received, he assumed I was in danger and tried to take me somewhere he thought I would be safe."

"Humor me. Tell me everything either of you did or said."

"All right," she sounded reluctant, and he guessed she thought it would be better for him to be out looking for Kelsey. When she finished her recital, Aaron hesitated, then taking her hands again, he asked her, "How did Slade know about the message on my answering machine? I didn't get that message until the day after the fire. By tracing the other messages on that tape, I know it was recorded early the same day Slade took you to the airport."

"But that doesn't make sense." Macady was clearly puzzled.

"I know it doesn't. That's why I have to find Slade."

"Aaron, you don't think Slade ...? Aw no, not Slade, he wouldn't ..." Macady was too shocked to finish her sentences.

"I've known Slade all of his life," Hazel protested. "So have you. He isn't capable of being mixed up in something like this."

"I'm not accusing Slade of anything, but I do have to ask him how he knew about the recorded threat. There are a couple of other questions I want to ask him, too."

Macady's back stiffened. "I told you I saw the man who shot

at me standing beside a green Ranger. Are you suggesting it was Slade's truck?"

"I don't know. We've received several reports that a large man driving a green Ranger is involved."

"Well, he's not Slade," Macady defended her cousin. "I saw the man who shot at me, remember? He wasn't Slade. He was as big as Slade, and he had dark hair, but that's where the resemblance ends." She drew as far away from Aaron as the narrow hospital bed allowed.

"I know that." He didn't like the way this conversation was going. "I'm not suggesting the sniper's Ranger and Slade's Ranger are the same truck. But something harder to explain is Slade's class ring."

"His ring? What does his ring have to do with Kelsey's disappearance?" Macady's voice rose, ending with a strangled cough.

"Nothing," Aaron snapped, "But it has a lot to do with the night we spent in the desert. Blacker found the ring beside a coke can and a little pile of cigarette butts a short distance from my truck."

Macady's cheeks paled. "Slade doesn't smoke," she whispered.

"I'm sorry, honey." Aaron tried to soften the shock he'd given her. "Slade probably has no connection with any of this, but I think he knows something. At least he knows something about that call on my answering machine. And he knows who the woman at the airport was who was so eager to pack for you and help him spirit you away."

"You want him to be guilty." She gripped her hands together in front of her knees and stared up at him. "You hate him so much you want him to be the one who set the barn on fire. You want someone to punish for taking Kelsey, and who better than the man who was in love with your wife? I understand your hurt and anger, even the hatred. I've felt it, too, but you're mistaken. Slade and Alicia were wrong, but Slade would never hurt me— nor Alicia's child." She dropped her head to her knees.

"Slade and Alicia? Macady, they were friends, nothing more."

"Slade loved her."

Was it possible? Had Slade been in love with Alicia? It would explain a great deal. A wave of pity for his old friend swept over him. Had he unknowingly hurt Slade by marrying Alicia? Slade had introduced them right after Aaron returned from his mission, and when he'd asked her if she was seeing Slade, she'd said they had gone out a few times but they weren't serious. Slade may have cared about her, but the feelings weren't returned. And no, there had been no affair. Alicia wasn't capable of caring deeply for anyone other than herself and her mother. She had also lacked the courage to take such a drastic step on her own. Helen wouldn't have approved, and that would have been reason enough for Alicia to walk the line.

His lip curled in a bitter twist. He was likely being unfair. Alicia was immature and spoiled rotten, but she might have grown up had she been able to break away from her mother. It was too bad in a way that Alicia hadn't loved Slade. It would take a force as formidable as the Jacksons to hold their own against Helen.

Aaron's silence made Macady nervous. Suddenly she remembered the shadowy couple she'd seen at the King Sol. Was Slade there the night Aaron's truck was vandalized? She shuddered. Was she beginning to doubt Slade too? No way! Aaron was right about someone needing to talk to Slade. But she knew Slade—he'd balk at cooperating with Aaron. She'd have to find Slade and talk to him herself.

CHAPTER NINETEEN

Macady stirred the ice in her glass and glanced toward the front of the restaurant, then looked down at her watch. Slade had agreed to return immediately and meet her at eight at a restaurant a few blocks from the hospital. She felt a stab of guilt. Honesty was a highly prized commodity to her, yet here she was sneaking behind Aaron's back. She should have told him that Slade had promised to call her every day he was away. His call had come through less than twenty minutes after Aaron left her room.

She felt certain her cousin's shock had been genuine when she told him of Kelsey's disappearance.

Her mother had tried to talk her out of checking herself out of the hospital, but had finally agreed that it would be better for Macady to talk to Slade than for Aaron to confront him. Reluctantly, Hazel had agreed to drop Macady off at the restaurant, leave her car, and go on home with David once Slade arrived.

Hazel had told Macady of the fight between Aaron and Slade that had been interrupted by the burning barn. The animosity between the two men saddened Macady. How had two people who were once the closest of friends become so angry and distrustful of each other?

"Hello, 'Cady." Slade pulled out a chair and settled himself across from her. "You look much better than when I saw you last."

"I'm fine." Slade looked skeptical and Macady rushed on,

"Thanks for coming. This is really important or I wouldn't have asked you to come."

"What about Kelsey? Has there been any word?"

"No, not even a demand for Aaron to drop his case." Her voice trembled as she answered.

"Why didn't he do something to protect her? If it had been me ... I guess you know what I tried to do to protect you."

"You were wrong, Slade."

"Yes, I know, but I'd do it again if I thought I had a chance of keeping you out of danger. I really thought you were the one being threatened."

"Would you like to order now?" A waitress interrupted their conversation. Without glancing at the menu, Slade ordered a steak. Macady shook her head. The best Chinese restaurant in town and Slade ordered American. When they'd given their orders and were alone again, Macady bit her lip and plunged right in.

"How did you know about the message on Aaron's answering machine?"

Slade looked startled. He picked up his water glass and drained it before answering. Macady knew he thought her question was stupid, but none-the-less, he decided to humor her. "Gossip, I suppose. I stopped for breakfast at the airport restaurant and heard a couple guys talking. I recognized Sid Ashcraft and asked him what he knew about it."

"Sid? Sylvia's brother?"

"Yes. He hauls drums of used oil and grease from the airport, so I see him occasionally."

"But who told him?"

"I asked him that. He said a couple of deputies had been in earlier and they'd been quite excited about it."

"Slade, will you do me a favor?" She bit her lip again and debated the best way to gain his cooperation.

"Probably." He leaned back to allow the waitress to slide his plate in front of him. Macady waited while he savored the first bite.

"Will you talk to Aaron? He has a lot of questions about that morning."

Slade stopped with his fork midway to his mouth and scowled. "Why should I tell him anything? After what he did ..."

"Slade! Let Alicia go. Her death was an accident. It's her daughter we need to be concerned about. Aaron didn't receive that message until after the fire."

Slade looked at her conveying the message he didn't believe her.

"It's true. He got called out in the early hours of the morning that day and never returned to his house until after he'd spent a night in the hospital and the following day with Kelsey and me. It was late the second night when he played his messages. No one could have known about that message except the person who put it there."

Slade chewed his food carefully, and he appeared to be digesting more than his dinner.

"Did Aaron tell you that?"

"He didn't have to. The sheriff, Mom, your brothers, and a dozen nurses can account for every minute of his time those two days."

"Why would someone leave a message like that, then go around telling everyone about it?" Slade raised a questioning eyebrow.

"I've thought a lot about that. Maybe someone didn't go around telling everyone about the message. Perhaps they told only you."

"You're not making sense. Why tell me?"

"I don't know." She pushed her dinner around on her plate. Her stomach revolted at the thought of eating, and she wondered if Kelsey's kidnappers were giving her anything to eat. She had to persuade Slade to talk to Aaron.

Without warning, Slade reached across the table and gripped her wrist. "Macady, what if I was right? What if you were the intended victim all along?"

"But Kelsey ..."

"No, think about it. It's you, not Kelsey who can identify the sniper. She's not a threat to anyone."

Macady shook her head. "Then why was she kidnapped?"

"Because they failed to get you. She's leverage, that's all, leverage. They want you and Westerman to keep quiet, and they know you'll both do anything to keep Kelsey safe."

"But there haven't been any demands. Besides, even if Aaron dropped the investigation, there are federal agencies involved. They won't quit."

"Then Aaron must be a lot closer than those other guys."

"But Aaron believes you're the one who can lead him to the drug runners—and to Kelsey."

Slade's face turned thoughtful. "What does Aaron think I know?"

"To begin with, you can tell him who the woman was in the charter service office the morning you took me there."

Slade lowered his eyes to his plate and ran his thumb absently across the rim of his glass. His thoughts appeared to be a long way from the dimly lit restaurant, and she wondered if he would answer.

"Maybe you should go call Aaron." She couldn't believe Slade had changed his mind so easily.

"Do you know something?" Macady asked hesitantly.

"Go make the call, then finish your dinner. You're nothing but skin and bones." Slade reached for a roll as though he hadn't a care in the world, but Macady saw the way a nerve jumped at the corner of his mouth. She pushed back her chair and hurried to the pay phone in the lobby.

"Sit down." Slade waved negligently toward an empty space at the table. Aaron never took his eyes from the other man as he carefully lowered himself to the chair. He avoided looking at Macady. She wasn't so different from Alicia after all. She'd known all along how to reach Slade, and the minute Aaron's back was turned, she'd rushed to warn him. He wasn't sure why she had called him. Her telephone call hadn't been particularly enlightening.

"Why is the lady at the airport important?" Slade went right to the point. The rigid line of his jaw indicated some deep emotion held tightly in check.

"A man died of a cocaine overdose last night." Aaron spoke softly, but with a hint of steel. "The coroner thinks he was murdered. A witness placed him with two men and a woman just before his death. One of those men is well over six feet tall and drives a green Ford Ranger. I think the woman is the same woman who helped you plan Macady's abduction."

"Careful, old friend. You're coming mighty close to making an accusation we're both going to regret."

"Slade, just tell him," Macady snapped out impatiently. "Alicia is dead. You're wasting time fighting over her now. Finding Kelsey is all that matters."

Slade sucked in his breath sharply and Aaron raised a sardonic eyebrow. "Your cousin thinks you were carrying on a hot affair with my wife."

Slade turned an agonized look toward Macady, and Aaron felt a doubt slip through his mind. In his heart he'd believed Alicia guilty of emotional infidelity, but had never questioned her friendship with one of his closest friends. He'd always known they occasionally met at the airport when Slade flew into Boulder, but he'd never once suspected there was anything more than friendship between them.

"You've got it all wrong, 'Cady. Alicia wasn't the one indulging in extracurricular activities." Slade's voice was tight and hard.

"Neither was Aaron." Aaron was surprised at the conviction in Macady's voice. "All those nights he was out late and the woman he spent so much time with were for work. Think about it. He was a cop, working alternating shifts, and his assigned partner was a woman. That doesn't constitute an affair!"

Slade turned frozen features toward Aaron. "Is that the truth?"

Aaron nodded his head, but his mind still worked to absorb

Macady's words. They'd hit him with a kind of shock. Macady had done more than defend his character; whether she realized it or not, she had proclaimed her trust in him. A flicker of hope warmed his heart. If Macady trusted him, there was a chance she could love him.

"What about you, Aaron? Do you think Alicia was unfaithful?" Slade's words bordered on being a taunt.

"No, not in the sense you mean." He held up his hand like a traffic cop when Slade would have interrupted, then quietly continued. He sensed it was important for Slade to understand. "Alicia was married to her mother. Helen wanted a lawyer for a son-in-law, so Alicia dumped you for me. When Helen discovered I meant to be a cop, she couldn't forgive me for what she considered ruining her daughter's life."

"I loved her, but I swear I never ..." Slade broke off, unable to go on.

"I know that."

"I was alone on this trip and I did a lot of thinking. And even more praying. Over Wyoming with nothing but blue sky as far as I could see, I felt the first peace I've known since Alicia died. It was as though I could finally tell her good-bye." Slade took a long swallow from his glass and visibly struggled to avoid exhibiting the emotion he was feeling. "How can you believe I didn't take advantage of your wife, but still suspect me of attempting to harm Macady and your daughter?" Slade asked the same question Aaron had earlier asked himself.

"For the same reason you believed I drove Alicia to kill herself. Somehow we've lost the ability to trust with the same innocent abandon we knew as children. We doubted our own instincts, listened to the words of others, and blew small pieces of evidence into giant sign posts." Aaron looked at Macady fully for the first time since he'd arrived at the restaurant and acknowledged to himself he had doubted her too quickly. As her eyes met his, he saw the hurt and he knew she'd seen his lack of faith.

"Speaking of evidence, just what were these bits of evidence that led you to suspect me of involvement with the people who set the barn on fire and stole your daughter?" There was still a defensive edge to Slade's voice.

"Ben said you were the only other person he saw near the barn that afternoon."

Slade's face registered surprise. "I didn't go near that barn until he said it was on fire. How could you think ...?"

"I didn't think that. I know your concern was real. You didn't fake being scared."

"Ben isn't a liar. If he said he saw me, then he must have thought he saw me—or someone he thought was me."

"There can't be many men who could be mistaken for you." Aaron's eyes narrowed their focus on Slade's face as the bigger man seemed lost in thought.

"There's one," Slade spoke so softly Aaron wasn't certain he'd heard him right. He leaned closer, waiting for Slade to speak a name.

Macady saw a hard expression on Aaron's face as he waited to hear what Slade had to say. Anxious to put doubts and suspicions between the two men to rest, Macady rushed into the next point she knew concerned Aaron. "Slade, Aaron found your high school ring where the drug runners had planned to ambush us that night in the desert."

Slade looked blank for several seconds, then a grim smile touched his lips. He nodded his head as though she'd just confirmed a point he'd made earlier.

"How did it get there?" She felt a growing tension as she asked.

"I gave it to an old girlfriend. She told me she lost it while we were hiking up to Balanced Rock years ago."

A picture of the huge ring on a much smaller hand rose in her mind. A thick wad of thread and pink fingernail polish kept the ring from sliding off a long slender finger. Nausea roiled in her stomach. No, it couldn't be.

"And the woman in your office?" Aaron prompted.

"Sylvia. Sylvia Ashcraft."

"And the man who is as big as you?" She could tell by Aaron's taut expression he already knew the answer.

"Sid Ashcraft, Sylvia's brother."

"I can't believe Sylvia would …" Macady's senses reeled. She'd known Sylvia all of her life. She'd been like a big sister to her when Macady had been a child.

"There's a lot you don't know about Sylvia." Slade's jaw was set and his eyes were as cold as ice. "Sylvia's been playing with drugs since our high school days. She got high at a party once, and we had a big fight. She promised she'd never do it again, but one night when I went to pick her up, she and her brother were both stoned out of their minds."

"Did you report them?" Aaron asked.

"How could I? She was my girlfriend." A hint of the anguish he'd suffered then crept into Slade's voice. "I wish I had. Perhaps all of this could have been avoided."

Aaron shook his head. "I should have suspected something when I saw an oil drum at the airstrip in the desert. But I'm so used to seeing those barrels at every service station, trucking garage and even the airport, I didn't think it was important."

Slade sighed. "Ashcraft Barrel and Salvage. Sid picks up used oil all over the city. It would be easy for him to pick up more than oil at the airport and slip it to prearranged trucks leaving Twin Falls."

"Why didn't either of us recognize him?" Aaron asked Macady. "Even though he's older, and I haven't seen him for years, I should have seen something familiar in him."

"You never saw his face."

"But you said you saw the sniper's face."

"I don't know Sylvia's brother. She told me once that he was five years older than she was. That would make him ten years older than me. Our paths never crossed."

"Do you know where Sylvia is living now?" Aaron asked as he rose to his feet.

"Yes, she's staying with Sid in their father's old house." He stood too, and reached for his wallet. "I'll go with you."

"No, take Macady to the ranch and watch her."

"Don't turn chauvinist on me now." Macady rose to her feet and planted her fists on her hips. "You're not leaving me behind. I intend to go after Kelsey, too."

"You should still be in the hospital. Besides, civilians aren't allowed to accompany law officers in situations where firearms might be used or arrests made. You'll both have to leave."

"In a pig's eye," Slade drawled. "Go make your calls. Call in every cop in the state, the feds too, but when you leave here, we'll be either riding in your truck or following you. You don't know Macady very well if you think she'll let a little thing like nearly getting killed hold her back, and I don't intend to take my eyes off her until your crooks are in jail."

Aaron gave him a dark look, then quickly stepped to a telephone in the lobby. His scowl deepened as he talked. After a hasty sketch of all Slade had told him, he hung up the phone and turned to face Macady and Slade.

"I assume Blacker told you to go home and leave it to him and the feds." Slade read his old friend's face accurately.

"You're off duty," Macady reasoned. "There's no law against just driving by the old Ashcraft place."

"Let's go. You know you intend to anyway." With that, they took off at a run for Aaron's truck.

CHAPTER TWENTY

They all three crowded into the front seat of Aaron's truck, and Macady found comfort in sitting next to Aaron. She knew she and Slade had pushed him pretty hard, but meekly going home was beyond her at this point. As much as she loved Kelsey and felt an aching need to find her and take care of her, she sensed Aaron needed her, too. If it cost her life, she would be there for Aaron when his daughter was found.

"Turn here," Slade instructed and Aaron frowned.

"He knows the way," Macady reminded Slade.

"Just making sure."

"I don't see any lights." Aaron peered ahead at a desolate old house that looked abandoned and stood at the end of a long lane.

Macady's heart sank. Was Kelsey here, perhaps tied up and locked in a room all alone in the dark? They would have to get inside to search. That would be breaking and entering, but at this point she didn't care. All that mattered was rescuing Kelsey.

She felt the truck slow, then come to a stop. Her heart felt like a bird fluttering to escape her throat. "Why are you stopping here?" she whispered. She'd expected Aaron to pull into the lane.

"Look." She followed his pointing finger and watched as lights came on in the house, first the lower floor, then the upper. Seconds later a faint gleam near the foundation of the house indicated a light had been turned on in the basement. Lights could be seen moving across the yard, too.

"Four cars!" Slade muttered.

"Probably that many more on the road behind the house,"

Aaron added. Macady could see dark shapes along the lane. Light bars across the top of each vehicle let her know the police had arrived ahead of them.

"Let's go," she urged Aaron to open the door.

"You're staying here ... and you, too," he turned to Slade. "I can get away with walking in on an investigation, but you can't. Blacker will order the both of you locked up for your own protection if he catches sight of you. Keep the doors locked." He slid out and moved quickly into the shadows.

Macady turned a questioning glance toward Slade.

"I think we better do as he says." He shrugged his shoulders.

Macady chewed her bottom lip and peered anxiously through the windshield, watching for any sign of Aaron. In minutes she was gnawing at her thumbnail. She couldn't see the house as clearly as she'd like, but nothing much seemed to be happening. Occasionally a shadow passed between a window and the light, and a few lights could be seen carefully bisecting the area around the house. Time dragged, and she started on her other thumbnail. Finally Slade put his arm around her.

"Stop fidgeting. I don't think she's here. Aaron would have let us know if they'd found her."

She'd already reached the same conclusion. "I'm so scared, Slade. Will you pray with me?"

"Yes." He took her hands between his.

They prayed, and they waited. Macady was ready to rip open the door and dash up the lane when a tap sounded on the glass beside her. She felt a surge of panic before she recognized Aaron and scrambled to open the door.

His face was pale and the shadows under his eyes were darker than they'd been before. He shook his head. "She isn't here. There's no sign they brought her here at all. Blacker is going to leave a couple of deputies in case anyone returns, but the house looks like they left quickly and without any plans to return."

"Do you think they have Kelsey with them?"

"I don't know."

"Is it possible they might be holding her at their warehouse?" Slade asked. "We could run by there and check it out. It's just a couple of miles from here, over by the sugar factory."

Aaron pursed his lips thoughtfully, then started the engine. "We might as well take a look."

The warehouse looked dark and deserted as they approached. A single pole light cast a pale swath of light across rows and rows of metal drums stacked three and four high across a yard the size of a football field. An eight-foot chain-link fence circled the salvage yard and two trucks and a front loader were pulled up against the garage doors of the long, low building at one end.

Aaron parked beneath a massive willow tree across the street from the warehouse. "Stay here and ..."

"Not this time," Slade cut him off. "The gates are padlocked. The only way you're getting over that fence is if I give you a boost. You can roll a barrel over to get back out."

"Okay."

Macady didn't speak, but simply followed the men across the street, taking care not to limp. They walked around the fence until they found a spot deep in the shade, and Slade helped Aaron over.

"I want to go with him," she whispered to her cousin.

"Let her come," Aaron spoke quietly through the fence. "There doesn't seem to be anyone around, and two of us can search more quickly than one."

Eagerly she stepped into Slade's cupped hands. At the top of the fence, she placed her hands carefully, then threw a leg over the wire. She felt her jeans catch. The fabric gave with a little rip as she slid down the other side into Aaron's waiting arms.

"Go back to the truck, and call for help if you hear anything," Aaron warned Slade. "If we're not back in twenty minutes, call anyway."

Together Macady and Aaron moved toward the end of the cinder block building that housed Sid's office. The night was eerily still and Macady felt goosebumps on her arms. Standing on their toes, they peered through two small windows, but couldn't see anything except a desk piled high with scattered papers and ledgers.

"I'll go this way," she whispered, indicating a truck-wide corridor through the barrels.

Aaron nodded his head and started walking in the opposite direction between the barrels and the warehouse.

The metal drums towering over her head gave her the creeps. It was easy to imagine the rows moving closer, the barrels on top tipping toward her. She'd be crushed. She shook her head and chided herself for letting her imagination distract her from her search. Strange, she should feel alone, but she didn't. The back of her neck prickled, and she experienced the illusion of dozens of eyes watching her. She wished she'd stayed with Aaron.

She came to an intersection where a smaller trail branched off between the barrels. She took a deep breath and peeked around the corner. An arm circled her throat and a hand slapped across her mouth. She felt something hard against her back. Instinct took over and she cocked her elbow to land a solid blow to her captor's midsection. She heard him grunt, but he didn't loosen his grip. Her teeth sought the fleshy pads of his fingers and she tasted blood. Still he didn't release his hold. His arm tightened against her tender throat.

She froze as off to her right a commotion erupted. Steel drums crashed together, and a man yelled. She could hear running footsteps. Another crash sounded, followed by silence. Suddenly spotlights cut across the yard and voices and footsteps were everywhere.

"Move it!" The man holding her eased his arm back and she heard a click as metal cuffs closed around her wrists. She considered trying to run, then decided to wait for a better opportunity. Slade had probably called the sheriff by now. There was no sense getting shot trying to escape when the cavalry would be arriving any moment.

Her captor marched her toward the light pole where a group

of dark-clothed men waited. Aaron stood in their midst. He appeared calm and slightly amused. Then she knew. She didn't have to be a genius to figure out they had stumbled into a stake-out. While the sheriff's department checked out the Ashcraft home, federal agents had gathered at Sid's business address.

The man behind her nudged her none too gently into the center of the circle. She stumbled against Aaron. He staggered back a step, and she realized he was cuffed, too.

"You okay?" She could see the concern in his eyes.

"Yes," she mouthed.

"That one have a gun, too?" someone asked.

"Not a chance," the agent who had captured her laughed. "There's no place to hide anything in those jeans." Macady felt her skin flush and saw Aaron take a protective step toward her.

One dark-clothed figure stepped forward. "You have the right to—"

"Skip it!" Aaron interrupted. "We know our rights. I'm a deputy with the Twin Falls County Sheriff's Office. There's I.D. in my wallet. Right hip pocket."

Macady saw someone remove Aaron's wallet. "Westerman? You related to the kid ...?"

"She's my daughter."

A shrill screech cut through the night. Metal screamed in protest and barrels began flying through the air.

"Stop!" two different voices shouted. A crack like a pistol shot sent agents scrambling for cover. Someone grabbed Macady's shoulder and jerked her behind a barrel. From there, she could see a gray pickup truck moving steadily toward them, and behind it the yard gates hung crazily from their metal posts. Slade had crashed the gate.

The truck stopped when it reached the circle of light. Macady watched with an open mouth as Slade opened the door of Aaron's truck. She stared in horror at the circle of guns silently pointed his way.

"No," she screamed.

"He's with me. Don't shoot." Aaron's voice cut above the confusion.

"Hold your fire," an authoritative voice barked.

Slade stepped from the truck and hoisted a bulky object to his shoulder before slowly walking toward the group. Casually he slid his squirming, wiggling bundle to the ground. "Next time don't send a girl to do a man's job." He spoke directly to the tall man standing beside Aaron.

"You're under arrest!" A high pitched voice came from the bundle at Slade's feet.

Macady's eyes widened at the sight of a woman with tousled auburn hair sitting in the dirt in the center of the group. She looked small for a cop, but there was nothing small about the anger spitting from her eyes as she glared up at Slade.

Slade grinned, and Macady expected the little spitfire to belt him. A belting he no doubt deserved.

"Cuff him," she snapped. When no one obeyed, she sprang to her feet and glared around the circle.

"Afraid not, Cara." The tall man stepped forward and released Macady. She could see Aaron was already free and deep in conversation with two of the men. "We got the wrong people." He spoke gently, like he'd no intention of running afoul of the woman's sharp tongue.

"Of course, now that I can see you better, you're welcome to try." Slade's face was covered with a silly grin and Macady could see the beginning of a shiner beneath her cousin's left eye. "If I'd had any idea a fed could look like you, I wouldn't have resisted arrest so hard."

Cara's clothing and coppery hair looked disheveled as though she'd wrestled with a bear, but there was no mistaking she was a beautiful woman. A shoe was missing and her holster was empty. Twin bracelets linked her hands in front.

Slade reached into the truck and pulled out a handful of the pretty young officer's tools, including her gun and shoe. "Is it safe to give these back to her?" he asked Aaron.

A snicker came out of the darkness, and Cara whirled to glare in the offender's direction.

"Enough!" The captain spoke sharply. "Collins, keep your team here. The rest of us ..." The wail of sirens cut off the remainder of his words. Seconds later, three sheriff's vehicles and two police cars screamed to a halt beside the mesh fence.

"Who invited them?" a disgruntled agent muttered as he set the female officer loose.

"I did." Slade grinned and handed Cara her shoe. She snatched it from his hand and marched away with her back ramrod straight.

It took the better part of an hour to exchange information and wrap up the investigation at the salvage yard before returning to the court house. Both FBI and DEA agents cornered Slade to demand a detailed account of his relationship with Sylvia, particularly since she'd returned to Twin Falls. He swore he'd only talked to her twice on the telephone and seen her once. She'd called him about six o'clock Saturday morning at the courier office to tell him she'd heard Macady was in danger and offered to help him get her safely away. Since he'd already heard of the threat against Macady, he'd agreed to Sylvia's plan. She'd come to the airport a couple of hours later with the clothes and supplies he and Macady would need.

Macady finally made her way out of the sheriff's office and walked through the double doors of the old court house. Her head ached and her throat felt raw. Slowly she sank down on one of the wide steps and leaned against the stone wall. They'd been right about the drugs. The DEA had found all the evidence they needed at the salvage yard to link Sid Ashcraft to the illegal traffic.

Sid was a minor operator in a large drug cartel, taking orders from a man who had arrived in Twin Falls from San Francisco about the same time Sylvia had returned to Idaho. Several others were involved, too, including a pilot who contracted independently with the ski resort and an employee of a local trucking firm. Blacker's office had concluded that the drug operation had switched to using legitimate flights once the concealed airstrip was closed down.

According to the DEA, the drugs were being leapfrogged up from Arizona, where they first entered the country, to Denver and Salt Lake, then on to Twin Falls. Slade roared with rage when he learned some of the businessmen he ferried around were carrying more than briefcases full of contracts and leases. Packages heavily wrapped in plastic had been dropped by the pseudo-businessmen into oil refuse drums at the airport to be hauled away by Sid.

Macady swallowed the tears threatening to surface. The Ashcrafts and their partners were just one link in a bigger drug chain, a chain that was coming unraveled, but there was still no trace of Kelsey. Her arms ached to hold the child, and she wondered how Aaron could bear it. His face and eyes were turning him into a specter, and deep in her heart she knew his pain was tearing him apart. She closed her eyes and pleaded with Heavenly Father, "Please lead us to Kelsey. Please keep her safe, and let her know we're coming."

"Macady. Honey, wake up." Aaron was beside her shaking her shoulder gently. She blinked her eyes and looked around. She'd fallen asleep leaning against the rock wall. "Slade said the morning he abducted you, the plan was to take you to a cabin near Magic Mountain Ski Lodge. We think they might have taken Kelsey there."

Macady struggled to her feet. She ached all over, but knowing there was a new place to search for Kelsey sent a surge of adrenaline pumping through her veins.

"I can drop you off at the ranch on the way."

"I want to go with you."

"You just got out of the hospital. I don't want you so exhausted you have to go back."

"Aaron, I have to go."

"I know. Blacker couldn't convince me not to go either." He placed his arms around her and drew her head back against his shoulder. "But we will have to stay back. I gave him my word we'd stay with the vehicles and not approach the cabin until he says we can."

Macady nodded her acceptance of the stipulations placed on them by the sheriff.

Slade joined them in Aaron's truck, and they took up the rear as a line of vehicles left the parking lot. Rodriguez and Brinkerman led the way with two FBI agents in the second seat of the extended cab, followed by the sheriff's truck.

Cara, who had been formally introduced as Agent Broschinsky, rode in the four-wheel drive Chevy just in front of Aaron's Ford F150. Macady noticed Slade's eyes frequently wandered to the pretty, young agent. Several times he rubbed the bruise beneath his eye and the corner of his mouth turned up in a faint smile.

"Does it hurt?" she asked him.

"Not really, but don't you think it's odd that with all the scrapes I've been in, the years I played football, and even the wrestling matches with my brothers, I've never had a black eye before? It took a half-pint fed to land me a shiner." Macady took a second look. The awe in her cousin's voice was for real.

"If I'd known about that upper right of hers, I would have asked the FBI to send her to Twin Falls a long time ago." Aaron gave his friend a sardonic half-smile.

"Why did they send her on a job like this? I could have broken her neck when I landed on her. She shouldn't be going up against Sid Ashcraft. He's about my size and plays rough," Slade grumbled.

"Don't underestimate Agent Broschinsky. The only reason you got the drop on her was because she saw some kids sleeping on the lawn behind the truck and chose not to draw her weapon."

"She's still a woman."

"A nineties woman, my dear chauvinistic cousin," Macady

joined the conversation. "When are you going to realize that today's woman doesn't scream and jump on a chair when a mouse appears?"

"I know, women like you pick up the chair and clobber the poor mouse yourselves, but the little fed isn't as big as you."

Macady stared at her cousin in surprise. "You're worried about her." Slade looked sheepish, and Macady hid a smile. Her cousin had fallen for the wrong woman twice—maybe the third time would be the charm.

Aaron turned right and no one spoke for several minutes, then Aaron asked Slade, "Where did you plan to land a plane up here?"

"Sylvia said there's a small strip about a quarter of a mile from the cabin. It's rough, but a small plane can set down on it. The people over at the ski lodge use it for their chopper."

Macady's eyes met Aaron's for just a moment, then she looked down to where his white knuckles gripped the steering wheel, and knew he was remembering the helicopter scouring the desert in search of them. Kelsey in the hands of those same ruthless people was a nightmare beyond anything she'd ever dreamed.

Aaron jerked the wheel and the truck left the pavement for a narrow dirt track. They lurched over tree roots and rocks until Macady thought her neck would snap. She clutched Aaron's leg with one hand and the truck seat with the other to avoid bouncing around. Slade wrapped an arm around her to anchor her to the seat.

"I thought we were supposed to stay behind the others," Slade growled.

"That was the plan until you mentioned the helipad. I know the spot and I'm just going to made certain no one leaves on a whirlybird." The engine protested and Aaron geared down as low as the truck would go. Tree branches slapped against the side of the truck and rocks scraped against metal. Finally Aaron pulled into a grove and cut the engine. Silence filled the night.

Both men rolled down the windows, and all three of them sat

scarcely breathing as they listened to the quiet. A helicopter, looking like a giant bug silhouetted against the lighter gray of the sky, almost hid from view the wings of a small plane tucked beneath the overhang of trees at one end of the runway. A fickle breeze wafted through the trees, then nothing. A faint whiff of campfire smoke drifted in the air, and Macady shivered.

"Do you think they bring cocaine in here?" she whispered to Aaron.

"No, it's too close to the ski resort, and there are too many campers and fishermen for a regular operation to go undetected."

A single pop sounded in the distance and Aaron grasped for the door handle. They strained to hear, and were rewarded by the sound of two more shots in quick succession. Then silence lay like a heavy fog across the mountain. Macady felt a tremor run through Aaron's leg where she still clung to him. Her own body trembled. Kelsey! Kelsey! The name beat through her heart, and she silently prayed for the child's safety.

"Look!"

Aaron's head snapped to the right at Slade's hoarse whisper. Two running figures left the trees, moving quickly toward the helicopter. Before he could react, a third figure broke clear of the trees.

"Halt, or I'll shoot!" The words carried distinctly in the still night air.

"That's Cara!" Slade jammed his shoulder against his door.

"Wait!" Aaron threw himself across Macady to grasp Slade's arm. "Don't distract her. That's how cops get killed."

"There are two of them," Slade protested.

Aaron reached behind him for a shotgun. "Don't you dare leave this pickup. I'll back her up. Now get down." He slipped from the truck, and Macady ducked her head. After a moment Slade slid down beside her.

Macady couldn't stand missing the action. Her head bobbed up for a quick peek. Cara stood in a shooter's stance. Aaron was positioned behind her with the shotgun leveled at the suspects.

Cara shouted something, and the other two people slowly flattened themselves against the ground. She moved cautiously toward them.

"Careful, careful," Slade muttered. His big hands were balled into tight fists, and his whole attention was focused on the action in the clearing.

"Need some help, Broschinsky?" Aaron's voice carried across the clearing.

"Cover me while I cuff them." Cara returned her gun to its holster before crouching beside the two people on the ground. Macady saw a flash of metal in Cara's hand as she reached toward the first suspect. A moment later she turned to the second.

The attack was so quick, Macady didn't see what happened, only that one suspect was running toward the trees and Cara Broschinsky was rolling on the ground. Aaron couldn't shoot. Cara was between him and the fleeing figure. The suspect disappeared into the trees just as Cara regained her feet.

"Stay with the prisoner," she yelled at Aaron as she sprinted toward the spot where the escapee had disappeared.

Seconds after she left the clearing, Deputy Rodriguez burst into sight. Aaron shouted to his fellow deputy to follow Cara. He'd stay with the prisoner on the ground.

Macady looked around and saw no sign of Slade. She hadn't heard him leave the truck, but she didn't doubt he'd gone after Cara. She wanted to go to Aaron, but remembered what he'd said about distracting an officer. In minutes, half a dozen deputies and federal agents joined the chase while two more hustled the man on the ground to his feet and led him away.

A few minutes later, Cara marched Sylvia into the clearing. Her long hair was down and straggling across her face, her arms were pulled behind her back, and she walked with a slight limp. Several men trailed behind the two women, but there was no sign of Slade until the truck door opened and he slid in beside Macady.

He didn't speak for several minutes, then he clasped his hands behind his head and leaned back against the headrest. "She's been out of my life for ten years, but because I cared about her once, it still hurts to see her come to this."

Macady leaned her forehead against her cousin's shoulder. "I know. It's a kind of betrayal. It's as though she repudiated all the fun and memories we shared. In a way, I feel the way I did when Daddy told me about Carol."

"I don't hate her." Slade's big arms hugged Macady tight. "More than anything I pity her, and I can't help wondering if I'd done something different all those years ago, could I have changed her life for the better?"

"There's no way you'll ever know. You'll also never know whether she might have ruined your life had you stayed with her. Perhaps I've finally grown up because I, too, feel more pity and sorrow than hate and anger."

Together they watched the figures on the tiny airfield until Cara and Rodriguez left the clearing with their prisoner. The other officers trailed behind. Only the sheriff and Aaron remained in the clearing.

"Hey, cuz," Slade scarcely raised his voice. "I think you might have the right idea. Perhaps I'll check it out myself."

"Check out what?"

"The arms of the law."

"Are you telling me you've fallen for the lady who blacked your eye?"

"Not just my eye. You ought to see the shiner Sylvia's going to be sporting. That little fed is really something."

"She didn't need your help?"

"She doesn't even know I was there. I arrived in time to see her make a tackle that I would have bragged about for a whole season back in my football days. When Cara stood up, Sylvia didn't. Rodriguez came along about then and helped Sylvia to her feet, but she was already neatly shackled and her left eye was darn near swollen shut. I figured I'd better just hightail it back here."

Macady started to smile, but the smile faded almost before it began. Slade was trying to distract her. Something was wrong. Terribly wrong. Where was Kelsey? As she watched, Sheriff Blacker placed a hand on Aaron's shoulder and shook his head. No! She formed a fist and bit down hard on her knuckles. He couldn't be telling Aaron they were too late. With a strangled cry she jumped from the truck and ran to Aaron.

"Kelsey?" She whispered as his arms closed around her.

"She isn't here. They captured Sid and two other men inside the cabin. The suspects fired several times at the officers, but no one was injured. Sylvia and the pilot were outside and saw what was happening, so they headed for the chopper with Broschinsky and Rodriguez right behind them. Sheriff Blacker questioned the men and they all swear they didn't take Kelsey." Aaron choked on the words, and his arms tightened around Macady.

"I spoke to Sylvia. She said they never touched my daughter, but when they heard she'd been kidnapped, they knew they'd be blamed, so they ran." Aaron held Macady fast in his arms. Gently he rocked her back and forth, as they fought the twin demons of grief and fear.

CHAPTER TWENTY-ONE

"Are you sure you want me to sleep in Kelsey's room?" Macady leaned against the door sill, looking gray and uncertain as she viewed Kelsey's bedroom. He couldn't very well say, "No, I don't want you in Kelsey's room. I want you in my room, in my bed." If he could hold Macady tight enough, perhaps her warmth and caring would push away the demons closing in on him.

He closed his eyes against the pain. He'd been so sure that when the drug runners were located, Kelsey would be returned. But they didn't have her. There was the possibility, of course, that they had taken her and gotten rid of her, but he had believed Sylvia. The four men they'd captured chose to remain silent, but Sylvia had plenty to say. She told the FBI interrogator she and her partners weren't stupid enough to risk kidnapping a cop's kid. She claimed she'd known nothing about the fire either, and that she and Sid had argued when she'd learned what he'd done.

"Will Sylvia be sent to prison?" Macady's raspy voice interrupted his thoughts. He glanced at her drooping shoulders and the eyes she could barely keep open. After the ordeal with the fire, he hoped the night's activities hadn't set back her recovery.

"Yes, she'll probably go to prison, though if she'll testify against the others, her attorney can probably get her a pretty good deal."

"I'm glad the sheriff let her talk to me for a few minutes." Macady's voice revealed both the physical and emotional strain she'd been under all night. "She said Sid called her that day from the desert. He told her that he'd found a cop snooping around the airstrip and that they'd all go to jail if they didn't prevent him from leaving the desert. The day we had lunch together, she guessed you were the officer he'd shot at. Then when you mentioned my hat, she had a pretty good idea what had happened and realized that if I saw Sid again I would recognize him. That scared her."

"I always liked Sylvia. She had a rough time growing up with a father whose whole life revolved around his business and making money. He let her know he considered a daughter a worthless expense. He was rough and crude, and Sid wasn't any better. Perhaps if her mother had stuck around, things would have been better." Behind his words was genuine compassion.

He recalled again the terror in Sylvia's eyes when Cara brought her back into the mountain clearing. Sheriff Blacker had read her rights and questioned her about Kelsey being at the cabin. Later, while she was being processed into the jail facility, she'd begged to talk to Macady alone. Blacker had permitted it, but insisted Cara stay with them.

"Is that all she said when she asked to speak to you alone?"

"No, she told me it was her idea to get Slade to take me to the cabin and keep me there long enough for them to wrap up their operation and leave. She was afraid Sid would kill me to keep me from identifying him, and she didn't want me hurt, so she concocted a scheme to keep me out of the way."

"I still don't understand why they were so determined to get me off the case." Aaron yawned and leaned against the wall.

"They knew you had my ring, and that it would lead you straight to Sylvia." Aaron hadn't heard Slade join them. The last he'd seen him, he'd been asleep on the sofa in the front room.

"Where's that pillow you promised me?" Slade rubbed his bloodshot eyes and looked around hopefully.

Aaron pulled a blanket and a pillow from the hall closet and tossed them to Slade. "How could they know I had the ring? And what was Sylvia doing with it after all this time?" he puzzled aloud.

"Beats me." Slade yawned. "She told me she'd lost it."

"Sylvia said she lied about losing the ring because she couldn't bear the possibility you might give it to another girl. Later, after her divorce, she ran onto the ring with some of her things, and she saw it as a symbol of a happier time, so she started wearing it on a silver chain around her neck for luck. When Sid ordered her to watch Aaron's truck that night, she refused at first. He grabbed the chain like he was going to choke her. It broke, and she wasn't able to find the ring again in the dark."

Macady yawned and sank down on the side of Kelsey's bed to continue her story.

"She knew about the initials on the inside of the ring. When she and Sid saw us in Sun Valley with Stuart and Sid told her you'd been visiting Steve Jennings, she remembered which friends you'd asked about that day at lunch. She suspected you were checking out former classmates with the same initials as those inside the lost ring. She figured Slade was next on your list, and he'd tell you she was the last person to have his ring."

"Being that transparent doesn't do much for my professional ego," Aaron remarked ruefully.

"I'm turning in." Slade covered another yawn. "You should have dropped us off at the restaurant. My truck is still there."

"Mom's car is, too," Macady added.

"Go on. Get some sleep." Aaron couldn't admit aloud the reason he'd insisted they stay at his house instead of driving to the ranch was because he couldn't face his house alone. He needed Macady with him, and the only way he could keep her over night was to keep Slade, too.

Aaron touched her arm to urge her to lay down. She looked like she was on the edge of total collapse. The night had been too much for her. When she turned her fatigue-glazed eyes toward him, he saw the sorrow and compassion in their deep, warm pools. She hadn't said the words, but he knew she loved him and his child. It was the only comfort he had to cling to.

"We'll find her tomorrow," Macady whispered.

"Yes," he let his mouth lightly touch her lips before turning away to enter his own room.

Methodically he peeled off his clothes. He had to get some rest. He knew that. Sleep deprivation wouldn't help him find Kelsey. Out of habit he placed his gun on the top shelf of the closet where Kelsey and Jackie couldn't reach it, then knelt beside his bed to make one more plea for his daughter's safe return. He felt his head jerk and spoke the essentials only. When he finished, he remained on his knees, staring blankly at the steady red light of his answering machine and wished his phone would ring and Kelsey's little voice would say, "Daddy, come get me."

His head jerked again. Fearing he'd spend the night on his knees with only his head against the mattress, he stood up stiffly and climbed between the sheets. His eyes stared through the darkness toward the ceiling, seeing Kelsey. Kelsey, laughing and snuggling her kitten; Kelsey, chasing Jackie across the lawn to meet him when he pulled into Matt and Denise's driveway; Kelsey, wrapped in Macady's arms stroking Tasha's neck.

A dark aloneness swirled through his heart. He'd missed something, some vital clue. It was right there at the edge of his mind, but he couldn't force it past the black abyss of fear that threatened to swallow him each time he attempted to piece together the facts of Kelsey's disappearance.

Was this his punishment for not really mourning Alicia? He'd felt regret for the loss of a young life, and he'd felt sorrow, more for Kelsey's sake than his own, but he'd never felt this deep gut-wrenching sense of loss for his wife.

His marriage hadn't been happy, and he'd blamed Alicia for her inability to "forsake all others and cleave only unto him." But it had taken falling in love with Macady for him to see Alicia and their marriage in a sharper light. At twenty, Alicia had been too young and too much under her mother's thumb for marriage. She'd married him with no thought beyond the perfect wedding and living happily ever after next door to Mommy. He'd fallen in love with her helpless airs and had seen himself as her protector and hero. He'd been hurt to learn she already had a protector and hero in her mother, and she'd wanted no other. Macady had made him see he didn't really want to be anybody's hero; what he did want was a full partner.

Alicia had been raised to believe her dependence on her mother was a virtue. She'd prided herself on the way she honored her parents, and she considered her mother the ultimate authority on life, the gospel, and her marriage. If he'd been more patient, perhaps his wife would have grown up and loosened the tie to her mother, but he'd never know now if that might have happened. Speculating on the future that might have been was just as futile as dwelling on the past.

He could see now that he'd been at fault too. He hadn't met her expectations any better than she had met his. He'd fallen in love with her because she was fragile and in need of care and attention. Then he'd fallen out of love with her for the same reasons when he'd discovered that marriage required the full-time efforts of two adults, and Alicia was more interested in being her mother's daughter than his wife. After marrying an insecure, dependent girl, he'd expected her to suddenly become a strong, competent woman and had shown no patience when she hadn't changed.

Slowly the bitterness and hurt drifted away toward the dark corners of the room, and he remembered her delight in their child. Once more he could hear her lovely voice singing softly to Kelsey. Alicia had loved Kelsey and been a good mother. It was time to let go of his own hurt and disillusionment and remember Alicia had good qualities, too. A quiet calm filled his heart, and he knew that wherever Kelsey might be, her mother was watching over her. Sleep crept closer. He closed his eyes and forgave Alicia. At last, he could let her rest in peace.

After less than four hours, Aaron met Slade and Macady in the kitchen. Macady called her mother to assure her she was fine, and he checked in with the sheriff's department to see if there was any news of Kelsey. There wasn't. No one was interested in breakfast, but he pulled a couple of cereal boxes from the cupboard. Macady mixed a can of frozen orange juice.

After a feeble attempt to eat breakfast, he got a note pad and pencil and set them on the table. He lined the pad up with the side of the table, carefully squaring the edges. Finally he cleared his throat and tried to speak. His voice cracked. He cleared his throat again, and got the words past the lump of fear blocking his throat.

"There must be something we've missed. Could Kelsey have entered the store from the family quarters and left through the front door without being seen?"

Macady shook her head. "I don't think so. I won't say it couldn't have happened that way, but it's not likely. Mary said they were busy that night, but the door is right next to the cash register and Mary is experienced enough that no matter how busy she is, she sees everyone who walks in or out of that door."

"Could someone walk into the family area without being seen?"

"I don't think so, but again I can't swear that would be impossible. But even if someone walked right into the family area, he couldn't walk back out with Kelsey without being seen."

"How about the back door? That's the one we all use," Slade joined the discussion.

"It was still locked with the dead bolt in place when I got there, and Ben said he went into the kitchen to check it before he started helping in the store. No one entered that way." Aaron ran his hand over the lower part of his face, and one corner of his brain registered that he hadn't shaved.

"The basement door is kept locked and barred from the inside, the windows all have security bars. I don't see how anyone got in to take her." Slade shook his head in puzzlement.

"I don't think anyone went into the house, found Macady's room, and just walked out with her." Aaron tried to piece together a possible scenario. "The kitten was outside. That's what alerted Ben that something wasn't right. Somehow that cat got out, and Kelsey went after it. Someone saw her wandering around alone outside and grabbed her." His knuckles turned white, and he felt the pencil snap between his fingers. Macady placed her hand on his shoulder.

"No one told me the kitten was outside. She probably went out my bedroom window."

"And Kelsey followed," Aaron groaned.

"But your windows have bars, too," Slade observed.

"They do, but they're different. The windows on the first floor can't be opened and the bars are welded into the window frame. Upstairs in my room the windows can be opened to let in fresh air and the bars are on a hinged shutter that can be opened and closed from the inside. Daddy had them installed when I was about ten and moved upstairs into a room of my own. He was afraid I might be trapped if there was ever a fire, so he had them built so I could release the lock and push the bars out of the way in an emergency."

"Would Kelsey have known how to do it?"

"She might. Mom keeps the windows in my room open a few inches to help cool the house during the summer. The cats have been in the house since the fire, and unless the door to the stairs is kept shut, I've no doubt they'd sneak out that way. A kitten could easily squeeze through the bars."

"And Kelsey must have released the shutter and followed Sandy right out onto the porch roof," Aaron added. He had no trouble imagining his tomboy daughter scrambling down the lattice-work on the end of the porch, straight into the arms of some twisted individual who saw his chance to snatch a child. A haze of red swam before his eyes, and he struggled to remain sane. He couldn't succumb to helpless rage. He had to think. As from a long distance, he saw Macady leave her chair and felt her arms come around him. Slade reached across the table to grip his arm.

"What kind of description did you get of the people in the store that night from Mary and the boys?" Slade attempted to keep their analysis of the kidnapping going.

"The only good descriptions were of people we've already eliminated as suspects. Ben gave us a description of almost every vehicle in the parking lot. When he described a white car with blue plates, I was sure it was the white Subaru with California plates we'd already associated with the drug people."

"Sylvia's car," Slade contributed.

Macady's fingers tightened on his shoulders. She spoke slowly as though reaching for her words. "Aaron, I saw Sylvia's car at the airport. Her license plate is white with an orange setting sun or something like that."

"California uses more than one style of license plate. No one mentioned which style the Subaru's plates were, so when he said blue ..." He could feel her nails pressing through his shirt.

"Ben is colorblind, Aaron. He can't tell blue from green."

"She's right. We all tease him about his mismatched socks," Slade concurred.

Aaron heard a buzzing in his ears. His vision tilted, then blurred. Hours ago his subconscious mind had tried to tell him. He'd stared right at the most glaring clue and seen nothing. With slow deliberation, he pushed back his chair and rose to his feet. For just a second his knees threatened to buckle, then with swift strides, he reached his bedroom. He stood in the doorway, his eyes fastened on a tiny red light. A light that never blinked.

"Ben saw a white LTD with green Colorado plates," Macady spoke in a whisper while tears streamed down her face, "not a white Subaru with blue California plates."

Aaron wrapped his arms around her and pulled her close. He leaned forward until his forehead touched hers. A deep shudder passed through him. He could hope again.

"Helen calls Kelsey every night. I couldn't reach her yesterday morning, so I left a message for her to call. There's no way she'd ignore a message concerning Kelsey or skip calling her two nights straight."

"Helen?" Slade nearly exploded. "I know you don't like her, but she wouldn't ..." He stopped and shook his head.

"I think she did," Aaron spoke softly.

"I think so, too." Macady agreed with Aaron.

"She's outspoken, even opinionated, but she sets great store in doing everything right. Where the Church is concerned, she goes by the book. There's no way she'd commit a serious crime," Slade argued.

"She wouldn't consider it a crime. She never considered me worthy of being Alicia's husband nor Kelsey's father. To her, taking Kelsey from me would be rescuing her. She has told me more than once that she considers it her moral duty to raise Alicia's child and protect her from me."

"But kidnapping? That's a federal crime."

"She's a woman crazy with grief," Macady spoke to Slade.

"Call her," Slade challenged.

"I will." Aaron crossed the gap between the door and bed with two long strides. Swiftly he touched the keys and listened to the phone ring on the other end. Theoretically there's no difference between the ringing of a telephone about to be answered and one that rings in an empty house, but he'd always sensed some kind of difference. The Colorado house was empty with no one there to pick up the phone.

His next call was to the sheriff. He outlined his suspicions, listened briefly, then described the route Helen was most likely to follow from Twin Falls to Boulder. Finally he nodded his head and agreed to wait until Blacker called him back.

Macady watched Aaron's face as he waited for Sheriff Blacker to call. At first there was hope and excitement that never quite erased the fear. Whenever he appeared the most confident Kelsey would be found with her grandmother, immediately black rage would clench his jaw and tighten his features. Macady shivered, glad she wasn't the one who would face his anger.

He paced back and forth across the bedroom. Each time he passed the telephone, he glared, willing it to ring. Macady's eyes followed him. She wished she could help him through this torture. She prayed the phone would ring. Most of all she prayed Aaron was right because, if he was, then Kelsey would soon be coming home. Macady had never wanted anything more than she wanted to feel Kelsey's little arms around her neck and know the child was safe.

"The next bite will draw blood." Macady lifted distracted eyes to Slade's sardonic figure propped against the door. She followed his pointed stare to her hands. Every fingernail on both hands had been reduced to a jagged stump. A flush of embarrassment touched her cheeks. She hadn't chewed her nails since she'd turned thirteen. Now look at what she'd done.

"This could take hours," Slade spoke to Aaron. "If your supposition proves right—and I'm not conceding that you are right—but just in case, don't you think you should be shaving and packing a bag so you can go get her?"

Aaron looked startled but admitted that Slade was right. He did need to be ready to leave as soon as he got word. He grabbed the telephone and headed for the bathroom.

"Wait a minute," Slade interceded and relieved him of the telephone. "Macady and I are in this, too, and we both need some clean duds. While you're in the shower, I'll call out to the ranch and have some of the boys fetch us some clothes and a couple of toothbrushes, then they can go pick up my truck and Hazel's car and take them home. I need to call the airport, too, to make certain my plane is prepped."

"You'll fly us?" Aaron choked on the words.

"But of course!" Slade waggled one eyebrow. "Did you think I'd abandon an old friend at this stage of the game?" Suddenly his facade crumbled, and he clasped his friend in a massive bear hug. Aaron returned the hug, then pulled away to land a playful slug on Slade's shoulder. Macady smiled around the lump in her throat. Aaron and Slade would be okay, their friendship would endure. They might have to feel their way carefully for a while, but they would make it.

Macady adjusted the shower nozzle and reached for Aaron's shampoo. She gave her hair a quick scrub before rinsing off. As she reached for the towel Aaron had set out for her use, she acknowledged she'd just taken the fastest shower of her life. Like Aaron, who had scarcely taken time to dry off before donning a fresh shirt and clean jeans, she couldn't bear to be out of range of the telephone. She jammed her legs into a pair of Aaron's sweats and pulled the matching shirt over her head. She'd certainly been wearing a lot of borrowed clothes lately.

She was still running a brush through her short curls as she hurried down the hall to rejoin the men in the living room.

Aaron sat in a deep chair, moodily staring out the front window. The telephone rested in his lap.

Slade was sprawled on the sofa, asleep again. She shook his shoulder. "The bathroom is all yours."

He mumbled as he slowly got to his feet, stretching and yawning.

The telephone rang with the impact of an exploding grenade. Macady's hand froze with the brush in midair. Her eyes met Aaron's for a wild, terror-filled second before he lifted the receiver. She couldn't breathe. His face was pale and his voice cracked as he spoke. Color returned to his face with a rush.

"Thank God," he whispered hoarsely. He listened for several minutes with silent tears running down his cheeks. "Thank you. Slade Jackson is flying us down. We'll leave within a half hour." After another pause he added, "I'm sure that will be all right. His plane is a four-seater." He hung up the phone and Macady didn't remember moving, but suddenly she was in his arms, laughing and crying.

"The Colorado Highway Patrol spotted Helen's car thirty minutes after they got the call. They followed her to her home where federal agents waited. Kelsey is fine, but she wants to come home."

"Well, let's go get her. Soon as I get one of those two-minute showers, we'll be on our way." Slade clapped Aaron on the back and started down the hall.

Aaron stopped his friend. "Sheriff Blacker asked if you'd have room for another passenger. Agent Broschinsky is being sent down to escort Helen back here."

"No problem," Slade grinned before disappearing behind the bathroom door.

CHAPTER TWENTY-TWO

"I can't wait to see Kelsey." Macady smiled through her tears. "For two days I've run from thoughts of every nightmare kidnapping I've ever heard or read about. I've been so scared."

"That makes two of us," Aaron sighed and Macady thought he sounded exhausted. "I don't remember a time when I didn't have a testimony of the power of prayer, but I've never prayed harder in my life than during this past week." He sank down on the sofa and pulled her down beside him. She leaned against his shoulder, and he brushed his freshly shaved face against her cheek. She could smell the clean scent of soap and a masculine essence that was his own.

"Macady, when this is all over and Kelsey is safely back in this house and you're well again, we need to sit down and really talk. I've harbored a lot of ill feelings toward Alicia because of what I call emotional infidelity, but I'm ready now to put that behind me. Last night as I lay in the dark praying for Kelsey's safety, I felt an assurance that Alicia was watching over her. That comforted me, and I feel that at long last, I can put the past behind me and begin thinking of the future."

Macady nodded. "It will be easier for Kelsey growing up if she doesn't sense any lingering animosity in you toward her mother." She was glad Aaron's bitterness was gone. He'd forgiven Alicia, but she couldn't help wondering if he could ever forgive Helen.

"Earlier this summer, when I first became aware I was beginning to care about you, I told myself I wouldn't get involved. You have a lot of family and you're close to them. The last thing I wanted …" The doorbell cut off his words.

"That must be our clothes." Slade poked his head into the room. Macady caught a glimpse of him standing in the hall with a towel knotted around his waist. He gestured for her to go to the door.

Aaron rose and stepped in front of her before she could move. He opened the door, then paused without speaking and took a step back. Her father stood in the doorway, a small suitcase in each hand. His face mirrored a strange mixture of hope and fear. Macady stood frozen, unable to think or move until she felt Aaron's arm circle her waist.

"I'll take those." Slade reached around her for the bags.

Spence looked expectantly toward her, and then at Aaron. Aaron turned his head to catch her eye. Slowly she nodded her head.

"Come on in." Aaron held the door wide.

Macady dropped her eyes to her hands. She didn't know what to say or do. A jumble of thoughts swamped her mind and tied her tongue. Her father's face tormented her. It struck her that as he'd stood on the doorstep, waiting for her to acknowledge him, he'd had the exact same expression on his face and in his eyes that she'd seen minutes ago on Aaron's as he'd answered the telephone. She'd seen the hope and the fear.

In her head, she heard her father's words in the hospital repeated and knew he'd been sincere. He was reaching out to her, but could she accept him back into her life? She didn't know. She didn't hate him anymore. The bitterness was gone. That realization was like letting go of a heavy burden. She felt lighter, more at ease. But no flood of warmth rushed in to take the place of the hate and anger. In its place was a vacuum.

"Thank you for bringing a change of clothing for us." Her voice sounded surprisingly calm.

"Are you all right?" Her father watched her closely, obviously waiting for something that wasn't there. She could see the disappointment in his eyes and felt a stab of remorse. She wished she could go to him and be his little girl again, but she wouldn't lie to him. Without the hurt standing in the way, she could recall her childhood and savor the good times, but she couldn't be that girl. Whatever the future held, it didn't include going back. But that didn't preclude forging a new relationship. In time, perhaps they'd even be friends again.

"I'm fine, Daddy." She saw the light in his eyes when she called him 'Daddy.' It twisted her heart. "Kelsey has been found in Colorado. Slade is going to fly Aaron and me down there to pick her up and bring her home."

"Thank God! She wasn't hurt?" He turned to Aaron and gripped his arm. Aaron shook his head, unable to speak. A look passed between the two fathers that touched Macady's tender heart and healed an old wound.

"Macady." She lifted her head as he addressed her directly for the first time in eight years. "I don't suppose you have much cash with you. If you're going to Colorado with Aaron, you better take this." He extended toward her a couple of folded bills and a telephone calling card. Her first instinct was to refuse the offer, then from deep inside her came the gentle warning. He needed to give. If she refused, she would be refusing much more than money. Hesitantly she met him halfway. His hand closed around hers for a moment, and their eyes met.

"Thank you," she whispered.

"Thank you." His eyes gleamed with a fine sheen of moisture.

The flight to Colorado was uneventful except for a steady stream of bantering between Slade and Cara. Macady managed to sleep part of the way and was glad Aaron had fallen asleep, too.

During the ride from the airport to the Randall home, Aaron sat on the edge of his seat. Macady reached for his hand, and he flashed her a quick smile before resuming his tense attention to the route the police cruiser took through the city.

She could feel her heart pound as Aaron bolted from the car almost before it stopped. He firmly gripped her hand and towed her behind him. Seconds before he reached the front door of the large two story home, the door was flung open.

"Daddy! Daddy!" Kelsey catapulted into his arms. Wet streaks left shiny tracks down Aaron's cheeks as he crushed his daughter to him. Macady wanted to allow them a few minutes of their own, but she couldn't resist stroking the child's back. She blinked her eyes to clear her vision and felt a tug of jealousy. She wished she had a mother's right to one of Kelsey's hugs.

"Macady! Did you come to get me, too?" Kelsey launched herself from Aaron's arms to Macady's. She wrapped her arms around Macady's neck and delivered a fierce hug.

Choking for breath, Macady whispered, "I'm happy to see you, too." There was no way to measure the joy she felt. Kelsey was the child of her heart, and though she hoped to give birth to other babies some day, she knew she'd never love a child of her own body any more than she loved this child.

"Are you all better?" Kelsey demanded to know.

"Just about," Macady answered softly.

"Did you ask her?" Kelsey released her stranglehold on Macady's neck as she turned to her father, and Aaron lifted her back into his arms. Sitting on his arm with a hand on each of their shoulders, Kelsey looked expectantly from one to the other.

"Not yet, punkin, but I will."

"When?"

"Soon, honey. Soon."

"This must be Kelsey." Cara Broschinsky stepped forward. Immediately Kelsey became shy and ducked her head against Aaron's shoulder.

"Kelsey," Aaron lifted her chin. "This lady is a police officer, just like me. She would like to talk to your grandmother. Would you sit here on the step with Macady while Miss Broschinsky and I go inside to see your grandmother?"

"I'll stay with you too, short stuff." Slade winked at her. "I'll just sit over here on the grass under this tree where it's nice and cool, and if you need me, you can yell, 'Uncle Slade'!"

Kelsey giggled. "Okay, Uncle Slade."

"Uncle?" Aaron raised his eyebrows.

"She's almost a Jackson, isn't she?" He glanced meaningfully toward Macady. Aaron pressed his lips together and shook his head, but Macady could see the hint of a smile trying to escape. That gave her an odd little lift she'd have to examine more closely later.

Kelsey seated herself on the step and Macady joined her. Aaron watched them for a minute, then quietly opened the screen door and stepped out of sight. Within minutes Kelsey was telling Macady and Slade all about climbing out of Macady's room to catch naughty Sandy and how she got caught on a sticker bush, but Grandma came and rescued her. Grandma said Kelsey couldn't go camping with Jackie, and that she'd have to go live with Grandma because barns don't burn down in Grandma's neighborhood.

Macady sighed and met Slade's grim expression.

"In her own way, she was protecting Kelsey," Slade muttered.

"I told Grandma, I wanted to tell Daddy good-bye and ask Ben to find Sandy, but she said there wasn't enough time."

The door opened and Macady's head turned in that direction. Aaron stepped out and reached for Kelsey. He didn't look toward Macady, and she couldn't hear what he said to his daughter before setting her on her feet and taking her hand. White lines framed his mouth, giving him an austere appearance, and Macady longed to go to him, to somehow soften his pain.

"Aaron's going to let her say good-bye to her grandmother before we take Mrs. Randall downtown," Cara explained. Macady hadn't noticed she'd joined them on the porch. "We'd like you and Aaron to leave with Kelsey before Mrs. Randall is brought out. It will be less traumatic for the child."

Macady agreed. She'd do anything to spare Kelsey and Aaron more grief than they'd already endured.

"What's going to happen to Helen?" Slade stood and walked over to stand in front of Cara. "Will she go to jail?"

"I don't think so, but that's up to the court. Her attorney and her bishop are with her, and they're talking about counseling. Our office will recommend leniency, considering that Kelsey was well cared for and suffered no harm. Besides, Mrs. Randall believed her granddaughter was in imminent danger and she was only protecting her. In spite of Mrs. Randall's animosity toward Aaron, he recommended her unresolved grief be taken into consideration. It won't serve any good to put an elderly woman who is no danger to the public in prison. I expect she'll go through a psychiatric evaluation, be put on probation, and possibly be assigned to do community service."

"Are you flying back with us?" Slade asked, and Cara answered in the negative.

"I'll follow later with Mrs. Randall."

"How about meeting me tonight for dinner? We won't be flying back until morning."

"I'm not sure."

Macady's attention wandered back to the house where Aaron was just emerging with Kelsey in his arms. He looked gray and haggard. Oblivious to her father's emotional state, Kelsey chattered happily. He lifted his head, and Macady met his eyes. Warmth replaced the bleakness there. He held out one hand and she went to him.

"Ask her now, Daddy," Kelsey whispered loudly.

"Ask me what?" She touched the tip of Kelsey's nose with her own.

"To be my mommy." Macady caught her breath and glanced down, unable to meet Aaron's amused grin.

"I think you just did," Aaron responded in mock exasperation.

"Did I?" Suddenly the little imp was all innocence.

"You did."

"Are you going to be my mommy?" Kelsey placed her little hands on either side of Macady's head and turned her face so she had to answer her directly. Macady felt her cheeks burn. Kelsey didn't understand the ramifications of her question, but how

Macady wished she could answer with a simple yes.

"Just a minute, punkin." Aaron cut short his daughter's demand for an answer. "I thought we agreed that I got to ask Macady to be my wife before you could ask her to be your mommy."

"Hurry up, Daddy." Kelsey had clearly run out of patience.

"Some things can't be hurried, Kelsey." He spoke to his daughter, but his eyes never left Macady's face. "I've got plans to put you to bed and leave Uncle Slade to babysit, while Macady and I find a place with candles on the table for dinner. I thought I'd buy her a dozen red roses and a box of chocolates. After a nice romantic dinner with music playing in the background, I'll reach across the table and take her hand in mine and ask her to be my wife."

"Couldn't you just pretend all that stuff and just ask her?"

"Could I?" Aaron wasn't speaking to Kelsey anymore. His voice was soft and low and slightly husky.

"I think you could." Macady answered with singing in her heart.

"I love you, Macady. Will you marry me?"

"Yes, Aaron." His arm tightened, drawing her closer, and his mouth slanted toward hers.

"Help, I'm getting squished!" Kelsey squirmed to be let down.

Macady drew back, suddenly aware of their audience. Slade and Cara were both grinning and a young patrolman, waiting to chauffeur them to their hotel, was smothering a laugh. Aaron set Kelsey on her feet and took one of her hands. The other he put around Macady's waist. Together they moved toward the waiting car.

"Daddy?" Kelsey suddenly stopped.

"What punkin?"

"Maybe we shouldn't pretend about the box of chocolates part."

"I don't think we should pretend about the 'Put Kelsey to bed and let Uncle Slade babysit' part either," Aaron responded with a slow, heart-stopping smile sent Macady's way.

"Hey, I've got a date tonight," Slade protested.

"Bring her along," Aaron winked at Cara. Then he tightened his arm around Macady's waist, and held Kelsey's hand a bit more snugly.

ABOUT THE AUTHOR

Jennie Hansen attended Ricks College and graduated from Westminster College in Salt Lake City. She has been a newspaper reporter, editor, and librarian, and is presently a technical services specialist for the Salt Lake City library system.

Her church service has included teaching in all auxiliaries and serving in stake and ward Primary presidencies. She has also served as a stake public affairs coordinator and ward chorister.

Jennie and her husband, Boyd, live in Salt Lake City. They are the parents of four daughters and a son.

Jennie has written two previous best-sellers, *Run Away Home* and *When Tomorrow Comes*.